I0891561

BUYING ON TIME AGAIN

Also by Antanas Sileika

The Death of Tony

Some Unfinished Business

Provisionally Yours

The Barefoot Bingo Caller

Underground

Woman in Bronze

Dinner at the End of the World

BUYING ON TIME AGAIN

ANTANAS SILEIKA

STONEHEWER
BOOKS

First edition published in 1997

ISBN: 978-1-7389933-6-9
eBook ISBN: 978-1-7389933-7-6

1 2 3 4 5 6 7 8 9 10

Cataloguing data available from Library and Archives Canada.

Author photograph (back cover) by Liudas Masys
Author photograph (interior) by Irmantas Gelunas
Set in Century and Abril by Ned Seager

Printed and bound by Friesens in Canada

Stonehewer Books | Victoria, BC
stonehewerbooks.com

Stonehewer Books is located on the traditional territory of the Lkwungen people on what is now called Vancouver Island. We acknowledge and are grateful for the unique contributions to our common well-being made by the Indigenous peoples of this land.

For Dainius & Gintaras again

None of this is true; all of this is true

Contents

A Few Words About This Book

BUYING ON TIME REFERS TO AN OLD-FASHIONED METHOD OF store credit. In the seventies film *Saturday Night Fever*, character Tony Manero sees a shirt he wants to buy to wear to the disco, but he can't afford it. So he pays a bit each week until he has paid in full and finally gets the shirt. These days, of course, we slap down our credit cards to get what we want right away and then pay later.

This collection is the story of a postwar immigrant family that needs to learn how to be 'Canadian.' It takes time, practically a lifetime. And why *Buying on Time <u>Again</u>*? Because this collection, first published in 1997, has continued to be popular — and I've added a prequel that wasn't there when the book first came out.

When I was writing *Buying on Time*, I thought I was depicting a couple of boisterous postwar immigrant boys growing up in a new Toronto suburb. But to my surprise, editor John Metcalf told me I was writing a book about their father, who loomed over all the action, even when he wasn't in the scene.

The 'Old Man' was a Displaced Person, or DP, as European refugees were called at the time. He wore a wool hat with earflaps in all weather, smoked a pipe, had a few gold teeth, and spoke English with an atrocious accent. Self-confident beyond reason, dictatorial in even the tiniest aspects of the kids' everyday lives, a heavy drinker and almost medieval in his understanding of

Catholicism, he should have been the tyrant the readers learned to despise.

Instead he was funny, even though he irritated his wife and children, and shopkeepers shuddered when he walked into their premises. Local authorities expected this East European immigrant to be some sort of dumbass peasant, and he could play the fool to win one concession or another.

He was terribly tight with his money, the kind of man who asked for a discount in retail stores to the embarrassment of his children. But he sometimes got what he wanted, acting against the norms of Canadian customs of the fifties and sixties. To his kids he seemed barbaric. They wanted to blend in, but there was no way this man could do that, an East European bull in a Canadian china shop.

In my childhood, this sort of father was not all that unusual among Baltic, Italian, Ukrainian, or other kinds of immigrants. This type of father might be somewhat rough, but was accepted and even loved as long as he kept the family together, paid the bills, and supported everyone in his own fashion without using a belt any more often than the teacher used the strap in school — very occasionally, and only for serious violations. And he was not the kind to hug very often, or to clap wildly at his child's piano recital. He might not even show up. Kid stuff belonged to kids.

In Hollywood films, I'd sometimes see adult characters who had been traumatized by their fathers' missing their childhood baseball games. I found this level of sensitivity ludicrous. 'Grow up!' I'd want to say to the wounded cinema adult nursing his trauma.

I was writing the book against the depiction of insufficiently tender men, of children as easily traumatized, of parental 'goodness' coming in only one flavour.

And I was writing against the increasingly common depiction, in movies and television shows, of the fifties and early sixties: naively prosperous in the film *American Graffiti*, patriarchal in *Father Knows Best*, lustful of conformity in the novel *Revolutionary Road,* and paranoically anti-communist in television ads for Voice of America.

Those films and novels reflected nothing of what I remembered growing up in that time period. Weston was a working-class suburb of Toronto filled with people who had been variously and truly damaged by the Second World War. My parents lost their East European families to lockdown behind the Iron Curtain. My friend Mike's Japanese parents had been interned and dispossessed in Canada during the war. My friend Alan's father had been prisoner of war in a Japanese camp after the fall of Hong Kong. When I knew him, he was always around because he was half-blinded by starvation and lived on a disability pension. He'd join us for a game of cribbage, but he needed to use large font playing cards. Years later, he would suffer flashbacks to his imprisonment.

Were these people supposed to be mindless conformists or silly materialists?

Money could be tight in that period. Factories laid off workers whenever orders were low. Pop was a rare treat and the twelve-cent deposit from six empty bottles was not something a kid on my street took for granted. Nobody was seriously deprived, but a broken hockey stick might not be replaced. You patched your bicycle's inner tubes and your father patched his rusty car. Mothers patched the knees of their children's jeans.

In postwar working-class Weston, people were trying to build lives for themselves — 'good lives,' as they understood them at the time. Much of this striving was hard, and much of it was funny. 'Keeping up with the Joneses' might involve not a white picket fence, but finally getting indoor plumbing.

It's so easy to sneer at the past. We look back to see times were more racist, more sexist, more cruel than our times now, and ridiculously unsophisticated in diet. It sometimes seems the people of the past were stupid to eat aspics and Velveeta cheese and to drink cream soda. As if eating avocados implies culinary wisdom, as if sushi trumps a jam sandwich. But this has to do with the narcissism of the present. We in the present will be seen as cruel fools in the future too. We're not sure what we are doing wrong now, but future generations will let us know.

Having come from an immigrant family, in my youth I felt like an underdog in the eyes of long-time Canadians, and believed I needed to prove something. With time, I became a long-time Canadian too, and a new generation of immigrants might feel about me as I once did about others.

In the stories here, the Old Man hangs over everything, much like the plume of smoke coming out of the Canadian Gypsum factory at the edge of the suburb of Weston. And he appears again in a prequel added at the end of this updated version of the book.

After finishing *Buying on Time*, which turned out to be the most popular of all the books I have written, I considered writing more stories about this immigrant family. But I decided to leave the family in this book in a kind of perfection of symmetry: beginning — middle — and end. With one exception.

A year or two after the publication of the stories, I wanted to write about how the family in this book found itself in the basement of an incomplete house. So I wrote one more story, a prequel, subsequently published in a Canadian literary journal.

It is called 'A House in the Country,' and it is a kind of origin story, background the reader might find interesting after completing the book. I also wanted to shower a bit more sympathy on an earlier generation of Canadians. Not all were as unkind as Mr Taylor, and many had been damaged in their own ways, either by the war or the Great Depression that came before it.

Since the prequel was written after the original publication of *Buying on Time*, it comes at the end of this volume. And in this new story, the character will not quite have become the Old Man yet. To his boys, he is still 'Father,' but never 'Dad.' The word *dad* was North American, and belonged in movies or on the lips of Canadian kids. A father, on the other hand, was a man in transition, someone on his way to becoming the Old Man.

Some minor changes have been made to the language to reflect our changes in sensibility over the last three decades.

Going Local

STAN WAS A DP LIKE MY FATHER, LIKE THE REST OF US, BUT THE outhouse in our back yard had made even him laugh. Not the outhouse itself, although it was the only one in the subdivision growing up in the old orchards, but the neat squares of newspaper my father had us stack beside the seat.

'You such fucking DP,' Stan said to my father, and he held his sides as he laughed like a character out of a cartoon. Stan only swore when he spoke English, a language that didn't really count.

My father went out and bought two rolls of toilet paper, but for half a year we used them only as decoration, like twin flower vases. Stan's advice on toilet paper and anything else in this foreign land was reliable. As for what the locals advised, one could never be sure.

'A fool is always dangerous,' my father told me, 'but a foreign fool is worse. You can't tell if he's an idiot or simply a foreigner.'

Mr Taylor was the only real Canadian we knew in the dawn of our subdivision, and we watched him as if we were anthropologists trying to fathom the local customs.

Mr Taylor was a special kind of Canadian, an 'English.' They were the only kind who really counted, and observation of them could pay a dividend. Mr Taylor was *our* English, the one who lived across the street and whose habits could be observed at will. We were astonished that he stayed in his dress shirt and tie as he read the evening paper in a lawn chair in his back yard. The lawn chair was just as astonishing. Who else but an English would spend good money on a chair that could only be used outside?

My father spat on the ground at this foolishness, but my mother sighed.

'These English are just like Germans,' she said. She meant not like us, not DP. We belonged on the evolutionary tree with the Italians, Poles, and Ukrainians. Our knuckles still scraped the earth.

'He's a banker,' my mother told us, and the word was heavy with meaning. It explained how he lived in a house that not only had proper brick walls and a roof, but a lawn as well.

Our street had half a dozen other houses on it, but none of the rest were finished. People dug the foundations and laid the basement blocks. Then they waited and saved. When a little money came in, they bought beams and joists and studs. Then they waited some more. The Taylors stood out because a contractor had built their house from start to finish. We stood out too. We moved in before the above-ground walls went up.

'You want us to live underground?' my mother had asked. 'Like moles? Like worms?'

'No,' my father said, 'like foxes.'

One day we had even woken to the smell of tar, and gone out to see that Mr Taylor was having his driveway paved.

My father snorted at this. It was 1953. Our street was still covered with gravel, and if a man had money, he laid crushed stones on his driveway. Everybody else had twin ruts in their yards. Asphalt was as unlikely as a skyscraper in the new suburb-to-be, where the apple trees from the old farm orchards still stood in rows all around us, their sad fruit unpicked. But Gerry and I were filled with envy. A paved driveway was a sign of sophistication — something so fine we never knew it was possible until we saw it.

'What a game of hockey you could play on this,' Gerry said to me one Thursday evening when we knew the banker and his wife were out shopping, and we knelt on the pavement to feel the smoothness with the palms of our hands. 'You could shoot a ball from one end of the driveway to the other, and it would almost score by itself. A ball on pavement moves faster than a puck on ice. My science teacher told me that.' I listened and I palmed the smooth pavement and the vision in Gerry's mind was seeded in mine.

When I wasn't hating him, I admired my older brother Gerry. He sensed the openings in this country faster than the rest of us, and he slipped through them. If we were quick enough, we could slip in behind him. Even on the ice, he could out-skate the other fast ones, and leave only the half-heard whisper of 'asshole' in their ears. The goalies feared him most, because the *Life* magazines stuffed in their socks did nothing to save their shins from the sting of his flying puck.

But to Mr Taylor, he was only a boy, and a suspect boy at that. The kind of boy who was sure to have matches in his pocket, if not a stolen cigarette as well.

When Mr Taylor crossed the street to speak to my father, we felt naked. We'd watched him carefully, but never guessed he might notice us. 'Your cat,' said Mr Taylor to my father, 'has been running across my lawn.'

My father glanced down at Gerry and me to see if he had understood the English correctly. Gerry shrugged.

My father pondered the words. The relationship between our cat and Mr Taylor's lawn was impossibly remote to him. What could the one have to do with the other? My father sucked on his empty pipe, and the sickening sputter of nicotine resin in the stem was the only sound. Clearly there was a problem, or this English would not be there, standing in his shirt and tie in the ruts by our subterranean home. My father strained to imagine the problem.

'It shits on lawn?'

Gerry and I were mortified. The colour rose in Mr Taylor's face as well, for in 1953, a man did not speak that way, not out in front of his house. Gerry and I knew it, but my father did not.

'No, no,' Mr Taylor said. 'That is not what I meant.'

'It pisses on flowers?'

'It merely walks. I do not want your cat to walk on my lawn.'

It was all that Mr Taylor could admit to without uttering the same sort of vulgarities as his neighbour. My father would never understand terms such as *defecate* or *urinate*. Mr Taylor's linguistic squeamishness had backed him into a corner.

My father sucked on his pipe and thought some more. He had negotiated with Red Army commissars and saved his sister-in-law from a Nazi labour battalion, but he had never heard an accusation such as this. This had to be an eccentricity. Banker or not, Mr Taylor was an idiot.

'I fix,' my father said.

Mr Taylor would have been happy to leave it at that, to take his victory against the foreigner and return to his evening paper, but my father gestured for him to stay where he was, and then went down the steps to our underground house.

He came out with the cat in his hand. He did not cradle the cat, for my father had come from a farm, and cradling was only for women or citified men. He carried the cat by a handful of skin behind its head, and he held it out to Mr Taylor.

'I told cat not walk on lawn, but it doesn't listen. Bad cat. You tell it.'

The cat hung in the air, its legs splayed and tense, but its face calm and inscrutable.

Mr Taylor's lips pursed.

'Really. If cat walks on lawn again, you can kill it.'

Mr Taylor stepped out of our ruts and onto the gravel street, and he strode back to his own home.

'I can kill it for you if you want. Tell me and I will do it!' He shouted at Mr Taylor's back, but Mr Taylor's back continued to recede.

That had been in the summer, but the memory of it must have stuck in Mr Taylor's mind throughout the months as it became clear that our pit in the earth was not going to have a proper house on top of it before the winter snows fell. The memory of it must have galled him as it became clear that the outhouse was not going to come down either, and his revulsion must have grown when my mother brought home the baby in November.

One February morning we heard the muffled thump of a foot against the snow on the cellar door. This was a real distinction. We were the only family in Weston that had a door you knocked on with your feet.

I looked up at the building inspector from the bottom of the staircase, a dark figure against a blue so brilliant that it hurt my eyes. Gerry and I stood beside our father in case we had to translate for him. Only my mother hung back by the woodstove because Tom was on her breast and the cold was always slipping down the stairway like an eager cat.

It was the woodstove that gave us away in the first place. That and the outhouse. He never would have found us after a new snow if it weren't for the smoking pipe above us. After every snowfall, my father dug out the stove-pipe so the smoke could pass freely, and from a distance you could always see the plume rising out of the ground at the top of the hill like a vent out of hell.

We had no doubt that the man at the top of the stairwell, the town building inspector, had been called by Mr Taylor.

'Come in!' my father shouted heartily. 'It is cold. My wife will make tea.'

My father was desperate to get the man to sit at a table. There would be no trouble then, not if he could see the inside was clean and we had a baby as well. A cup of tea at best, or a couple of drinks and ten dollars at worst, would get rid of the problem. But the inspector would not come down the steps.

'The law says you can't live like this,' the building inspector called down the stairwell as if he were looking down into the hold of a slave ship. 'The roof doesn't have any pitch, and the snow could crush every one of you! Besides, it's not decent.'

'Wait. My English bad.'

This was another tactic in my father's strategy for life in a foreign land. He could deny he had understood anything, and an order not understood never existed in the first place.

'It's for your own good.' We could not make out his face. He was like an angel at the top of the staircase, surrounded by painful blue light.

'We have baby,' my father said expansively, as if showing off a new heifer. He motioned to my mother and she stepped closer into the cold air that came down the steps.

'The baby'd be the first to go when the roof collapses.'

'Danger?'

'For the baby. Yes. You must move out for the sake of the baby.'

'Then you take baby.' My father took Tom from my mother's arms, and she did not complain, did not hesitate.

'You take baby and bring him back in April when snow gone. If you want, bring him back in September, after we have walls and roof.'

A crunch of snow as the inspector left, and then a quick return. 'Are you Catholic?'

'What?'

'Your religion.'

'Church of England.'

The inspector slammed the door down on us.

How could my father have known there was a Catholic Children's Aid? An admission of religion would have brought them down on us. He was in seas only partially charted and, where he was ignorant of how to act, he navigated by dead reckoning.

Dead reckoning could be a problem. Sometimes it was dead wrong, and this time my mother was not sure my father had his bearings right.

'You were ready to give him the baby.'

'So why did you hand him to me?'

'I thought you knew what you were doing.'

'I do. He won't be back.'

'But what if he does come back? What if they make us leave? We have no place to go.'

'I know what I'm doing.'

'Just like you said we'd have the roof on by the end of September.'

'We ran out of money.'

She knew that. She had calculated how many nails he would need, so there would be none left over — no extra money spent for nails that would lie uselessly in a box for years. She knew the butcher gave a free piece of liver if she bought a pound of bacon — double the savings because she could use the bacon drippings on our sandwiches instead of butter. She knew the matters of money very well — the cost of condensed milk for the baby and counting the tins of it on the shelf each day because Gerry might snatch one and suck it dry.

And this problem of money was not a new one for her, because even in the house where she had lived before the war, the men who came to cut the hay were paid in eggs or meat or beer and as little money as possible. She knew the value of money even from up in the tower of the white frame house that was gently sinking into the mud below. A shallow pit had to be dug so the front door could swing open. The problem of money had always been there. She was the one who had brought home fifteen cents' worth of lamp oil each day, so her father could read to them from Shakespeare for an hour.

They were sent to bed when there was still a little oil left in the lamp, and her father stayed up alone to read Voltaire in translation. He put the book behind others when the priest came to visit. Voltaire was their secret — they knew not to talk of the book — it was their father's weakness, like a need for liquor or pornography. He was enlightened enough to read Voltaire, but his Catholic heart demanded penance. Not to be paid to the priest, that fool. He paid for his vice by teaching Shakespeare to his daughters. They already learned German in school, so he was edifying them, arming them with another language. It never occurred to him that any other book was necessary for their English. If he could only afford to own one book, then he wanted it to be the best.

She memorized and repeated Hamlet's speech. The sisters spoke to one another in Shakespeare's English at the dinner table where their mother silently watched the servant girl dish out the mashed potatoes and listened to the foreign sounds, no more perturbed than a cat on a windowsill. Even their father had been self-taught. Father and daughters spoke to one another, innocent of the rules of English pronunciation.

And so years later, she became the English teacher in the DP camp in Hamburg, in the British zone, and when the English colonel came on an inspection visit, she was the one who had trained the children and had them repeat in a chorus:

Now is the Winter of our discontent
Made glorious summer by this son of York;

> And all the clouds that lour'd upon our house
> In the deep bosom of the ocean buried.

But the English colonel heard the rhythmic beat of foreign vowels and consonants of what he guessed was some folk poem. It was only months and years later that my mother and her now dispersed English students were bewildered in front of immigration officers on the piers of Halifax and New York and Sydney as their words made no impression on officialdom, which scowled or smiled on them depending on their luck but which clearly understood nothing of the winter of their discontent.

Now my mother was marooned with her children in the underground dwelling, a victim of my father's dead reckoning. Yet he assured her that the way ahead of us was clear. We could go on confidently until spring, when there would be enough money for the walls and a roof. If only the inspector did not return, that emissary of the English Mr Taylor, that scuttler of our dreams. For the bank was only a hundred yards down the road from the town hall. To us, Mr Taylor and the inspector were practically the same man, and to make an ally of one would make an ally of the second.

'I'll bake them a napoleon cake,' my mother said, and my father approved the expenditure on a pound of butter, a dozen eggs, sour cream, flour, sugar and vanilla.

'It would be cheaper to kill the cat. Then he'd be happy for sure.'

Gerry and I looked at one another, panic stricken, but my mother just shook her head swiftly at us. It meant either that my father was joking or she wouldn't let him do it.

She chopped the butter into the flour with a knife.

'Don't let the butter get too warm, or it doesn't form into grains. There's another way of doing this whole thing, a method of folding over the pastry to make puffs. That's the way the French do it. After all, this is a French cake. But we have our own special way. We chop the butter into the flour until the pieces are the size of small peas.'

'If we burnt his house down, we'd be rid of him sooner.'

Gerry was walking around the room, rocking Tom in his arms as my mother made the cake. He looked funny to me, his face all fierce and twisted and the baby in his arms. I laughed.

'Don't think I wouldn't do it.'

'It's a brick house. How are you going to make it catch fire?'

'Toss a bottle of gasoline through the window.'

'You'd be in jail in a minute.'

'They'd never catch me. I'd go north into the woods.'

'Stop that talk,' my mother said. 'You're beginning to sound like your father.'

That shut us up.

'Roll out each leaf right on a round metal pan. Don't try to lift the rolled leaf from the counter onto the pan. It has to be thinner than a pie crust, and it'll break as you move it.'

Our basement room was sweltering with the heat from the woodstove. Gerry and I were in our T-shirts.

'You have to be just as careful when you take the leaf out of the oven. It's supposed to be very thin. You need at least twelve of these leaves. If one does break, crumble it up and use it as a garnish on the very top layer.'

'What are you telling us this for?' Gerry asked. 'We're never going to bake cakes.'

'I don't have any daughters.'

'Well, I'm not going to be one for you.'

'You look like one already with that baby in your arms,' I said.

'You take him. Catch!'

'Toss that child and you will not be able to sit down for a week, I promise you.'

Gerry scowled.

'Make a custard with sugar and a dozen egg yolks and a little milk and flour,' my mother said. 'Make sure you let the custard cool. If you add butter to hot custard, it melts and separates. Beat the butter into the custard, and spread a little between each of the leaves.'

'I said I'm never going to bake one of these.'

'This is a napoleon cake. Do you know who Napoleon was?'

'Yeah,' Gerry answered, but he did not sound sure of himself.

'He was a French general who became the most warlike man France has ever known. He knew how to use artillery — big guns, and he marched across most of Europe. This cake is named for him.'

'But I bet he didn't bake it himself.'

'Don't be so sure. Napoleon was a man who knew all weapons.'

After Gerry suggested we put a dead mouse in the middle of the cake, my mother selected me to take the gift across to the banker and his wife. The beaten snow path to the road was slippery, and half an inch of water lay on the icy road. We were in the middle of a warm spell, and icicles hung off the eaves and the sound of running water came from under the snow. The cake was heavy, placed on a board covered with wax paper, and I had to hold it out in front of me with two hands.

Mrs Taylor answered the door.

My mother had made me rehearse the whole speech twice, about neighbours and friendliness and helping out, but I froze when I saw her in her perfection. Short hair, red lipstick (lipstick at home!) and a dress with short sleeves and cuffs and a blue-checked apron. She looked like she had stepped out of an ad in the household section of the Eaton's catalogue.

'You're beautiful!' I said, and then regretted it, and felt ashamed of the grey wool mittens that she could see holding up the cake. They were scratchy, like everything else I had to wear in the wintertime, but worse, they were wet and had a patch where I'd poked my finger through once and my mother had repaired it with pink thread. Pink thread and grey mittens came from across the road, in the basement where we lived, and I hoped then that we *would* be forced to move, because I couldn't bear the shame of being across the road from her.

Mrs Taylor laughed, and asked me what I had in my hands.

'A cake. We baked it for you.'

Mr Taylor was behind her in a moment.

'We can't take that.'

'Oh, Harvey, they're just trying to be nice.'

'It might not be sanitary.'

'Hush. Thank you, dear, and say thanks to your mother. Wait a minute.' And she disappeared back into the house.

Mr Taylor stood there glowering at me. I looked down and away from him, and studied the lower walls of his house, where the concrete blocks came out from the ground to meet the bricks. I saw a step-shaped crack there, and I stared at it until Mrs Taylor came back.

'There's a piece of fudge for you and one for your brother. Now remember to thank your mother.' I took the two pieces, each wrapped in a square of wax paper, and stuffed them into my pocket and went back home.

'Thank God for women,' said my mother as she nursed Tom in the armchair.

'You say they had a crack in the basement wall?' my brother asked.

'Yeah.'

'We could pour acid through there and it'd turn into gas. We could poison them.'

'A boy exactly like his father.'

The uncharacteristic February thaw kept up with much dripping of icicles and gurgling in ditches still covered with snow. Three days later, the temperature dropped way below zero and the neighbourhood became a treacherously shiny surface. Gerry and I skated over the crust of ice that had formed on the snow in the abandoned fields beyond our subdivision. We skated down the long aisles between the drooping trees, kicking frozen apples with the toes of our skates. Gerry could always last longer than me, and he came in one night after dark, when the rest of us were already finishing our supper at the kitchen table. He was carrying a strange bundle of newspapers that he pulled apart before anyone could say a word. The napoleon cake fell from the newspaper wrapping and clanged onto the floor like a piece of iron.

It was frozen from sitting outside. No piece had ever been cut from the cake.

'Where did you get that?' my father asked.

'It was wrapped up in newspapers in their garbage can. I thought you wouldn't believe me if I told you about it, so I dug it out and brought it home.'

'Did they see you?' my father asked.

'They're out shopping.'

'What do you think people will say about us if they find out you've been lifting the lids off garbage cans?' my mother began, but my father cut her off.

'He did the right thing. Now at least we know what the locals think of us.'

'I've got a plan, Dad,' said Gerry, and my father turned to him to listen. Gerry had just earned the right to speak.

'There's a crack in their basement wall. Dave saw it. We get some kind of acid, you know, something poisonous, and we pour it through the crack, and then at night the fumes rise up through the house and kill them both.'

My father sucked on his unlit pipe, and the nicotine in the stem made the sickening slurping sound.

'What crack?'

'The crack in their basement wall.'

'Did you see it too?'

'Yeah, I checked. We could get this little pipe or something and do it at night. We'd just have to cover our tracks in the snow and nobody'd be the wiser.'

'You say they are out shopping?'

'They go every Thursday.'

'And you could show me this crack?'

Gerry couldn't believe my father was taking him seriously. He was getting more and more excited, stepping from side to side in the puddles from the melted snow on the concrete floor.

'Why are you letting him go on like that?' my mother asked. 'He's morbid enough as it is.'

'I want to see this hole,' my father said, and he rose deliberately from his chair and carefully stuffed his pipe before going to put on his coat and hat.

Gerry looked back triumphantly at my mother and me before the two of them took the steps up and out of the cellar.

'Are they going to kill them?' I asked her.

'Nothing would surprise me from your father. Nothing at all.'

'You mean he'd do it?'

'What?'

'Kill them.'

'He can't even bear to prune a tree. He's all talk, talk, talk, and it all winds up being no more significant than farting in the bathtub.'

I didn't like it when she spoke like that. She had told me again and again about the house with a tower, and her childhood there with a view over the fields and woods. A woman from a white house should not talk about farts.

That night, Gerry whispered to me in the bed.

'We're on,' he said.

'You mean you're going to kill them?'

'Father smiled like a Cheshire Cat when I showed him the crack.'

'What's a Cheshire?'

'It's a cat, stupid.'

'So what's the difference between a cat and a Cheshire?'

'Clean out your ears during science class and you might learn something, like how to make poison.'

I had visions of Mrs Taylor in her apron, falling to her knees in the kitchen as the poisonous fumes rose up. She'd be at the stove, frying fish sticks, and when she fell unconscious, the grease would catch fire, spread to the curtains, and soon she'd be surrounded by flames. Mr Taylor's cigarette would fall from his lips as he was reading the newspaper. If I watched the house carefully, I could break through the door just at that moment and carry her out to the back yard. I thought about her size for a moment, and then decided I could drag her if I had to. By then it would be too late to save Mr Taylor, and when she woke from unconsciousness, she would wrap her arms around my shoulders and cry.

The imminent destruction of Mr Taylor was beginning to seem less appalling.

'I have to take Tom to the doctor for his shot,' my mother said when Gerry and I came back from school. 'Gerry, you come along too. I need to buy some things and you can carry them for me.'

'Why can't Dave go?'

'You're stronger.'

Gerry nodded sagely. He reminded me to peel the potatoes and put them on to boil.

I hated potatoes. My father bought them in fifty-pound bags in the fall, and by February the eyes were growing right through the burlap. I was picking potatoes out of the bag in the pantry under the steps when my father threw open the door above me and came down in his snow-covered boots.

There were no separate rooms in our cellar yet. I stayed where I was, the only real hiding place, and watched him.

'Forget the potatoes and come with me, Dave. Hurry up.'

It was frightening how much he sensed. I was afraid to think about him in case he smelled out my mutinous thoughts.

Mrs Taylor opened the door to the two of us. The pipe in my father's pocket was still smoking, and intermittent clouds escaped from around the pocket flap as if he had the Little Engine That Could puffing away inside. He held his hat in his hand and smiled with his yellow teeth. Mrs Taylor went to get her husband.

'Use your nose,' my father whispered, 'what do you smell?'

'Liver and onions.'

'That's right,' and he smiled as Mr Taylor came to the door.

'Big problem with house,' my father said, pointing to the crack. 'I see. I think, tell or not tell?'

'Yes, a crack. I see. I'll get the contractor to come around and patch it when the weather warms up. Thank you very much.'

'No patch.'

'I beg your pardon?'

'Three days warm, and already your footings shift. Bad foundation. When real spring comes, crack will open much more. Foundation move — walls move. Walls move — doors and windows break — roof shift. Very bad. Very expensive to fix. You tell contractor dig out everything. I check for you — make sure he do good job.'

'And we just laid the lawn in the fall!' said Mrs Taylor from the screen door. 'I wanted to put in a garden this spring.'

We left them then, and walked back across the road to our cellar.

'Get the potatoes on. I'll make the soup.'

He whistled tunelessly to himself. I couldn't understand what he was so happy about.

'The neighbours are taken care of,' he said to my mother as soon as we sat down to dinner. He began to slurp on his soup, using a big European spoon, the size of a small ladle.

Gerry froze.

'You mean you did it without me?' Gerry asked.

'Of course. This was no business for a boy.'

Gerry slammed his own spoon down on the table.

My father told the story.

'Like trying to pull a goat by its horns,' my father said of Mr Taylor's reluctance to come outside. 'He started to tell me his contractor would come back and do it, but I know a man who worked for that contractor. He's bankrupt. Mr Taylor is going to have to pay oh, I don't know, maybe six hundred dollars to have the job done, and he doesn't have the money.'

'He told you that?'

'No, but we figured it out. Tell her, Dave.'

'I don't know,' I stammered.

'Sometimes I wonder what they teach you at school. What were they eating?'

'Liver and onions.'

'What kind of liver?'

I stared at him blankly.

'Pork liver. That means they're broke. They spent all their money on asphalt and rolls of grass. He'll have to save to get his foundation fixed. It should take him a year or two to get the money. Unless the building inspector catches sight of it and makes him do it right away.'

My mother put her hand on his arm and she began to laugh.

Gerry was glum at the rink that night, and got into two fights. On the way home, he finally said, 'I don't like it. It's not a sure thing. If that inspector shows up at our house again, I'm going to do it myself.'

We waited over the weeks that followed, as the first true thaw came in late March, and just as my father had said, the crack in Mr Taylor's basement wall grew wider.

By April, we had lumber and several squares of bricks stacked in the muddy back yard. My father whistled often and my mother took Tom out to be in the sun during the occasional warm day.

Only Gerry sulked that spring.

The Coat

POCKETS OF DANGER LAY BOTH WITHIN THE ABANDONED APPLE orchards and beyond them, in the no man's land between the approaching suburbs and retreating countryside. A derelict farmhouse floor might give way beneath a troop of boys out to break the last windows. The creek and pond surfaces glittered with rainbow colours from leaking oil drums buried in the dirt, and boys had been known to climb into the culverts by the Humber River to chase rats, and never be heard of again.

'Never talk to the hobos,' my mother warned us before she got sick and stopped talking. But hobos appealed to us, and we went looking for them. They were always near the horizon, furtive men who huddled in groups, but disappeared when we drew closer. Like the spoor of elusive animals, proof of their existence appeared in smouldering cook-fires, empty tins, cigarette butts, and the occasional mickey of rye whisky emptied so thoroughly that no drop remained for us. Even the odour had been consumed, so we could smell nothing when we inhaled deeply from the stubby necks.

'Never talk to the man with the cat,' my mother said when she was still of sound mind. He walked the streets each evening with a dog on a leash and a cat sitting on his shoulder. A leather patch had been sewn into the shoulder, so the cat could dig in its nails, find purchase, and then sway gently in rhythm like a rider on a camel.

The man with the cat on his shoulder was a magnet to children and anathema to parents. In that suburb, a beard was enough to condemn a man to the ranks of the crazy and the dangerous. Even Bicycle Bill was suspicious, because a man should walk to the bus if he did not have money, and use a car if he did.

As the weather warmed, my mother took to sitting out on the front yard with Tom in the baby carriage or a homemade playpen that my father had nailed together out of leftover two-by-fours. It looked like a prison for infants.

'There's too much dust in the house,' she said, and it was true that our basement ceiling shivered and dropped sawdust as my father and his friends slowly raised the walls above us and partitioned the space into rooms.

'The days are fine now anyway, and it's better for the boy to breathe fresh air into his lungs.'

The work on our house went slowly, because my father could only do it on Saturdays and free evenings. He wouldn't work on Sundays. Sometimes one of his friends or his cousin Stan would come around to help out, but my mother always considered the arrival of help as a mixed blessing. The men might work for nothing, but they expected a bottle of liquor to be split among them after the sun had set, and then my father drank too much and snored through the night.

People came around to look at the construction after we had the walls framed and roof on. It was as if we lived in a public park, with strangers walking through the maze of upright two-by-fours and commenting on the design. The stove-pipe from our woodstove still came through the floor, and when my mother cooked, the smoke rose up through the wall studs and huddled under the roof until it seeped out the sides.

'We'll have to take out the pipe soon,' my father said. 'Otherwise, the inside of the roof will smell like smoke for years.'

'You won't be finished for years anyway,' my mother said.

'I'm doing the best I can.'

She did not answer that. She spoke less and less, punctuating her silence with strange speeches.

'I was in medical school before they closed down the university. Even after they closed the school, there were still operas at the theatre every night. Sometimes, when the air raid siren went off, the musicians and singers wouldn't even bother to leave the theatre, and they turned off the lights and we sat in our seats and listened to *Libiamo* in the darkness. My old biology professor had the seats in front of us, and he always said that as long as the music was playing, there was still hope.

'In the darkness, we could see none of the flashes from the explosions, but we could feel them, and for all we knew, our homes and our parents were being blown to pieces, but still we sat there. "Sing from *Carmen*!" somebody shouted out when the act ended. The priests had forbidden *Carmen* on the stage because it was immoral, but with the bombs whistling around us in the darkness, who was going to call in the clergy? For all we knew, the bishop might have been sitting up in the mezzanine. For all we knew, he might have been the one who called out for it. The orchestra could not have seen the music, even if they had it, but in that darkness, they managed it somehow, and we heard part of the first act of *Carmen* before the all clear sounded and the lights came back on.'

My father's psychology was elementary, and at this rare speech, he went and turned up the radio, and he could not understand the sudden outflow of tears when Patsy Cline whined through the basement and some more sawdust from between the floorboards salted the hamburgers on our table with fine grit.

'Your mother came from a good family,' my father said to us out back one day. 'She's not used to living like this.'

'This' was normal to me and Gerry. Anything else would have been strange. It was true that others lived in houses that were already built, while we lived in the basement as the house was being raised above us. But normal houses belonged to that other race of people, Canadians, who wore suits to work. Before the basement, we had lived in a rented flat and before that in a wooden shack on the edge of a farm. Earlier there had been the DP camp in Germany, which I couldn't really remember much, except for all the bomb craters filled with water where children fished hopelessly all day.

The shack had been pretty much the same, with wooden walls and a wooden floor and a woodstove. Sometimes we fed it with coal if the winter night was very cold and we could afford to splurge.

My mother talked about the other house, the one she had lived in before the war. It was white and had a tower, but there were no photographs of this past before we were born. 'Tell us about the princess in the castle,' we used to say, and sometimes she would tell us some tale of Hoffman, and other times she would tell us of her life with her sisters in the white house where servants cleaned the rooms and served dinner. Most of all, we wanted to hear about the tower, that high white room with windows on four sides, where the girls played in the summer. The room was not heated, and they closed it up over the winter, and there was always some forgotten toy — a doll, perhaps, that had to spend the winter up there covered in frost, until the girls rescued it in the spring and wiped off the mildew that had started to grow on its porcelain face.

But my mother's voice had started to fade like the volume on the radio. She became quieter and quieter. Soon she hardly spoke at all.

My father was not surprised. Women were finicky creatures, given to unusual actions. He took over. He even prepared our lunches. The sandwiches that Gerry and I brought to school became one of only two types: cold hamburger with hamburger grease spread on the bread, or else baloney. Cold, sweet tea in bottles whose tops always leaked. Gone were the pieces of fruit from whatever was in season, and gone the slices of sweet yellow cake that she used to bake once a week.

We lived in an awful silence with occasional edicts from my father, who understood none of the rules of life in Canada. He might accuse us of dallying on the way home from school, and then keep us in the basement all weekend, unless it was to go to church on Sunday morning. No more radio serials were allowed. They were all too morbid, except for Amos and Andy, whose southern drawl he could not understand, but whose intonation reminded him of the slow-talking farmers from back home.

In the morning, we rose to find my mother already in the scrubby front yard, with Tom in the carriage or playpen. Usually, my father had already gone to work, but he made sandwiches for my mother and two Thermoses of warm condensed milk so she merely had to fill the empty bottles for Tom. She watched us depart down the street towards school, and she was still there when we came back at the end of the school day. It was our job to count the empty bottles when we came home from school, and to make sure that there had been at least three given to Tom during the day. That was my father's line of measurement. As long as Tom was fed during the day and his diapers were changed, there was no need to call the doctor and pay him four dollars for the visit. After we counted the empty milk bottles, I carried Tom, and Gerry held my mother's arm and walked her inside.

'Turn on the radio as soon as you come in,' my father said, 'but don't turn on any of the serials. Make sure she has music, fun music, dance music. I don't want to come home and find her crying over some sad song.'

She hardly ever talked to us. Usually she just stared into the distance like a sailor marooned on a desert island. Her absence marooned us as well, but we were not exactly alone on a desert island. Living with my father in charge of our lives was like living with Captain Bligh on a spaceship — he may have understood nothing of the workings of the world he was in, but he still commanded with an assurance that was all the more dreadful for his ignorance.

'Why do I see you catching baseballs with your left hand?' my father asked Gerry.

'Because I don't have a glove.'

'I know you don't have a glove, but that doesn't answer my question.'

'Because if I had a glove, it'd be on my left hand.'

'But you don't have a glove.'

'Dad.'

'If you don't have a glove, then catch with your right. That way, you won't have to waste time transferring the ball to your right hand.'

'Dad, you've never played baseball in your life. There was no baseball in Europe.'

'Don't argue with me. I don't want to see you catching the ball with your left hand any more.'

The frightening part was that he actually might check up on us. We could be out in the flatter parts of the abandoned farm fields where we played baseball, and he might show up from among the apple trees, sucking on his pipe and making sure Gerry was catching the baseball with his right hand. Then he would bring us home for a dinner of fried hamburgers and fried potatoes. Hot hamburgers for supper, cold hamburgers for lunch, and baloney and eggs fried in hamburger grease for breakfast.

*

One morning my father roused Gerry and me from bed.

'Boys, your mother isn't feeling well.'

My father was still wearing his wool hat with the earflaps bent down even though it was already mid-June. He was usually out of the house before we got up for breakfast, but the contractor who picked up him and the other men for work had to run a few loads of lumber in his pickup truck first. It was a warm morning. My mother and Tom were already outside on the scrub front lawn.

'No kidding,' said Gerry. We could smell the hamburger grease on our sandwiches all the way from the kitchen table.

'I'm going to pick you boys up at lunch, and we're going to buy your mother a surprise.'

'I've got a big ball game planned for lunch,' said Gerry.

'You'll have to miss it.'

Gerry scowled.

'Just don't come to the classroom, okay? We'll meet you at the school gate when they let us out.'

'I'll have to talk to your teacher to tell her you'll miss the afternoon.'

'I'll tell her.'

'What are we going to buy, Dad?' I asked. 'A dog?'

'Not a dog.'

'A dog would make her feel better. It could look after Tom when she went to the store.'

'I said we're not buying a dog. It's a surprise.' He lumbered up the steps with his pipe in his teeth when he heard the contractor beep his horn at the roadside.

'What do you think he's going to buy?' I asked Gerry on the way to school.

'Something stupid.'

'Like what?'

'Like a housecoat. I just hope he doesn't come anywhere near the school. I can't stand it when he talks to the principal.'

Gerry was mulling over a fight he had had on the way home from school the day before. He had bloodied the nose of his opponent, and then done the same to another kid who had tried to help the loser.

My father was sitting in the principal's office when we walked past it on the way out for lunch. He was wearing his grey baggy pants with the patched knees, a grey wool coat, and had his hat on his knee. The earflaps on the hat were still turned down, and the hat sat on his knees like an awkward cat. Sawdust clung to the back of his coat, where he could not see it, and he had his unlit pipe between his teeth.

'Oh, shit,' said Gerry.

It was the first time I had ever heard him swear in the school building, and it made me nervous. School was not exactly the same as church, but it was not far off. A picture of the Sacred Heart of Jesus hung in the hall, and Mother Leone had a massive cross hanging on the wall behind her. This small black-robed nun in the gold-rimmed glasses was leaning towards my father, trying to understand what he was saying through his thick accent.

'Three years old, you understand? When shooting and bombing start, we take little one, Dave, and we go into ditch. "Gerry," we shout. What he do? He climb on back of horse and talk in its ear so it don't get scared. Bullets fly, hitting road from planes, and all refugees in ditch crying and shouting, and little boy right in middle talking to horse. He afraid of nothing but me.'

'The janitor has some boxing gloves,' said Mother Leone. 'Maybe Gerry could burn off a little of his energy by boxing with the older boys after school.' Mother Leone was a modern nun. She had seen

The Bells of St. Mary's, and *Boys Town*. From these movies she had learned a troublesome boy could be saved by music or sports, and Gerry did not have much of a singing voice. They had thrown him out of the choir loft when he farted after each of the repetitions in 'Holy, Holy, Holy! Lord God Almighty.'

'Good idea. We think about it. Bye, bye, Mother.'

'Where are we going?' I asked.

'To the bus. Let's cut through here.'

There was an empty lot on the way to the bus stop, and my father took us in there, and made us walk behind a high mound of dirt. He picked up a thin stick, and told Gerry to turn around. My father ran one of his monologues as he switched Gerry across the rump.

'Get into fights after school, will you? That crazy old nun wants to get you into boxing gloves so your face will be smashed up by the time you're sixteen. With the face on you then, you'll turn out to be a criminal. No more fighting, you hear me? Next time there's trouble, you run. Call it practice for track and field.'

Gerry was white at the jaw from clenching his teeth together in fury. The thin stick hardly did any damage against Gerry's rump, but there was a chance someone from school might see him getting beaten.

We walked the rest of the way to the bus, and my father told us to eat our sandwiches as we rode downtown. I wanted to eat as fast as I could, so I would be finished before we passed the meat-packing plant. Now that the weather was warm, you could gag as you passed it, and if there was a little kid on the bus, he might puke. Gerry stuffed his bag between the seats and left it there in protest, but my father didn't notice. If he had, he might have eaten the sandwiches himself.

We knew the Eaton's department store, because we went down there at Christmas to look at the window displays. My father made all three of us get into a single wedge of the revolving door so we did not get separated, and then he marched forward into the women's wear department.

'Hey, Dad. This place isn't for us,' said Gerry. He would have liked to maintain his silence, but he was not going to walk into women's wear with his father. It was bad enough whenever our mother took us into one of those stores and made us wait on a chair as she tried on bra after bra in the change room. It seemed indecent to us. But it could have been worse. We could have had an older sister. Gerry and I had been in houses where we were horrified to find nylon stockings hanging from the shower rod. To us, it had seemed immoral, as bad as having a bathroom without a door.

'Come on, come on,' my father said. 'I'm going to need your advice.'

It was bad through skirts, worse in blouses, and almost unbearable in women's underwear. But the worst was yet to come. There was a fake trellis set up in the corner of the room, and cloth roses were twined through the grille in the entrance to women's furs.

'I can't go in there,' said Gerry.

'You can, and you will.'

My father still had on his hat with the earflaps down, even though Gerry and I were already sweating in our spring jackets. Bits of sawdust fell off his pants. I walked behind him and tried to step on the flecks of it on the floor. I hoped it would stick to the bottom of my shoes so the woman behind the fake marble desk would not see it. She wore a dark pink dress, and she had a corsage of gold-coloured roses pinned to her lapel. There was no one else in the showroom, but she did not look up from the pad on which she was writing figures.

My father stood for a while, but when the saleslady still did not look up, he sat down in the white wrought-iron chair across from her.

'Hello, Mrs! You busy?'

'Miss.'

'Vas?'

'Miss Trethewey is my name. Can I help you?'

Of all the mysteries of English, the pronunciation of 'th' was the most arcane to my father. He said it was a silly, effeminate sound, and he refused to say it.

'Okay, Miss Trudy, we want mink coat.'

'I see.'

She studied us for a while, and tapped her pencil on the table as she did so. The damned sawdust kept rising up off my father's coat and hovering in the air. Miss Trethewey watched the flecks in quiet amazement, as if they were lice that had learned to fly.

'These coats are very expensive,' she said finally, and I sensed a hint of kindness in her voice. Anyone else would have sent for the security guard.

'How much?'

'They start at several hundred dollars.'

'Not cheap ones. No rabbit fur for my wife. How much good fur coat?'

'It all depends. You might have to pay about a thousand dollars.'

Gerry and I looked at each other. On the radio serials, men killed for that much money.

'No problem.'

We looked at each other again. Maybe our father did not cut wood for a living. Maybe he murdered carpenters.

'And would you pay in cash?' Miss Trethewey was trying not to smile, and that was one thing that Gerry could not bear.

'My dad wants to see some coats. Haven't you got any?'

Miss Trethewey wavered for a moment, and she even put her hand on the white telephone on her desk. The phone impressed me. I had never seen a white phone. She looked at him carefully. He was sitting in the chair like an English gentleman in the lobby of the Waldorf Astoria. His clothes seemed out of place, but he smiled confidently.

'Just a moment,' said Miss Trethewey, and she stood up and walked through the satin curtains over a door in the back of the salon.

'How come they don't have any racks of coats?' I asked.

'It's almost summer,' my father said. 'Maybe they're sold out.'

'Just buy the most expensive coat, okay, Dad?' Gerry said. 'And if she gets smart with us again, I'll kick out her legs from under her, and we'll be out of the store before anyone knows the difference.'

My father cuffed Gerry affectionately across the head just above his ear.

'You can't kick the legs out from under a woman. Save that for the hockey rink.'

Miss Trethewey returned with a model in a white fur coat.

'Send her back,' my father said with a dismissive wave of his hand. 'White is too hard to clean.'

Miss Trethewey's face began to look a little haggard. 'What colour would you like to look at?'

'Fur.'

'Yes, but what colour fur?'

'You work in a fur store and you don't know what colour fur is?'

'Just a moment.'

My father had Mona the model walk past us in half a dozen different coats before he saw one that he liked. He made the model stand where she was, and stepped out to the ladies' underwear department beyond the rose-covered grille. He picked a thirtyish woman with blond hair who was looking at camisoles.

'Hey, Mrs. Come here please.'

It astonished me when she let go of the silk that she had been running through her fingers and came up to my father's side. Maybe it was the lack of doubt in his voice that made her do it. That and the knowledge that she was safe in an Eaton's store.

'Your husband buy you this coat — you like?'

'I'm not married.'

'He wants to know if you like the coat,' Gerry translated into more understandable English.

'Sure I like the coat. Does he want to buy it for me?'

All of the women giggled at this, and my father smiled widely to show his tobacco-stained front teeth and the gold ones at the side.

'It's for my mom,' Gerry said fiercely.

'Lucky woman,' said the blond. 'She'll love it.'

'Okay, wrap up,' my father said.

Miss Trethewey called my father's bank manager to make sure his cheque was good. I half expected the police to show up and take us all away as frauds, but Miss Trethewey hung up the phone and asked Mona to wrap the coat.

'Now, boys,' said Miss Trethewey, 'your father has just bought your mother a wonderful gift, and it will be up to you to help your mother take care of it. Does she speak English?'

Gerry bristled.

'She speaks English and German, and French, and Italian, and Latin, and Greek, and...'

'English alone will do. Just in case she has any difficulty reading the fur-care booklet that comes with the coat, I want you boys to remind her that a fur should always be kept in cold storage over the summer.'

'We live in a basement,' I said. 'It's never too hot down there, even in the summer.'

'You live in a basement?' The question was polite, but Gerry could read undertones.

'Yeah,' he said. 'It's freezing down there this time of year. The only thing is, we have mildew growing up the side of the wall. Do you think it'll affect the coat?'

'Mildew?'

'I guess we could get mom to scrape it off the wall, if that would help,' said Gerry.

Miss Trethewey looked to my father for guidance through this conversation, but the words were whipping by too fast for him to understand. He just smiled, and stuck the pipe between his teeth and sucked on the empty bowl until the nicotine in the stem made a sickening gurgle.

The box was big and heavy, but Gerry wanted to carry it. Miss Trethewey slipped it into an Eaton's shopping bag for us before we left.

On the way back home in the bus, Gerry sat with the box on his knees, and wouldn't even let me hold it for a while. He thought of something to ask my father just as we came upon the meat-packing plant, but it smelled so bad, that he breathed through his mouth until we had passed the foul odour.

'Hey, Dad,' he said.

'What.'

'Did you ever kill anybody?'

My father thought about it for a while. 'I'm not sure. I had a gun during the war, and I fired it a few times.'

Gerry winked at me, and he nodded towards the box that held the coat.

That night, my father added some canned peas to the dinner, so we had something besides potatoes and meat to stir around the hamburger grease on our plates. Gerry was trying not to give away the secret, so he kept his face in a scowl that all of us were used to. Tom was starting to crawl around the floor, and all of us had to sit still at the table in case he was somewhere near the legs of our chairs. My father was telling stories about the idiots he worked with, and my mother, as usual, was stirring the food on her plate into one big greasy mass. It was only when we had finished and my father leaned back to light his pipe, that he nodded to Gerry to go and get the box. I moved the dishes out of the way, and Gerry brought in the bag and set it on the table. The Eaton's shopping bag looked so good that he never bothered to pull the box out first.

'What's this?'

My father just puffed away at his pipe.

'It's a present for you, Mom,' said Gerry.

'A present?'

'Open it up.'

My mother was in some distant place. Gerry pushed the bag closer to her.

'Open it up.'

She stared at the package for a long time, and then slipped the box out of the Eaton's bag and folded it carefully as she studied the lid.

She reached forward tentatively, and then fumbled with the box. Gerry took the folded bag out of her hands. Then she could not untie the ribbon. Gerry offered to cut it with a knife, but my mother persisted in working at the knot. When she opened the lid of the box, she stared at the fur uncomprehendingly.

'Take it out, Mom,' said Gerry.

'What is it?'

'A fur coat. You can't really tell what it looks like until you take it out.'

We studied her face for signs. I expected a beatific look, something like the face on the Blessed Virgin Mary as she ascended into heaven. But Mary's hair was always hidden under a shawl like the nuns wore. My mother's hair was pinned at the sides, with loose strands hanging out. My mother did not take the coat out of the box. Instead, she just looked at it for a very long time, and the only sound was my father sucking on his pipe and blowing out great clouds of tobacco smoke.

'Mom, you've got to take it out of the box,' said Gerry, and he reached forward to help her.

My mother's hand shot out and held Gerry's fingers away from the surface.

'Don't touch it,' she said sharply, and pulled his hand away.

'How much did this cost?' she asked my father.

'I can't tell you. It's a secret.'

'One thousand and forty-two dollars,' Gerry said proudly. 'Can you believe it?'

'Are you out of your mind?' my mother asked. She was so agitated that she stood up and began to walk around the basement floor. When Tom held up his hands to be carried, she swung him up to her hip and kept on pacing.

'Nobody touch that coat. Gerry, you wash your hands and put the lid back on. That's right, don't look at me with that ridiculous face of yours. Now you,' she said, and she turned on my father, 'God must have been having a bad day when he created you. Do you want us to be paying this off for the rest of our lives? The children don't even have any decent summer shoes, and you're throwing money around as if you'd just made some big black market deal. This is so stupid, that I don't even know what to say. Why I had to choose such a lunatic for a husband is totally beyond me. It must have been all those bombs dropping on the city day in and day out that addled my brains. What was I thinking of? I mean, just look at how we live! It's sad to be poor like this, but what you've done tonight is so scatterbrained, so moronic, so deranged that I might as well call up the asylum and have them take you away. But before I do that, you're going to take this box right back where you got it and get that money back. Then you're going to march right back to the bank and take the mortgage off this house.'

'Who says I took out a mortgage?'

'Where else could you have gotten the money?'

'Anyway, the lady at the store won't take it back.'

My mother froze.

'What do you mean?'

'She said they wouldn't accept it back if we returned it. That's why I was so careful about getting the right size.'

'Simpleton. You bought this at Eaton's, didn't you? Every idiot knows that they take their goods back.'

'I can't do it. The woman in the store would laugh at me.'

'You incompetent. I'll take it back, and I'll get an apology out of her as well for dealing with the simple-minded.'

'I think you should keep it,' my father said.

'Not another word, or I'll really blow up.'

She had spoken in the loudest voice we had heard in weeks, but my father had sat through it all unperturbed. She went on calling him various names until he stood up, buttoned the collar at his neck, and went out to the shack out back to do a little maintenance work on his tools. With him out of the way, my mother turned on us.

'You two clear the table. Gerry, you wash the dishes and Dave will dry. Put some water on the stove as well. I want to wash your hair tonight.'

Later that evening, my mother sent us all out to buy some mock chicken loaf for our sandwiches the next day. My father whistled tunelessly as the grocer cut eight slices off the square loaf. Why was he so untroubled? Gerry looked angry, but that was normal. I drifted to the cash counter at the front and looked at the candy display: white roman nougats with jellies embedded in them, big two-cent jawbreakers, and waxed tubes filled with sweet, coloured water. The real mystery lay in the three-cent grab-bags that the grocer filled himself. Sometimes he even slipped in small chocolate bars. Gerry read my mind.

'You ask him,' he said. 'Maybe he still has some of that mortgage money in his pocket.'

I waited until he had his wallet out to pay the grocer, and then I asked him for six cents.

'Nope,' my father said, as he slapped his wallet shut, 'money for candy is a waste, and I never waste my money.'

The Man Who Read Voltaire

Gerry and I were marooned on the concrete front porch in long sleeves and ties. We weren't allowed to roll up our sleeves because we might lose the cuff links, and besides, the sleeves of our starched shirts would look wrinkled when we rolled them back down again. My mother bought the neck sizes big enough to last two years, so the collars drooped low and showed the white crew-neck T-shirts below. We had clip-on bow ties, but no jackets. We looked like a tap dance team at the church basement amateur night.

'They're only boys,' my father had said. 'What do they need jackets for?'

'I want them to look nice.'

'Just clean their fingernails and make sure they don't talk too much when the guests get here. I don't want them yapping the whole day.'

'I can get two jackets for twenty-seven dollars at Bi-Rite.'

'Money again. That's all you ever talk about.'

My father had stuffed his pipe, and that was the end of the conversation.

That morning, my mother fell purposefully to her knees with a painful thud. Painful to my ears, anyway. She was wearing an old flowered cotton dress that I still remembered on her at church only two years before. Now it looked like a nightgown she had been wearing too long. She hunched over the floor with the rag in one hand and the paste wax in the other, and started to rub the floor in tight, angry circles.

'Go sit on the porch and wait. If they show up early, God forbid, you run right in here and let me know. Otherwise, stay out of the house. And don't step on the yard either. I don't want your shoes to get dirty.'

It was hot on the porch.

'What if he's just like the Old Man?' Gerry asked. He had started to call our father the Old Man, but I couldn't bring myself to do the same. Gerry was like that. Starting things that worried me a bit, and then looking to see if I'd follow, ready to sneer if I didn't.

'There can't be two like him,' I said.

'But they're brothers, so how different could they be? A younger brother is just kind of an imitation of the older one, so the odds are that he's going to be like the Old Man, only more.'

My father was puttering around the shed in the back because he too had been banished from the house. My mother had caught him sneaking shots of whisky right after breakfast.

'Eight years you haven't seen your brother, so you want to be dead drunk when he arrives. What a genius you are.'

'I only had one drink.'

'Liar.'

'Two.'

'Liar.'

His face became a mask of hurt forbearance. She nicked the label on the bottle of Five Star whisky with her thumbnail, and then she checked the seal on the other bottle to make sure it wasn't broken.

But she expelled him from the house for his second misdemeanour, the salting of cabbage.

'You don't even know how to cook,' she said, wagging a wooden spoon like a long finger.

'What's to know? Turn on the oven and put in the food. Add salt.'

In some arenas, very, very few, my father could not win against my mother. He tucked his suit pants into the tops of his black boots and went out to the back yard.

We stayed in the front yard, where off-cuts of lumber still lay around, and the thin wild grass and weeds had been beaten down to dust by me and Gerry. The only other house on the street belonged to the Taylors, and theirs was an oasis of lawn and garden. The rest of the street was being dug up by contractors as they built houses in our new subdivision. Small contractors appeared at the dusty lots with pickup trucks of Italians, and Ukrainians, and Poles. Sometimes the men would show up at our door to ask for glasses of water. The clipped green lawn of the Taylors' yard was as good as a No Trespassing sign to them.

Our town of Weston lay in the shadow of Toronto, and our new suburb fattened itself on the old farms and orchards as Toronto loomed, waiting for us to gain enough weight to be taken to the slaughter.

My father had finally finished the shell of the house, and then he rushed to make sure the hardwood floors were in and the walls painted. He ran out of money for the interior doors. We all moved up from the basement where we had been living for almost a year, and Gerry and I shared a small bedroom beside my parents' room on the ground floor. The second floor was going to be rented, and we were not allowed up there in case we put smudgy fingerprints on the walls. He managed to buy one door for the bathroom when he found out our uncle was coming to visit, but he had lost the pins to the hinges and slipped in straight nails instead. There was no need to lock the door because half the time it wouldn't open properly anyway.

Gerry and I sat on the concrete front porch for two hours, as the sun swung around and put our east-facing porch into the shade. My mother brought out sandwiches once. She almost caught Gerry urinating off the porch into the dust of the yard.

'I wish they'd get here,' I said.

'Yeah, but Detroit is a long way away.'

'Six and a half hours.'

We still did not have our citizenship papers, and could not hope to go to Detroit to visit my uncle for years. In the grit of our new suburb, Gerry and I longed for America. That was where real life happened. All of our favourite radio shows came from there. Kids in the radio serials ate candy bars we never even saw in the stores — Fifth Avenue and Three Musketeers. It was the kind of place where a man in a cape could fly over the city. In Weston, a man in a cape would be arrested.

Gerry's teacher let him borrow the class atlas for one night, and together with my mother we had found Detroit.

'It's so close on the map,' I said.

'Everything's close on the map, stupid,' said Gerry. 'Look, I can walk my fingers down to New York and see the Yankees. Down the coast to Florida and get some oranges, big juicy ones that I pick off the tree. Across to Texas where I wrestle a couple of longhorns.'

'To California,' my mother continued, 'where I stand on the beach and look across the Pacific to Hawaii and China.'

'You could swim all the way to Japan,' my father said from his armchair. He didn't bother to look at the map with us. 'Right to some other DP camp outside Hiroshima.'

We'd been sitting on the front porch a long time when our mother came out and joined us after she locked the back door to make sure my father could not sneak in for another drink. She had changed into a new dress and imitation pearl earrings and a hat she usually wore to church. It was a straw hat with a white veil folded up above the brim.

'You going out?' Gerry asked.

'No.'

'What's the hat for?'

'I want to look nice.'

'You going to wear the hat indoors?'

'Just until your uncle gets here. I'll take it off when we go in.'

'That's stupid.'

'If you were a girl, you'd understand.'

'If I was a girl, I'd cut my throat.'

'You know something? A pipe would suit you.'

Gerry didn't get it, but I laughed. She looked down the street where a perpetual haze of dust hung in the air from the construction that went on during the week. It got so that the taste of it in my mouth made me think of home on my way back from school. It was a strange kind of dust that was so light it never settled, but it was scratchy too, and I could always feel it between my collar and my neck, especially now that I was wearing a tie.

'When your uncle gets here, I don't want you to badger him,' said my mother. 'I want you to entertain your cousins.'

'Yeah, yeah,' Gerry said. 'Just our luck that the only cousins we have are girls.'

'Tease those girls once, and I'll spank you right in front of your uncle.'

Gerry sneered.

'Besides, the girls are both a couple of years older than you. They could probably beat you up if they wanted.'

Gerry ground his teeth.

'Just be thankful you've got anyone at all. Your uncle and aunt are the only relatives you have on this continent, and if anything happened to your father and me, they're the ones who would take care of you.'

'So what could happen?'

'Anything. One night during the war, your father answered the door and someone stuck the barrel of a rifle inside.'

'What did he do?'

'Your father had a revolver in his other hand, so he fired through the door.'

'Did he kill the guy?' Gerry asked.

'No. The man ran away.'

'Too bad.'

'Your father and his brother made a deal during the war,' my mother went on. 'If something happened to them, we'd raise their girls, and if anything happened to us, they'd raise you boys. It almost happened too.'

'What?'

'They got caught in Dresden.'

Neither of us knew if Dresden was a city or a country, but I didn't care and Gerry hated to ask questions. We'd heard the war stories a hundred times.

But I wondered what it would be like to have sisters. Older sisters probably did not beat you up. If they were old enough, they might even buy you things. I had a vision of blond sympathy that would take all my share of the housework.

The heat was rising up off the street in wavy lines. Between the dust and the heat, I felt like I was in a dream when the brown car with the running boards glided up beside the ditch at the end of our yard, and stopped as silently as a ship slipping into anchorage. The woman in the passenger seat wore a hat with a veil lowered over her face. She turned to look at us from under her veil, and she raised a gloved hand against the window in a gesture so small it could hardly be called a wave.

'Go around the back and get your father,' my mother said to Gerry.

'Why can't Dave go?'

'Just do it.'

Gerry spat into the dust at the side of the porch, dropped his head between hunched shoulders, and went around the back, kicking up as much dust as he could onto his new leather shoes.

There was no crunch of gravel under his shoes as my uncle stepped out of the car and waved at us over its roof. Thin as the Thin Man, he wore a white shirt and tie, but a long one, not a bow tie. He walked around to the passenger side of the car and opened the door. A slim woman in a suit came out of the car. Both of them had cigarettes in their hands.

My father came round the corner of the house with Gerry at his heels. He had not bothered to take off his rubber boots, and his pants were bunched up at the knees.

'What, so old?' my father shouted across the yard as he approached them. 'Can this be my brother, this old man who's losing his hair? And what happened to the girl he married? Who's this stocky matron he brought along? You must have to tie two belts together to make it around that waist.'

Beneath the veil, a masked frown played over my aunt's face.

'Look who hasn't changed at all,' my aunt said. 'Eight years and one war later, and he's still talking like a smart-mouthed peasant boy.'

She was not fat at all, but my father never cared what he said. My mother told us that God was going to be in for an earful when my father died.

'Where are the girls?' my mother asked.

'Measles. We had to leave them at home with their grandmother.'

'Poor girls.'

I could feel their weightlessness. Their feet were only lightly fixed to the ground, and I was afraid that if I breathed too hard they would blow away like angels.

'So these are the boys,' my uncle said. He walked up to us and kissed us both on the lips. His smell of tobacco was different from my father's. The American cigarettes left an exotic aroma, as if he'd just come back from Egypt.

'Do you smoke?' he asked.

I hesitated, but Gerry nodded immediately.

My uncle walked back to the car, and took two packages of Lucky Strikes off the seat.

'Here you are, boys.'

I looked anxiously at my mother and father, but they were both smiling, so I ripped off the cellophane and opened up the package. Chocolate cigarettes. Gerry and I put them into our mouths, and we all walked into the house.

Visitors to the house had always been a mixed blessing. It was the only time there was ginger ale in the house, reserved for the highballs of rye and ginger that the women sipped while the men took their shots neat. But the women were generous, and they let us pour glasses of ginger ale for ourselves, although some of them clung to the notion that ice cubes were bad for the throat, and one of my mother's friends had dug the cubes out of my glass with her red-painted fingernails. The 'mix,' as they called all pop, was a double blessing, because we could sneak some of the bottles to the store when the adults were all hung over the next day, and get the refund.

The men were less predictable than the women. They might come bearing gifts of Schneiders salami or boxes of chocolate-coated cherries that ran a sticky liquid onto our hands when we bit them in half. The fools among them, as far as Gerry and I were concerned, brought flowers. The happy drinkers might give us money for ice cream after the meal, or send us out to buy cigarettes and let us keep the change. But most of the men ignored us altogether, indifferent to our merit, indifferent to our longing for gifts. They told long and boring stories about adventures with the Red Army, or clashes with the Nazi labour battalions that combed the refugee columns for able-bodied men and women to dig earthworks against the Russians. Deep in their cups, the men banged on tables to show anguish over the families they had left behind, or else they described in infinite detail the hunger of everyday life in the refugee camps before the British or Americans arrived. These stories were boring enough in themselves, but sometimes a man might begin to cry at the memories enlivened by alcohol, and then Gerry and I despised them with all our hearts. What did we care for the sorrows and longings of grown men who could not recognize the longing of children who sat at the same table?

But my uncle and his wife were not ordinary guests.

My aunt walked beside me as my father showed them the rooms he had built, and as she walked, she rested her hand gently on my shoulder, and I did not dare to look at it for fear that she might take it away. Women all smelled of powders and hair spray and perfume, but the scent of my aunt was different from all the others. It was powerful but elusive, and I did not want to take myself away from it. It smelled faintly of citrus, as if she had driven through an orange grove in an open car, yet smoky too, as if she had spent the night in a jazz cafe where Black men blew strange sounds though horns that said nothing about our lives in Canada, or the lives of our parents in Europe.

My aunt refused to laugh at my father's lame jokes, and she walked into each room as if she could own it if she chose. Her hips swung more than the hips of Canadian women. She had raised the veil of her hat to kiss us all, but then let the veil drop again as we walked through the house. I did not dare to look at her full in the face, but I stole glances at her nevertheless, and she seemed far younger than any mother I had ever known. This was a woman who must have been lucky enough to work in an office. She neither cooked nor cleaned, nor made things with her hands, but went to a place that was clean and sat at a desk all day and answered the phone and got paid for it.

Back downstairs, after the tour, my aunt pinned up the veil of her hat, and then I took my father's matches to light the first of many Parliaments that she smoked in the house. Even Tom fell under her spell, and he crawled across the floor and pawed at my aunt's legs until she lifted him onto her lap. Tom reached up for the gauze veil on her hat and pulled it back down over her face. Like a child before God, he had no fear, and he stared at her face through the veil with his lips turned into a tiny 'o'.

Gerry talked all the time until my father told him to shut up. As usual, he grew sullen, but he did not leave, because he too had fallen under our visitors' spell. The adults talked without stopping, mostly in our language but sometimes with English incantations like 'Singer,' 'Ford,' or 'Westinghouse.' Sometimes I just watched my uncle and aunt as they gestured with movements far smaller than the European ones we knew, yet firmer and more knowing than the flapping from the elbows that was the Canadian norm. My uncle had brought a bottle of cognac from America, and he showed my father how to make a *Nikolashka* by putting a few grains of sugar and coffee on a lemon wedge, and then biting down on it after taking the cognac straight up.

When my aunt went up to the bathroom, I waited for her at the bottom of the stairs so I could have a moment alone as she came back down. When she was done, I heard her try the door, but it was stuck.

I was at the top of the stairs in a moment.

'The door sticks sometimes,' I said. 'You have to lift it up a bit as you pull.'

I could hear her trying, but it did no good.

'Stand back,' I said, and I twisted the knob with my hand, lifted as much as I could, and threw my weight against the door. It resisted for a moment, and then gave way suddenly with a splintering of the veneer where it met the jamb. The door came open and I flew into the arms of my aunt. She caught me with both arms and held me to her breast, and I could feel the movement in her as she began to laugh.

'My hero,' she said through her laughter, and she held me back at arm's length. 'My hero,' she said again, and she led me into her bedroom and let go of my hand. From her purse she took an American dollar and placed it in my palm.

'Father's going to be furious about the door.'

'That's nothing,' she said, shrugging. 'I'll tell him I did it.'

I was ready to march into hell for her.

After dinner, my uncle took Gerry and me out in his car, and the two of us sat up as straight as we could so any kids on the street could see how fine we were.

'How many horsepower?' asked Gerry.

'I'm not sure.'

'It's got to be close to two hundred. Just listen to that purr. Eight cylinders or six?'

'Six.'

'That's okay for now. You can get eight in your next car.'

'Six is enough,' I said.

'Shut up,' said Gerry. 'Can't you see I'm talking to my uncle?'

My uncle spoke in English as soon as we stepped out of the car, and Gerry winked at me, appreciative of his linguistic wisdom. In public, we spoke English. We walked in together to Kresge's, and he stood for a moment on the dull wooden floorboards, getting his bearings.

'Come on, boys.' He led us straight to the glass candy bins, but there was no one there. My uncle took out a Parliament and lighted it, and then rapped on the glass bin with his wedding ring. An old woman with tight white curls walked purposefully to her place behind the counter. She wore a blue smock and an expression unsweetened by the candies she sold.

'Thank you, madam,' said my uncle. 'How are you this afternoon?'

The stern face softened a little.

'My feet are killing me, if you want to know the truth.'

'It's almost the end of the day. Please give the boys a pound of candy each. You boys choose what you like.'

He stood back and finished his cigarette as Gerry and I agonized over our selection, and after he paid for us, he saluted the woman with a finger brought loosely to his forehead.

She smiled.

'Where did you learn your English?' Gerry asked in the car, where we held on to our pound bags of candy, afraid to open them because we had never had so much wealth before. We were now speaking in our own language again.

'I studied in Germany and France when I was a student,' my uncle said, 'and once you have those two languages, English is not so hard. You just put German and French into a bag, add some absurdity and ridiculous spelling, and English comes spilling right out.'

Back home, they ate, and they smoked, and they drank right into the evening and on into the night. As it grew dark around nine o'clock, my father's voice became louder and louder and his face more flushed. They talked of prewar politics, and the coming war between Russia and America, and at nine-thirty my father stood up from the table and walked away. My mother and uncle and aunt talked on, and an hour later my father returned to the table, but he did not sit down. He was dressed in his boxer shorts and an undershirt that looped low under his arms. He looked dazed.

'What, still up?' he asked.

'Go back to bed, or put on some clothes,' my mother said.

'Like drunks, all of you, sitting up into the small hours. Everybody go to bed!'

It was the voice that Gerry and I knew all too well. He was taking control of the situation again, like a madman who takes over a sinking ship.

'Nice underwear,' my aunt said.

'I told you all to go to bed. I won't have this house turning into a den of drunkards.'

I was afraid for my aunt. If she provoked him, he would rage even more.

'You go back to bed right now,' my uncle said sharply. 'You heard me. To bed. And not another word out of your ridiculous mouth.'

My father swayed as if he had been punched.

'To bed!' my uncle repeated, and my father turned on his heel, and walked through the dark kitchen to his bedroom.

Gerry and I stared at one another in awe.

In our new small bedroom, Gerry and I had separate beds, and when we talked, we had to do it very quietly, because if our father heard us, he would come storming in. He had once caught Gerry with a flashlight and a book under the covers, and he had thrown the flashlight across the room in a rage, and broken the glass and the bulb. Gerry said he was an idiot because it was cheaper to replace the bulb than the batteries, and who needed the glass on the front anyway?

'He told off the Old Man,' I said, rolling the words around in my mouth because they gave me so much pleasure.

'Yeah. When push comes to shove, the older brother is the one with the authority.'

'You said he was going to be just like the Old Man.'

'Naw. The Old Man must have been adopted or something. Maybe he was raised by wolves, and they found him in the fields when he was a little kid.'

'I wish I could go back with them.'

'He's got two daughters. You want to live with girls?'

'I'd put up with it.'

'You'd like it. You could try on their nylons.'

I threw my pillow across the room in the darkness.

'Great! Two pillows,' said Gerry.

As we lay in the darkness, we could hear the talk that still came from the dining room. My father's snoring from the next bedroom was loud and irregular, and sometimes he muttered in his sleep, as if he knew they were saying evil things about him.

Gerry was up first, and I came into the kitchen to find him washing the crumbs of a napoleon cake off his lips.

'Are you nuts? We have to go to communion.'

'Shut up.'

He washed the crumbs from his face just as my father came into the kitchen. His hair was standing up in tufts, and his eyes were bleary, and he was still in his boxer shorts and undershirt. He nodded at us, washed his face and smoothed his hair with his hand, and then started towards the stairs.

'Dad,' said Gerry, 'you better put on some clothes if you're going up there.'

'They're family,' my father said. 'What do they care?'

He went heavily up the steps, like Frankenstein's monster. We could hear him stop and stand at the open doorway.

'So what, are you living or dead?'

Gerry and I heard everything from the bottom of the steps. There was hardly any furniture upstairs, and the sounds bounced off the empty walls. We could hear the springs creak as my father sat down on the edge of their bed.

'What time is it?' my uncle asked.

'Seven-thirty,' my aunt said.

'I thought maybe he'd grown out of this by now.'

'He never changes, no matter what continent he lives on.'

'Enough philosophy,' my father roared. 'Get up and dress. We have to be at church by nine.'

'Why the early mass?' my aunt asked.

'Because we have to take communion, and I get too hungry if we go any later.'

'I'll go to mass for your sake,' my uncle said, 'but I'm not taking communion.'

'You have to,' my father said. 'Think of the two boys down there. They like you. They admire you, and if you don't go to communion, you're going to make them fry in hell.'

'I wish you'd stop with all that superstition. You sound like someone out of the last century.'

'I won't argue with you,' my father said. 'I don't argue on Sundays. Just do as I say for the good of the boys.'

Gerry and I raced away from the bottom of the steps as our father came down. He whistled tunelessly in his dry mouth.

Oh, the agony of Catholic hangover on a Sunday morning before communion. Not even water passed the lips of my father, although I suspected that my aunt and uncle drank freely from the tap after they had closed the bathroom door behind them.

Gerry and I were used to hung over adults. Our lives were filled with them, for all of my father's friends drank the same way he did — to oblivion — to the bottom of any bottle on the table. We grew wise in avoiding them on mornings after, especially on Sunday mornings. My mother claimed that aspirin and water were not food, but my father did not believe it.

In the alcove between the door and the bottom of the steps, my uncle whispered to us, conspiratorially.

'When you get older, promise me you will do one thing.'

'Anything,' Gerry whispered back.

'Promise me you will read Voltaire.'

He paused, and looked worried, as if he had said too much.

'But promise me another thing. Wait until you are twenty-one before you do it.'

My father was uncommonly gay that Sunday morning. He looked as if he had snatched two savages for the faith, and he held his hand lightly on his brother's back as the two of them lined up for communion. I watched carefully to see if the wafer would fly from my atheistic uncle's mouth, but it went inside his lips just as it did for all the others.

My mother had managed to hide half a bottle the night before, so when they sat down to eat after mass, the reinjection of alcohol brightened them again, and I willed them to sit there until I could summon my courage. When it came time for them to leave, Gerry and I volunteered to put their bags in the trunk, and my uncle gave us the keys to do it.

I told Gerry my plans.

He went red in the face as soon as I explained.

'I'm going too,' he said.

'You can't. Who's going to close the trunk?'

'Then I'll go instead. I'm the one who's older.'

'I thought of it first.'

'I don't care. The Old Man is going to be pissed off, and he's going to take it out on whoever gets left behind.'

I left the trunk open, and walked back towards the house. Gerry came running after me.

'You can't do this. I'm the one who thinks of things like this. You're supposed to be the good one.'

'Either you close that trunk after me, or I'll find a piece of string and do it myself.'

'So what do you think will happen even if you make it? They'll just send you back.'

'At least I'll get a look at America. Maybe they'll let me stay.'

'What happens if you die in there?'

'Why should I die?'

'There could be a hole in the floor. Exhaust could seep in from a hole in the tailpipe.'

'It's not an old car. There won't be any exhaust in the trunk.'

'But it's hot today. You could cook in there — you could die of thirst before you got to Detroit. The car might break down and they would have to leave it in a garage overnight.'

'Will you close the trunk after me or not?'

Gerry chewed on his lower lip. It looked like he was going to cry. I knew I'd won when the sullen look returned to his face.

My uncle and aunt were already standing in the living room. I had to move fast. I hugged them and kissed them, but all the adults I knew took forever to say goodbye, so there was still time. Gerry and I returned the keys, and then we shot back outside. There was plenty of room for me in the trunk. Gerry slammed it down. He waited a few seconds, and then gave two raps. I gave two raps back as an all clear.

My aunt's dresses were on hangers, and I lay down on the mat deep in the trunk, and pulled the dresses over me in case someone opened the trunk before they left. It took a long time for the car to start. They had to be wondering why I wasn't standing next to the car to say goodbye. I imagined my father's rage at this impoliteness, but then I would never have to worry about his rage any more. I did not want to think about my mother.

The engine finally started, and the car jerked away from the side of the road. I pulled off the dresses, and looked carefully in the darkness for pinpoints of light in the floor of the trunk, just to make sure that there was no way the exhaust from a leaky tailpipe could get inside. There were no lights, but I kept sniffing for the tell-tale gas, and wondered if my aunt and uncle would hear me if I rapped on the inside of the trunk. I sniffed, and I could smell many things; it was difficult to tell what might be poisonous. There were gasoline and oil in the background, the smell of the clothes under me, and my aunt's perfume in them. Sometimes I thought I could smell something burning, and hoped it was only the Parliaments that my aunt and uncle smoked.

I had prepared myself for the thirst and the heat that I soon came to feel, but I had forgotten to go the bathroom before we left. Not that I had to go yet, but the knowledge of it was worrisome to me. The car started and stopped often, in those days before highways, and the rocking motion and the heat that began to fill the trunk made me dozy. I half slept and then dreamed, and awoke to wonder if I had died from poisonous gas, and then I slept again. I finally came fully awake when the pressure in my bladder grew unbearable, and then I rocked myself back and forth to ease the need to urinate. I thought that if I let out just a little — not enough to be noticeable, the pressure would go away, but when I began to urinate in my pants, I could no longer stop, and for a moment the relief was too delicious for words. Then I thought of my girl cousins greeting me, and there I would be with my pants all wet, like an infant. They would hate me then, and my uncle would turn away in his shame.

I had no watch, and I could not have seen it in any case, but it seemed we would go on forever. Twice, the car stopped, and each time I thought the trunk would open and we would be in front of my uncle's house in Detroit. When finally the trunk did open, all I could see in the brightness of the late afternoon sun was the outline of a military hat.

'It's Dave,' I heard my aunt say.

'So you do know the boy,' the man in the hat said.

'Of course I know him. He's my nephew.'

'Most of the time, people claim it's some kid they've never seen before in their lives. You'd better come along with me.'

It had never occurred to me that trunks were sometimes opened when people re-entered their country, especially the trunks of men with accents. The American customs officers took us into a low row of offices.

My father met me at the bus station in downtown Toronto late that night. I got off the bus with the wet pants in a paper bag, and a new pair of pants that someone in the customs office had found. They were adult pants, and looked ridiculous with the cuffs rolled up to fit my legs.

In silence, we rode back to Weston on the last bus. My mother did not look up at me as I walked through the door. She was knitting something, and she stared resolutely at the knitting needles just above her lap. Gerry was already in bed. My father directed me straight down to the basement. I could hear him working to get his belt undone as we went down the steps.

I stood in the customary corner, and he talked as he let me have it across my buttocks.

'We had the police here all evening. They had dogs to sniff around the bushes in the fields in case someone had killed you and stuffed your body in there. Your mother was crying the whole afternoon. Let me tell you something. That uncle of yours works on the assembly line at Ford. He works a blowtorch, and every day he welds the same joint. Hundreds of times a day — day in and day out. Your aunt is a saleslady at Kroger's, and all day long she sells socks. Now if you think their life is so much better than ours, you can go and live there if you want. But you'll have to wait until you're twenty-one, and then as soon as you cross the border, they'll draft you into the army and they'll send you to be killed in Korea, or some other place where they kill American boys. Until that time, you'll live here and you'll like it, and you'll listen to every word I say or we'll come down here again and again until you learn.'

Gerry whispered to me after we heard my mother and father go to bed.

'Does it hurt?'

'Kind of.'

'He gave it to me too.'

'You told?'

'After the police came around again and told him where they found you. He didn't believe you closed the trunk yourself.'

'Yeah.'

He was quiet for a couple of minutes.

'They said you actually made it to the American side of the bridge.'

'I guess so.'

'So you're the only one in this family who's ever been to the States.'

'Yeah.'

'Was it beautiful there?'

'I couldn't see much. But when he drove me back over the bridge to the Canadian side, I looked out the window. It's this huge bridge — so high it feels like you're going to shoot right into the sky. There's a wide river, and Detroit is on the other side.'

'What does it look like?'

'All these factories along the river, and barges and ships, and behind that these skyscrapers.'

'How many?'

'A lot. All packed together, and tall as the bridge — maybe taller.'

'How many storeys?'

I thought for a while.

'Hundreds, I guess.'

He whistled low.

'But the Canadian side was different. I didn't see any factories at all. Just green, you know? Like a lot of lawns that come down to the water.'

'Nothing ever happens on this side of the border.'

'Nothing ever will.'

We talked for a little while longer, but it was late. Gerry fell silent. He must have fallen asleep, because he did not say anything when the door to our room opened and my mother walked in. It was dark, but my eyes were used to it and I could make out the white nightgown.

She sat down on the edge of the bed and stroked my hair for a while.

'I know you're awake,' she said. She didn't sound angry at all. Maybe just a little sad, and that was worse. She was quiet for a time.

'There's just one thing I want to know,' she said. 'Was it beautiful?'

Buying on Time

THE APPLE TREES IN THE LAST OF THE ABANDONED FIELDS CAME down, cut so they all fell neatly to the right. Soon the truck would come to haul them away. We were treeless in our new suburb, except where some cherry or apple had happened to grow conveniently at the perimeter of a yard-to-be. The sky was somehow very big over the neat new houses, and the vast blue canopy was only cut by a constant white plume from the Canadian Gypsum Company at the fringe of the neighbourhood. Not for us the dark houses of the city on tree-lined streets, where there were no driveways and the wretchedly small windows left the interiors in perpetual gloom. We had large picture windows in the living rooms, and on the smaller windows of our bedrooms were curtains with pictures of cowboys on bucking broncos.

The Lymes moved into a tarpaper house down the street. (Nine children. They were not even Catholics!) They never bothered to seed their lawn, or even to level the mounds of earth left over from the construction of their house. Now that our outhouse was gone, we had someone *we* could look down on. Father Lyme brought home two Model T Fords that he intended to restore, and left them parked between the mounds of earth on the front yard. There they stood for months. On Sundays, the father spent the day working under the hoods of these cars, and he scandalized the neighbourhood by keeping a beer bottle in easy reach. The Baptists, whose girls and women always wore hats and gloves on Sundays, looked away from Mr Lyme as they passed him on their way to church.

'We'll have to see if the town can do something about Lyme's yard,' Mr Taylor had even said to my father, who nodded sagely and puffed on his pipe in mute assent. My father's English had failed to improve, so I was not even sure he understood Mr Taylor's words, but he sensed the camaraderie of the outraged neighbour. Now that we no longer lived in the cellar of an unfinished house, and my father had covered the ruts in our driveway with gravel, Mr Taylor began to speak to us.

It did not matter to Gerry, whose hatred continued to burn fierce and strong. It did not matter that Mrs Taylor waved to us from across the street.

'I'm going to make so much money when I get a job, that I'm going to buy that house of his and get a bulldozer to knock it down.'

'No sense in knocking it down if you own it.'

'It'll be worth it. I'll send him an invitation to a party with his old address on it, and when he gets there, I'll be standing in the rubble and laughing at him.'

We were learning about Canadian domestic life from the Macvittys who had moved in upstairs. Mr Macvitty was a Canadian version of my father. Every morning we heard him clump down the steps in his heavy work shoes, black lunch pail in hand, on his way to drive a grader. My father clumped up the steps from the basement with his tools to work as a carpenter on the new houses springing up in suburbs and towns like ours. The men came and went, but the women stayed behind.

'Want some chicken gumbo soup?' Mrs Macvitty asked me when I was up there one day at lunch time. *Gumbo.* I didn't know what gumbo was, but I suspected the sound, even if it did come out of a safe can with 'Campbell's' on the label. Gumbo, gum, gumby, glue — It sounded bad. Maybe it was just flour paste and water and carrots. Everything seemed to have carrots in it. I turned down this strange offer, but I thrilled to the taste of her margarine. She took two white sticks and beat them together with a little butter, and then squeezed the colour tube and stirred the margarine some more. Sometimes she squeezed in too much, and the margarine took on the deep sickly yellow of a Kresge's five-and-dime birthday cake. If Tom was upstairs with us, he might dart his finger into the bowl and swallow a teaspoonful of the yellow stuff before Mrs Macvitty could stop him.

We asked our mother to buy margarine too.

'I can't do it,' my mother said. 'Your father and I ate so much of the stuff during the war that I gag whenever I put it in my mouth.'

'They made it out of used motor oil,' my father said.

We longed for margarine, and almost anything that came from a can. My father put slabs of roast meat on his bread, but we refused to eat anything besides Spam, baloney, and mock chicken loaf.

Once a week, Mr Macvitty brought home a pizza for dinner. My father was offended by the smell.

'It looks like vomit on bread,' he said.

The only toilet in the house was upstairs, so we had an excuse to go up as often as we liked. The Macvittys had a fourteen-year-old daughter who slept on the pull-out couch in the living room, and a small boy Tom's age who slept with his parents. When I heard Tina's light steps on the floorboards above me, I ran up to the bathroom and dawdled on the landing. Sometimes Mrs Macvitty would give me a piece of fudge or Mr Macvitty might ask me to stay to listen to the hockey game on the radio. I took the fudge or stayed and listened, but I was only there for Tina.

She always lay on the couch with her head on one hand and her eyes staring at the ceiling. She blew enormous bubbles with her chewing gum, and showed me a trick — if I pursed my lips at the right time when I blew, I could create a double bubble. After I learned the technique, the boys in the school yard gathered around me and tried to do the same. Gerry learned the trick as well. He blew his bubbles at the back of the classroom when the teacher's back was turned.

Mother Leone, the principal, saw him once through the open door of the classroom, and in a frenzy of discipline, she rushed in on him and burst the bubble with her hand. The class and teacher watched dumbfounded as the gum stuck to her hand and found its way onto her habit. The thin, pink membrane twisted into strands, and as she plucked at them, they spread across the black wool. Gerry had to do a week of eight a.m. masses for that. But as it was Lent, he also won the prize of a picture card of Saint Anthony for the most morning masses attended. He should have been disqualified because he was only there on Mother Leone's orders, but she had a forgiving side. She slapped him heartily on the back after she presented him with the card, like a boxing manager congratulating his pugilist. And why not? Mother Leone wanted soldiers for Christ.

If only she knew. Gerry burned his Saint Anthony card to prove that God didn't give a damn. The kids right up to grade eight were aghast, yet they admired him too. The strength of their admiration showed in no one's betraying him to Mother Leone. The repercussions would have been too great, even for the small, mean minds of the tattlers. For all we knew, it was the kind of act that might warrant a letter to the bishop.

Even the toughest kids gave up something for Lent, but Gerry swaggered and said he was going to chew gum every day until the purple bags were taken off the statues at Easter. We were in awe of him, but we still wrote JMJ on the tops of all the pages in our scribblers and on all our tests. Even if divine intervention did not take place to save us from a lack of studying the night before, at least the red pencil hands of the marking teachers might be stayed by our piety.

'If you want to get a job just so you can buy more rags in downtown Weston, then go ahead, but don't think we need the money,' my father said. He rose from his armchair and gestured wildly with his pipe. I was waiting for the glowing knob of tobacco to come flying out of the bowl the way it had when my mother let Gerry sleep over at a friend's house.

'If you go out to work, the children will become gangsters from hanging around in front of drug stores. We'll never eat properly again in our lives, and we'll become thin and waste away. Don't smile your smile at me — it happened to Anatole. His wife goes to work and six months later the man dies!'

'He was an alcoholic. He pickled his own liver.'

'Because his wife wasn't there to make sure he got some food in his belly. He sat around waiting for her with a bottle, and by the time she got home, he didn't feel like eating any more.'

'So that was her fault?'

'Of course it was her fault. Did the Virgin Mary work? Did you read anything in the Bible about her putting on a hair net and packing food into boxes? Did you read about her selling underwear at the five-and-dime? The only woman who worked outside the home in the Bible was Mary Magdalene, and she gave that up.'

'Did you ever read about Christ getting drunk?'

'Now you're blaspheming. I won't have that in this house.'

My mother had found a job packing cookies in a bakery, but she had had to lie about her education. She told them she had dropped out of high school.

'You haven't earned a cent in three weeks,' my mother said. She had both her hands on her hips and she was leaning into him like a woodpecker aiming at a striking point.

'House construction has its ups and downs. You know that. I'll make it up on the next job.'

'But food and clothes don't have ups and downs. I can't wait to feed the children and I can't send a boy to school without a spring jacket.'

'You see? You've become a slave to fashion! You'll rip this family apart to make some money-grubbing designer rich! If you weren't wasting money all the time, we'd be better off.'

'Just where do I waste money?'

'You took the kids to the dentist.'

'Their teeth hurt.'

'So give them a hot water bottle or else tell me. A bit of string and a swinging door and I'd save us five dollars.'

'Are you saying we don't need the money? Is that what you're saying?'

'I'm saying I make enough money for us to live on. I do my part of the bargain. You're the mother. You should be willing to keep up your side.'

'You haven't answered my question.'

'What question?'

'Are you saying we don't need the money?'

'That's right.'

'Then I'll take the job, but keep the money.'

'You'll have a week's wages spent by Monday. You'll be borrowing money from me by Tuesday. And anyway, who's going to take care of Tom?'

'The Macvittys will do it for ten dollars a week.'

'Hah! Spending money you haven't got already.'

*

Breakfast dishes were laid out for us in the morning, and breakfast itself was left warm in the oven. When we came home for lunch, my father was often there if he was out of work. He had loose-fried hamburger and fried potatoes waiting for us. Sometimes he fried baloney until the round discs ballooned in the centre and he flipped the disks and filled the pockets with scrambled eggs.

'What did you learn this morning?'

'Nothing.'

'Well, I'll just have to keep my tools in good shape for you. When they throw you out of school for stupidity, you can get up at six with me, and then saw lumber and nail shingles all day until dark. We'll be a team. The three of us will build houses.'

When my mother came home at five-thirty, Gerry and Tom and I jostled to get the bag out of her hand to see what kind of broken cookies she had brought home. She started giving orders before she had her coat off.

'Dave, you set the table. Gerry, peel the potatoes.'

My father waited in the basement until we called him up for supper.

'How come we always eat fried food?' my father asked.

'Because that's all I have time for when I get back from work.'

'Hah! The whole family has to suffer because you want to buy some rag picker's goods downtown.'

'So why don't you start something before I get home?'

'It's a mother's duty to cook.'

'Boys, I don't want to tell you to get the food on after I'm home. From now on, I want the table set and the potatoes ready by the time I arrive. As for you,' she turned to my father, 'any time you're not working, you can have the meat ready. Just put it in the oven in a roasting pan, cover it, and turn it on to three-fifty. Think you can manage that?'

'Hah! I know all there is to know about cooking.'

Gerry and I loved to hear her boss my father around.

As the weeks passed, miraculous things began to happen. When the blade of Gerry's hockey stick cracked, she bought him a new one. He taped the cracked one up carefully and used it for road hockey, and he saved the new one for use on ice. She even bought a rubber knob that Gerry could stick on the end of the hockey stick instead of making one out of tape. Sometimes Gerry loaned the knob to me, and I always scored more goals whenever I had it.

My father made us write out Carpenter Available notices, with our phone number on tails of paper at the bottom, and then he tacked his notices on supermarket bulletin boards and waited for the calls to come.

One week my mother bought a carton with six small bottles of Coke. Gerry, Tom and I got two bottles each, and we even gave her a sip to show our gratitude.

'So how much money do you make?' my father asked, eyeing the empty Coke bottles.

'It's just pin money — you said so yourself.'

'Sure, pins, and clothes, and Coca-Cola and hockey sticks. Why don't you spend the money on something useful?'

'Like a mickey?'

'Sure, a mickey of rye once every couple of weeks to show your appreciation.'

'Why don't you buy it yourself?'

'Who's paying the bills here?'

'You said you didn't need my money.'

'I don't, but I can't stand to see all this waste.'

'I'll make you a deal. I'll buy the groceries every second week, and I'll pay the water bill. You take the electricity.'

'Now you're talking! I'll put the extra money aside for important things.'

'Like what?'

My father searched desperately for something to say.

'Like shoes.'

'Shoes?'

'That's what I said.'

'Both the boys need new shoes now. Hand over ten.'

'I haven't got it.'

'What about all this cash you were supposed to be saving?'

'I mean I haven't got it with me. I'll need to go to the bank.'

'I'll save you the trip. You can put in the ten dollars towards this week's groceries. Then you can pay the whole bill next week.'

Towards the end of March, my father was working on house construction, and at the same time he started to get calls for indoor renovations of the kind he had been looking for all winter.

'Cupboards? You want cupboards now, in March? Mrs, I waiting all winter for you to call, but now I build houses. You wait until November, I build you cupboards. Why you need cupboards in summer? Go to beach in summer. Go swimming in summer. I give you cupboards in November.'

A new couch and chair appeared in the living room. My father came in from work later than my mother, and she stayed in the kitchen as he walked back and forth in front of the couch to examine it. He ran his hand along the fabric of the armrest and shook his head.

'At least a hundred and fifty dollars!' my father said. 'Did you get a raise or something?'

'I bought them on time.'

My father sucked on his pipe. The nicotine in the stem spluttered in anxiety.

'You mean you borrowed the money?'

'I didn't go to the bank or anything. The store does it.'

'And you pay interest?'

'A little.'

'Aha! You're dealing with usurers! When I tried to put a mortgage on the house, you made me take it off. No debts, you said. Now you're selling your soul to some greasy furniture salesman.'

'This is how the world works here. I'm not selling my soul, I'm just buying on time.'

'How much time? A lifetime?'

'Fifty weeks.'

'What if you get fired?'

'Why should they fire me?'

'Factories open and close all the time.'

'Then they'll take back the furniture.'

'I can see it now, the bailiff at the door with a truck. All the neighbours standing around as they take our goods away for auction. The next thing you know, you'll be sending the boys out to sell newspapers to buy yourself dresses.'

It was a silent dinner that night.

My father's working hours were unpredictable. He would leave early and come home late for weeks at a time, but suddenly he might be home when we came back from school. When we were alone with my father, we tried to find the corners of the house where he was least likely to be, or else to slink outside into the empty lots and look through the leftovers of construction for sticks with which to build forts. If we ever let ourselves be found, he might seize the opportunity to improve us.

My father never knocked on doors. He simply swung them open. Luckily he had a very heavy step so we could always hear him coming. One afternoon, Gerry was doing his homework before dinner so he could go out and play ball hockey later.

'What are you doing?' my father asked.

'My homework.'

'With a pen?'

'The teacher said we could practise with a pen on some of our homework if we wanted. Next year, everything except math gets done in pen.'

'You're holding it the wrong way.'

'Huh?'

'The cap. You're supposed to put the cap back on the end to get the right balance.'

'I don't like the cap on the end. It makes the top of the pen too heavy.'

'Let me see your writing. Hmm. Looks like hell. Looks like caveman writing. Put the cap on the end. I never want to see you writing without it.'

'Dad.'

'No discussion. I'm telling you, when you get older, you'll thank me for it. And stop grinding your teeth! The dentist is costing me a fortune.'

Our worst days with my father were the ones when my mother did not come home directly after work. One day, she had to go to a friend's baby shower.

'Gerry, you wash the dishes,' my father said after supper. 'Dave, you get little Tom's jacket and shoes on. Meet me outside. I've got to get the wheelbarrow from the shed. We're going out.'

'Is it garbage day?' I asked Gerry as soon as my father had left.

'I don't think so. Maybe he wants to pick up something at the lumberyard.'

My father had shamed us both when he picked up an old wooden ladder from the Reidys' yard down the street. The kids had called us garbage pickers for a week after that, until Gerry bloodied so many noses that no one dared to say it any more. My father was waiting for us outside.

'Where are we going?' Gerry asked.

'Downtown Weston.'

'What for?'

'None of your business. Let's go.'

It was a mile to the hundred yards of shops that made up downtown Weston, and my father picked up the handles of the wheelbarrow and we set off. The wheelbarrow was homemade, with stains from mixing concrete inside. My father had set a newspaper at the bottom which meant he was getting something that he wanted to keep clean.

Walking to town with a wheelbarrow was not much better than going there in a housecoat. I stared at the ground all the time. Gerry kept his head up just in case some neighbourhood kids dared to make a comment. He could not beat them with my father there, but he could remember their faces for later. When, halfway to town, little Tom could not keep up with us any more, my father set him in the wheelbarrow. Tom was happy about it, but Gerry and I were even more embarrassed.

'Going to plant the boy in your garden?' an old man asked.

'No, no,' my father answered. 'We take him to market to sell him to gypsies.'

Tom started to wail as we continued up the sidewalk.

'Stop crying, for heaven's sake,' my father said to Tom. 'How much do you think we'd get for you anyway? It wouldn't even be worth it.'

My father wheeled the wheelbarrow with Tom inside right down to Weston Road, where the sidewalks were filled with people coming home from work and making a few last-minute purchases before the stores closed. Men and women stepped aside to make room for us. At every curb my father had to turn the wheelbarrow backwards to haul it up onto the sidewalk. We stopped outside the appliance store.

'Gerry, you wait here. I don't want anyone to steal the wheelbarrow. Dave and Tom, come with me.'

'How come I have to wait outside?' Gerry asked. 'I want to go in too.'

'You're the oldest one. You're the one I have to rely on.' Gerry nodded and crossed his arms, watching everyone pass by the sidewalk as if they were prospective wheelbarrow thieves. Tom and I went in.

'Ah, you're here. I was afraid you weren't coming.' The salesman wore a dark suit and black-rimmed glasses. He was leaning on a wringer washing machine as if he owned it. We didn't usually go into showrooms. There was no use looking at things we could not have. The salesman took out a gold-tipped pen.

'All you have to do is sign here, and we'll make the delivery tomorrow.'

'No. I want tonight.'

'I'm afraid our delivery men have finished for the day. I'd do it myself, but I don't think the box would fit in my trunk.'

'We take. You give two dollars off.'

The salesman smiled a condescending smile.

'Delivery is free, you know. You can take it if you want, but that makes no difference in the price.'

'You pay delivery man. You pay gas. You pay truck. I save you money, so you save me money. Two dollars off.'

'This is highly unusual.'

'Two dollars off. Go speak to boss.'

'He's busy right now.'

'I wait five minutes. After five minutes, three dollars off.'

The salesman capped his pen and hurried to the back. He returned in under five minutes.

'The owner says all right, but the papers have already been written up. I'll give you two dollars from the till.'

'Good. Dave, you take Tom and wait outside.'

I hated it when he bargained. I wished he would just pay the price and shut up.

'What's he buying?' Gerry asked.

'I don't know, but we're taking it home in the wheelbarrow.'

'If it's a washing machine, we'll have to carry Tom, unless we put him inside.'

Two men in blue smocks came out with a large cardboard box. It had RCA printed on the outside.

'Is it a TV?' Gerry asked the men.

'Sure isn't a radio.'

Gerry and I were dumb with amazement. My father did not buy cakes or juice when he bought food, or toys or sports equipment or anything else we might ever want. It was understood that we went to my mother for those things.

'Does Mom know about this?' Gerry asked.

'It's a surprise.'

'She'll really be able to get into hockey now,' said Gerry. 'She just couldn't picture it on the radio. You're doing her a big favour.'

'Your mother deserves this,' my father said. 'She's worked hard raising you boys, and now it's time she got something nice.'

Tom started to wail when he saw he could no longer ride in the wheelbarrow.

'It's a television, Tom,' said Gerry, but Tom did not stop wailing. 'A television. You'll be able to watch cartoons on it.' Tom did not know what cartoons were. 'It's like comics, except ones that move and talk.' Our parents disapproved of comics, and Gerry and I only saw them at other kids' houses. 'A moving picture book!' Gerry finally said, and although Tom was still not sure what that was, he wiped his nose, and put his hand on the side of the wheelbarrow. Whatever the thing in the box was, it belonged to him.

The trip back home with the wheelbarrow was far better than the trip into town. Instead of being ignored or getting dirty looks, absolute strangers smiled at the box. 'I'll have to get one of those soon too,' a man in a suit said to us as he passed. It was incredible to us that we now owned a television, something a man in a suit did not already have. We weren't just catching up, we were leaping ahead.

When we got to our street, all the other kids were outside playing, and Gerry called out to them that we had a TV. Soon a ragged procession of children was following us, and Mrs Bryant ran off from her front porch to phone the neighbours. If anyone else on the street owned a television, we did not know about it, and we knew everything, right down to who used a belt and who used a hand to beat the children.

Mr Macvitty was sitting on the front porch, smoking a cigarette, when we came up to the house, and he helped my father carry the box inside. All of us except Gerry had to wait in the yard until they got the television set up.

'What are you going to watch?' one of the kids asked.

'I'll see *Howdy Doody* and stuff, but mostly my dad bought it for my mom to learn about hockey.'

'Wow. Your dad must really love your mom.'

And then Gerry opened the screen door and let all of us inside. The Macvittys were already sitting there in the darkened room, and the kids got to sit on the floor or stand in the dining room with the shorter ones at the front. Mrs Macvitty took Tom on her lap, and Tina tapped her lap for me.

I was already too big to sit on women's laps, but I sat on hers gladly, and she looped her arms around me and rested them on my legs. I could feel the movement of her jaws as she chewed gum right beside my ear, and the sweet smell of bubble gum wafted from her mouth. Mr Macvitty turned off the rest of the lights and my father turned on the TV. We waited, and a dot of light illuminated the centre of the screen, and then the screen lit up with ghostly figures. Mr Macvitty adjusted the rabbit ears, and suddenly we could make out the picture.

A fat man was dressed in a clown costume, and Tom laughed as soon as he saw him. Through the makeup on his face, we could tell that he looked exasperated, the way my father did when he saw us cut the fat off our meat.

'Alice!' he roared. 'Alice!'

'What is it, Ralph?'

The woman carried a dishcloth in her hand, and she looked the way my mother did when she found my father sneaking shots of whisky on a Saturday afternoon — disappointed, but not surprised.

The people on the screen were like us, but far funnier, and whenever we laughed, I could feel Tina's breasts move across my back, and I wanted the laughter to go on and on.

The front door was still open, and neighbours came in without knocking and crowded around the doorway to look over one another's heads. When the commercial for Ipana came on, I ran my tongue across my teeth. I wanted mine to look like the teeth on the screen, which were white and straight. My desire for the onscreen riches mingled with my desire for Tina, whose sweet bubble gum breath worked on my senses more powerfully than any perfume.

We watched show after show without any interruption, except

when Tom wet his pants on Mrs Macvitty's knee, and she took him away to change him. My mother came home. Some of the faces, white from the glow of the television tube, looked to her, and then turned back to the television again. She was uncommonly quiet, and she slipped into the place where Mrs Macvitty had sat.

'Where did this come from?' she asked of no one in particular.

The glow from the television absorbed us, and there was a pause before Gerry answered.

'Dad bought it. A gift for you so you can learn to appreciate hockey.'

She nodded, but abstractedly, and smiled at the man on the television. The man sat at the piano and sang songs even though he had an arrow shot through his head. Miraculously there was no blood.

'How did you pay for it?' my mother asked.

'On time,' my father answered.

'How many payments?'

'Forty. We'll have it paid off before the furniture.'

The days had been getting longer, and that night the street should have been full of kids playing in the mucky ditches, and being shouted at by neighbours trying to keep them off newly seeded lawns where the grass was starting to rise up in thin shoots. But it was quiet out on the street, and it was only long after dark that the neighbours drifted back to their houses one by one, and we were left in front of the television. When the news came on at eleven, my mother switched off the television to put us to bed. In the harsh light of the lamp, we blinked and yawned, and rose slowly to go back about our lives. We felt we had looked into a magic well, and we would come back to it again and again to peer into worlds that were far more wonderful than ours.

We moved the television to the end of the dining room table so we could watch it during dinner. My father no longer seemed as angry when we cut the fat off our meat, and we only had to put it on his plate for him to be satisfied that we were not wasting food. Mr Macvitty told us that we could catch more channels if we had an antenna, so my father drilled a small hole in the window frame, and he ran a wire up to the chimney. Sometimes, when the weather was good, we could get the shows from Buffalo.

From *Ozzie and Harriet*, my father learned to wear a cardigan, and from *I Love Lucy*, my mother learned of steak knives. On Saturday nights we all watched *Hockey Night in Canada*, and the only penance the children had to pay was watching *The Lawrence Welk Show* first. Even from that we learned something. Gerry mixed soap and water and made a funnel out of newspaper so Tom could blow bubbles. Tom had his *Howdy Doody* on Saturday mornings, and Gerry football on Sunday afternoons, and my father laughed uncontrollably through most of the wrestling matches, once even dropping the burning pipe from his teeth.

The neighbours came less often as the televisions filled our street, and at certain times, during *Lassie*, say, ghosts could have walked up and down our neighbourhood for all anyone knew. Together we watched Ed Sullivan on Sunday nights, enduring the crooners our parents loved so much for the circus acts and puppets and the rubber man who could be twisted and folded up as if he were a doll.

One night I had just fallen asleep when Gerry shook me awake.

'What is it?' I asked groggily.

'Come with me, but be really quiet. It's a secret.'

We crept through the kitchen in our bare feet, and Gerry stopped me where we could see the back of the couch. My mother and father were sitting together, watching a television programme. He had his arm draped around her shoulder and she leaned in towards him.

I looked at Gerry in wonder, and he put a finger to his lips. It was amazing to see my father with his arm around my mother, and a little disgusting as well. They were grown-ups, and had no business touching each other like the teenagers we saw in the park.

Gerry and I were spies in the secret world of adults, and we settled silently on the floor to watch them and listen to them talk.

'I got another job offer,' my mother said.

'What is it?'

'Filing clerk. Ten dollars a week more than I'm making now, but it's in downtown Toronto.'

'You should take it,' my father said. 'Get yourself out of that factory and into a clean job. If I had a car, I could pick you up at the bus stop. We could buy it on time.'

We fled silently when my mother bent over to kiss him. We didn't stay long enough to be sure, but it looked like she was aiming for his lips instead of his cheek, and that would have been just too indecent to behold.

Shale

THE MAN WORE BAGGY PANTS, A WRINKLED BROWN JACKET AND a hat that might have been crushed a few times and then punched back into shape. He had his back to us and was looking across the train trestle that spanned the Humber River.

'We finally found one,' said Gerry.

'What?'

'A hobo, you idiot. He must be waiting for a slow-moving freight.'

Gerry and I had scrambled up the crumbling shale that made up the sides of the Humber Valley, through the thorn bushes and up to the tracks of the trestle. We each had leather satchels on our backs that the Old Man had brought along from Germany, with sandwiches and bottles of sweet cold tea stopped with wax paper held tight by elastic bands. The tea always leaked and the bottles became heavy after we'd only walked a little way, so we drank the tea well before lunch, and then had to beg for glasses of water when we became parched in the afternoon.

It was worth it. The Old Man hardly ever came around the river, and we were free of household chores or having to take care of Tom. The only trick was to get away from Tom without being seen, because he started to cry and run after us any time he saw us leave the house. Being seen by the Old Man was even worse. He'd make us stay home in case he thought of anything for us to do later in the day.

The river marked the frontier of our town, and up on the opposite bank the world was more wondrous than ours. The banging and hammering that went on in our suburb was echoed there, but the houses that came up from the mud of Etobicoke were far more magnificent than ours. No little brick boxes rose up there, but wide-slung houses with only one storey that miraculously held three or even four bedrooms. The roofs of these houses were low, with long lines that made the buildings look as if they were wearing berets tugged smartly down over one eye. The garages were big enough for two cars. Our beachhead on the Etobicoke side was the Weston golf course. The head caddy told us we could work there when we turned thirteen, and in the meantime we combed the roughs for golf balls, which we sold from the woods on the eighth hole, always careful to gauge our customers to distinguish between those who might buy and those who would betray us to the groundskeeper.

The Humber River Valley was the no man's land between Weston and Etobicoke, a place where the locks had been cut off the grates of the storm sewers embedded in the banks. We hunted rats with slingshots deep into the drains, using candle stubs to light the way.

'Hey, boys,' the hobo at the trestle said. He hadn't turned around, and Gerry and I looked at each other to figure out how he had seen us.

'Mirrors on the brim of his hat,' Gerry whispered. We walked down to where he stood. He looked like many of the men my father worked with, olive-skinned and wrinkled with a few scabs round the neck from where he'd nicked himself shaving with a worn Blue Blade.

'You boys have watches?'

We shook our heads.

'See a clock anywhere in the last little while?'

'No.'

'Not much use to me, boys, but I might be of some use to you. Do you like pop?'

'Maybe,' said Gerry. He had his chin up, the same way he jutted it out when he was working up to a fight.

'I've got six bottles over at my camp on the other side of the river. Two bottles apiece.'

'What do you want for it?' Gerry asked.

'Well, I was hoping you might be able to tell me the time, but I guess you're no good for that.'

'Are you a hobo?' I asked, and Gerry kicked me quickly and sharply in the ankle. It hardly looked as if he had moved. Gerry had had a lot of practice.

'I've travelled a bit. Been to Alaska and California. I could tell you about it.'

'We're not interested in stories,' Gerry said.

'Suit yourselves. I've still got those bottles of Coke at my camp. Over on the other side.'

The man continued to stare across the river to the far bank.

'You going across the trestle?' Gerry asked.

'I was thinking about it. Wouldn't have to wade the river and get my feet wet. Wouldn't have to climb down this side of the valley and up the other. Knees start to bother a man my age.'

'Every couple of years somebody gets killed crossing over here.'

'They don't know the schedule. I do. On Saturdays, the only train that comes across here is a fast passenger train at one-fifteen.'

'Is that why you wanted to know the time?'

'Right.' He butted his cigarette. 'What do you think, boys, is it later than that?'

'I don't know.'

'Neither do I,' he said.

He looked across the trestle a while longer.

'You want those Cokes, you can come over with me. If you're scared, go around the bottom and look for my camp on the left side, just below the new house construction. I'll be waiting.'

He stepped onto the trestle and started to move across in an odd walk with very short steps. The ties were set too far apart to take two at a time. He did not run, but he was not strolling.

'What do you think about those Cokes?' I asked Gerry when the man was out of earshot.

'I think he likes boys too much.'

I nodded. I wasn't sure what it meant.

'But he doesn't look too strong or too smart. We could get the Cokes and take off.'

'Want to do it?'

'Maybe. Put your hand on a rail.'

'What for?'

'Just do it.'

It was late September, but the sun was still hot and the rail was painful to touch.

'It's humming,' I said.

'Jesus, a train's coming.'

We shouted at the hobo, but he did not turn around. We stepped back from the rail, but it wasn't easy to stand on the slope because the shale was broken into pieces the size of silver dollars, and it kept giving way under our feet. It was a thirty-foot tumble down the slope if we slipped.

The hobo was more than halfway across the trestle when we heard the train coming up in the distance behind us. It took so painfully long for the sound to draw close that I was sure he would make it, but the train was upon us suddenly, a thrust of air and a pounding of pistons that deafened me. We put our hands to our ears and watched the hobo. He did not look back and he did not run. He just hastened the fast walk on those short steps.

It was not a passenger train. It was one of the old steam engines, some relic on its way to the scrap yard, and it had a string of empty flatbeds behind it. But it was moving fast. The engineer could not have seen him because no whistle blew, and the engine closed the gap with terrifying speed. The wind caught the hobo's hat and it flew off behind him, but he did not turn around or reach for it. Step, step, step, and he was across the trestle with ten feet to spare when the train roared past him.

'Jesus Christ,' said Gerry. 'He's one cool number. Anybody else would have shit his pants.'

After the flatbeds had passed, the hobo walked back onto the trestle a few yards and retrieved his hat. He shaped it with his fist and then waved to us before turning and disappearing into the bushes on the other side.

'We'll go across at the bottom,' said Gerry, and he started down the steep hill. The flood plain at the bottom was a mass of thin trees and scrub bushes, and I had to stay far behind Gerry or the branches whipped me in the face when he let them go. Horseflies and mosquitoes buzzed around our heads, and we had to watch for logs and broken beer bottles at our feet.

It was easier to pass in the spring. Then all the saplings stood naked and we could search among the roots for junk that had been trapped when the spring high waters came down. It was mostly liquor bottles and pieces of clothing that wrapped themselves around the tree bottoms or got caught in the dead long grass of the year before, but it was always worth looking carefully. Gerry found a gas engine model Spitfire in the branches of a low tree that year. The engine was soaked and useless, but the body of the plane was sound and the paint still miraculously fresh, and Gerry had hung it by a wire from the ceiling in our room.

Some people said wolves came down the Humber Valley when the winters were cold, and sometimes we could see creatures skulking through the brush, but we could never be sure if they weren't only dogs. All the talk on the radio that year had been about rabies, and the teachers at school told us to keep away from friendly animals. Packs of dogs ran loose in the neighbourhood, and that summer a couple of kids had been mauled by them, but nobody got rabies. They were just regular maulings where some kid lost an ear or a finger.

The brush opened up at the river's edge where Gerry was already sitting on a rock and untying his shoes. The Humber ran shallow for most of the year and it was only a foot or two deep in most places by the end of the summer. There were deeper holes that held suckers and carp, and Gerry and I fished for them and gave them to our mother — she used them for fertilizer under the roots of her rose bushes. Nobody but a fool ate a fish that came out of the Humber. Sometimes we swam in the holes, but we had to do it secretly. When they weren't talking about rabies, the teachers and parents went on about polio. We figured we were safe as long as we kept our mouths shut while we were swimming, but sometimes my mother could tell we had been in the water by the smell that clung to us when we came back home.

Gerry tied his shoelaces together and slung his shoes over his shoulder. He rolled up his pants, and I did the same. We carried sticks to brace us up in the water because the rocks on the bottom were slick with slime and we had to feel each spot with our toes before we put any weight on our feet. The bottom was littered with broken glass and crayfish snapped their tiny pincers on our skin if we disturbed their holes beneath the brown water.

The water hugged the steep river-valley bank on the other side, and there was barely room for us to sit on the bottom and put our shoes and socks back on. It was strangely cool in the shade of the west bank. There was little vegetation on the slope of broken shale above. Gerry had chosen a bad place to cross. The trestle abutment blocked us from searching for an easier way up unless we wanted to go back into the river, and there was no more forgiving slope upstream. No wonder the hobo had taken his chances on the trestle.

'Look at this.' Gerry was holding a piece of shale the size of a cigarette package. It had the perfect outline of some kind of large water bug on it.

'It's a troglodyte,' said Gerry.

'What's that?'

'A big old water bug. Say the word after me.'

'What for?'

'Just say it.'

I repeated the word.

'That's how you learn things. Improve yourself, or you'll end up like the Old Man.'

'He knows stuff.'

'Nothing important. This bug got squashed in the muck a million years ago, and here it is. What do you think's going to be left of you in a million years?'

'Nothing.'

'Exactly. I'm taking this in to school,' and he put it in his satchel.

We surveyed the slope above us.

'You see that ledge about twenty feet up?'

'Yeah.'

'I figure we run like hell until we reach it, and then worry about the rest once we're there.'

'Okay.'

Gerry went first, and I stood aside because the bits of shale went flying down behind him and onto my head. The trick was to get enough momentum to make it all the way to the ledge. The only way for Gerry to stop from tumbling back down was to drive his feet deep into the broken pieces of shale, but if he did that, he lost the momentum. Gerry made it up less than halfway on both his attempts. Then he got that look on his face, the one he wore before he smashed some kid in the face or knocked over the defencemen on the hockey rink. On his third run up the slope, his feet barely touched the shale and he used his hands to help him scrabble to the side of the ledge. He grasped the bottom of a thin bush and pulled himself on top.

'Now you do it,' he called down to me.

I wouldn't even have tried if Gerry were not already standing up on the ledge, staring down at me with his hands on his hips and a smirk on his mouth. I was going to make it up there, and I was going to make it on the first try. I backed up as far as I could go, and then tore up the shale slope quickly so my feet did not sink in and slow me down.

Gerry knelt down on the ledge and held out his hand, but I was not going to take it. I reached for the same branch he had, but I was already slipping back down and I grabbed at some thin roots that came through the bottom of the ledge. My feet were no longer on the slope at all, but hung away from the sides.

'Grab my hand,' Gerry said.

'I can't let go,' and Gerry could not reach down far enough to get at my wrist. As the thin roots began to break free, I thought of nothing but the Hardy Boys, and what they would have done. They would have had a rope with them, coiled in one of their sacks, but their father seemed to have money for coils of rope whereas ours had money for nothing. Gerry was saying something above me, but all I could think of was the cost of rope, three cents a foot at the hardware store, and what length we would have needed to save me.

Maybe fifteen feet. I was going to crack my head open for lacking forty-five cents.

I had no clear sensation when I fell, just a confusion of speed and then a sharp pain in my foot and a wetness on my head. I lay for a moment, thinking that I was feeling my wet brains run down my neck. That worried me less than the pain in my foot.

Then two faces appeared above me.

'Is he dead?' It was a kid's voice, but I could not tell if it came from a boy or a girl. The child wore a red-checked Hudson's Bay shirt, and so did the man who stood beside. It was a girl. She had pigtails behind, but the hair was pulled back tightly at the front of her head.

'Are you hurt, son?'

'My foot.'

The man reached down to under my neck and raised me up to a sitting position. The back of my head had been lying in the river.

A shower of shale came down on our heads as Gerry ploughed down the slope above us.

'That was incredible,' he said excitedly. 'You bounced off the slope twice and then went flying out into the air. I thought you were dead for sure.'

I could not put any weight on my left foot.

'Not broken though,' said the man. 'Just a bad twist. We should get some ice on it fast.' We told him where we lived. 'You'd better come back to my house. We'll put some ice on it and give you a ride home.'

He made me get on his back, and then he and the girl went up a long narrow path that Gerry and I had never seen. It felt odd to be on the back of a strange man. I could smell the Burma-Shave on his neck and my face was uncomfortably close to his ear and the thick black arm of his eyeglasses. At least he didn't have any hair growing out of his ears.

It was a long way to go to their house even after we got up onto the streets. The bricklayers and the carpenters working on the houses stopped to look at us as we walked by. My only fear was that my father would be among them, and that he would descend on us with his broken English.

The man on whose back I rode was called Mr Lots.

'Lotsa luck,' said Patsy beside him.

'Patsy talks a lots,' said the man. He was breathing hard.

'But that's your lots in life.'

'Thanks a lots.'

'Dave's getting heavy. How'll we choose who carries him next?' The man asked.

'We'll draws lots,' said Patsy, and the two of them laughed. Gerry looked at me, but it was hard to tell if he thought they were crazy or if he liked them.

'You boys get down by the Humber often?' Mr Lots asked.

'Whenever we don't have chores,' said Gerry.

'Do any fishing?'

'Sometimes. We hunt rats most of the time.'

'What's your record?' Patsy asked.

'Huh?'

'How many you get in a day?'

'I don't know. A couple.'

'Patsy once got four. She's a good shot.'

'The trick is to use a ball bearing,' said Patsy. 'A stone just doesn't kill them dead.'

'A marble works pretty well,' said Gerry.

'They're okay. The problem is, a rat's got a tough skull, so a marble can only be used once. Ball bearings are forever.'

Gerry nodded sagely.

It felt like we'd been walking for a long time before we came to a street that curved down to a row of new houses backing right onto the slope to the river. Mr Lots carried me around the house to the back yard where he had some patio furniture, and he made me lie down on a long chair that kept my feet elevated.

'You boys wait here,' said Mr Lots. 'I'll go in and get some ice. Patsy, you bring out some lemonade. They must be thirsty after all this.'

'What do you figure?' I asked Gerry after the other two had gone in.

'It's not Cokes, but at least it's something,' said Gerry. 'If you hadn't been so stupid, I'd've dumped that hobo over the cliff and we could've had three Cokes each.' He ruminated for a moment. 'At least you didn't die on me. That would've really pissed off the Old Man.'

The yard had a long lawn that ran down to a chain-link fence where the slope dropped off sharply to the Humber River below. There was a sugar maple at the end of the yard, and a treehouse in the branches that overhung the river. Patsy came out with a tray of glasses and lemonade.

'Your dad make the treehouse?' Gerry asked.

'Nope. I did. Mostly, anyway. He cut the boards but I nailed them in.'

'A girl nailing boards?'

'So what?'

'I bet the thing's going to fall right into the river.'

'Come here.'

'What?'

'Come on and try it if you don't believe me.'

Gerry stood up and followed her to the ladder nailed to the tree trunk. Patsy ripped a handful of mountain ash berries from another small tree before she climbed up the ladder after him. I could hear Gerry jump up and down on the boards a few times. Then there was silence. Something hard whacked me in the forehead, and then plopped down on my shirt. It was a broken mountain ash berry.

'Right between the eyes!' said Gerry.

'I never miss at this distance,' said Patsy.

I began to look around for an escape, but Mrs Lots came out with ice cubes wrapped in a tea towel. She was wearing a flower print dress. Every mother I knew wore a flower print dress, but each one fascinated me more than the last. The material seemed so thin, as if the whole dress would fit into the palm of my hand. I used to touch the dresses, secretly, whenever I went to Kresge's in Weston, and wonder at the near nakedness of the women who wore them.

'I'm a nurse, dear. Let's take a look at that foot.'

'You're not dressed in white.'

She laughed.

'I don't usually wear the uniform at home, dear. Not unless I'm expecting an emergency.'

She undid the shoelaces and pulled off the sock. I winced as she felt my foot with her fingers.

'I don't think it's broken, but you can't really tell without an x-ray. You might have a hairline fracture in one of those bones. Maybe Andy could drive you over to the hospital.'

'I'll be okay.'

'It wouldn't be any trouble.'

'My dad wouldn't like it.'

'You mean the cost?'

'Well, yeah, the cost would bother him some. He just doesn't like it when I take stupid chances.'

'How's the foot?' It was Mr Lots.

'I think the boy needs to keep it on ice for a couple of hours to hold down the swelling. He won't really know until tomorrow. What time do you boys need to be home?'

'By five, for dinner.'

'He'll be bored. Maybe you could bring out the crokinole board. I'll make some sandwiches to tide them over.'

'Don't go in,' I said to Mr Lots.

'Why not?'

'They're shooting stuff at me with their slingshots.'

'Oho!' said Mr Lots. 'Taking unfair advantage of a fallen enemy. We'll just have to flush them out.'

It was quiet up in the treehouse. Too quiet. They could have dirt clods or crab apples stored up there. Mr Lots took out his garden hose, turned it on, and walked towards the treehouse.

'Oh Patsy! Why don't you and the other boy come down for a while? We're going to play some crokinole.'

'I don't want to.'

'I'd really like you to.'

'Not now, Dad. There's a rat way down there by the river. We want to get it.'

Mr Lots put his finger on the end of the hose and the water rose up in an arc and shot through a window of the treehouse. The two came tumbling down, shaking the water off their heads and wiping it out of their eyes.

'Couldn't we shoot some tin cans instead?' asked Patsy.

'Sure.'

Mrs Lots went inside and her husband brought out a .22 from the garage. It was a single-shot bolt-action rifle.

'You shoot that off in your back yard?' Gerry asked.

'We're high up on the bank here. I use a short bullet, hardly more than a pellet. It pretty well drops harmlessly into the river.'

Neither Gerry nor I had ever held a real gun before. Mr Lots put up some tin cans on the fence and showed us how to hold the rifle. It was heavier than I thought it would be, and harder to hit tin cans than it looked in the Westerns.

'What we need is a machine gun,' said Gerry.

'They're not very accurate,' said Mr Lots. 'A machine gun is made to spray bullets around, not hit a specific point.' Gerry nodded.

By four-thirty, my foot was so numb from the ice cubes Mrs Lots kept putting on that I almost felt I could walk home, but Mr Lots offered to give us a drive.

'I'll drop you off a couple of blocks from home, just so your parents won't think you got into some kind of trouble. Where do you live?'

I told him.

'You two can come over here any time you want,' said Patsy. 'You're fun.' Patsy waited, but we didn't say anything. 'So can I come and visit you some time?' she asked.

'It'd be kind of a long walk,' said Gerry doubtfully, 'and my mother had polio, so she's always getting a little flustered whenever someone comes over to visit.'

'Does she wear leg braces?' Mrs Lots asked.

'She tries not to. Usually she just relies on a couple of canes, but she's tired all the time. Don't you worry though. We'll drop by here to say hello.'

Mr Lots dropped us off not far from the house. By then the numbness was going out of my foot and I had to rest my arm on Gerry's shoulder to make it back.

'What did you tell them that polio story for?' I asked.

'That Patsy's okay, but I don't want any girl dropping by the house. Think what the Old Man would say.'

I did think about it. He'd try to make a joke or something, but she wouldn't understand a word he said because his English was so bad. He might ask her if she wanted to marry us.

'She's a good shot with the slingshot, though,' said Gerry. 'I'm going to get some ball bearings and go back into the sewers with her.'

'What about me?'

'You won't be walking around much for a while. Besides, you're a lousy shot. You'd scare them off before we were in range.'

My father was already sitting at the head of the table when we got home, waiting for my mother to serve dinner.

'You're almost late,' he said.

'Dave hurt his foot. He can hardly walk.'

My father grunted. 'Eat something first, and then we'll look at it after dinner. If your belly's full, it won't hurt as much.'

My mother didn't say anything as she put the food on the table.

Spinach borscht, sausages, sauerkraut, beet salad and boiled potatoes. The food disgusted me, partially because the ache in my foot made me nauseous, and partially because I knew that the Lotses were sitting down to a dinner of roast beef. We never ate 'English' food except for hamburgers and baloney. We ate pork roasts and ham if there was money, sausages and pork chops in between, and hamburger the rest of the time. Cabbage soup and borscht. Gerry had been right. Patsy would have been sickened by the food on our table.

My mother still didn't say anything. Her eyes were red and she hardly ever looked up. It was quiet at the table except for the slurp of soup from the spoon that my father always used. It was the size of a ladle.

'So how come you're home so early?' Gerry asked our father.

My father slammed down his spoon.

'You want to know why? You want to know? Because that damn contractor who drives around in a Buick all week has decided to go bankrupt! He gets together with his pals from the bank, declares bankruptcy, and then buys a new house, a new car, and starts all over again. Meanwhile, men like me don't get paid for the work we did last week. What's that to Mr Buick-Man? Nothing. We don't exist for people like him. Just a few weeks left to the building season, and I have to waste a couple more days looking for another job. Where's the money for the food going to come from? Eh? Are you going to make it?'

'Stop shouting at the boy,' my mother said. 'You only have yourself to blame.'

'Myself? Now it's my fault?'

'If you just got a factory job like everyone else, this wouldn't happen to you.'

'And what's to prevent a factory owner from doing the same thing?'

'They don't fold up so quickly.'

'No, they just lay you off for a few weeks whenever things are slow. It's all the same.'

Tom started to wail at the table. The kid had it down perfectly. Every time my mother and father started to fight, he broke out in tears. It was the best trick he knew. As for me, my head was beginning to swim and I thought I might get sick. The ache in my foot was spreading through my whole body. I suddenly found my face among the potatoes and cabbage in my plate. It was strange. I could still hear everything they were saying.

'What's the matter with him?' my father asked.

'You've driven him crazy,' said my mother.

The swelling went down the next day, but I still couldn't put any weight on my foot. My father spent Sunday afternoon down in the basement, and when he came up in the evening he held a crutch that he'd carved out of a two-by-four.

'I don't want you to miss any school. You can start early tomorrow and use this.'

I felt like Tiny Tim.

Gerry wasn't around after school on Monday, so I hobbled home alone. I didn't have a cast to sign, so some of the kids had written their names on my crutch. Gerry was late getting home.

'I went to Patsy's after school,' he said.

'Why didn't you tell me?'

'You think I'd haul a cripple that far? She has binoculars, and we saw a couple of people making out down by the river.'

'The hobo?'

'No, stupid. A couple of high school kids. It was disgusting.'

'Any rats?'

'No time to hunt them. We'll do that tomorrow.'

'You might want to give me a hand getting home. This foot's still pretty bad.'

'You hurt it, you get home yourself. It's time you grew up a bit anyway.'

By the end of the week, I didn't really need the crutch any more, but I still brought it along. The teachers were softer on me that week. So was my father. Gerry went to Patsy's house every day, but he could only stay a little while if he wanted to be back in time for supper. He told me about the archery set she had, and the go-kart they pushed down a hill. She was almost better than a boy.

In the week that I used the crutch, the last warmth of summer expired suddenly and the days became cool and grey. On Saturday I would have been well enough to walk slowly to Patsy's house, but our father left us the job of uprooting the garden and breaking up the soil for the winter.

At least the hockey games had begun. We sat in the living room as my father puffed on his pipe and my mother sewed, and we watched the Leafs race back and forth on the ice. We made popcorn on the stove, and even my father ate it, the only new food he put in his mouth since the war.

'Like little sponges to hold the butter,' he said.

The next day we were tied down because there was an archdiocese rosary festival at the Canadian National Exhibition grounds. First we had to go to mass as usual, and then we had to sit out in the drizzle as the parishes marched down the centre of the field one by one, displaying their shiny banners of Saint John the Baptist or Our Lady of Sorrows. Some of the parishes had marching bands and they played favourite hymns that we had to sing from a song sheet. I didn't have any favourite hymns, and my father watched us carefully to make sure we weren't just mouthing the words. Finally thousands of rosaries clacked out of pockets as the main event began. Down on the field it was like a football halftime show. Fifty-nine girls in red and white long dresses stood down on the field in the shape of a rosary. Beside each girl stood two more, and as the multitude completed a Hail Mary or an Our Father, the two girls in attendance on the rosary bead girl pulled her wide and long skirt up from the ground between them, so that it looked like a rose opening as each prayer was said. Gerry sniggered. I knew his mind well enough. He was hoping for a gust of wind to flap up the dresses and show the underpants on the rosary bead girls.

'It's beautiful,' my mother whispered between the prayers. My foot began to ache because we stood through the entire rosary. There was no place to kneel in the tight, concrete stands, and I leaned into my father for support.

'Good boy,' he said. 'Just don't sit down. Think of the Holy Spirit.'

All I could think of was Patsy.

On Monday, Gerry had his first football practice, and I took a chance with my foot and hurried across the footbridge down from Lawrence Avenue, and made it over to Patsy's house. She was waiting in the back yard in blue jeans that zipped up at the side and she wore the same checkered Hudson's Bay shirt that I had first seen her in.

'Where's Gerry?'

No other words could have wounded me so much. I reached suddenly towards my foot, as if I had just had a sharp pain there.

'You won't be much good for pushing me around in the go-kart. Let's go into the treehouse.'

I had wanted to see the inside of her garage first. I imagined the go-kart in there, surrounded with dart boards, hockey sticks, and the archery set. For all I knew, she might even have had a hockey game, the kind with the black wooden disk for a puck and six long wire handles to control the players.

'I've already got the binoculars up there. Come on.'

The ladder nailed to the tree trunk hung out over the river. I put my hand on the windowsill of the opening that looked down and across the river, and I steadied myself to still the vertigo that came from looking at the moving water below. There was a breeze on that grey day, and the slight swaying of the tree heightened my feeling of suspension in the air. It was wonderful.

Down below us the river had risen slightly in the autumn rains, and beyond that we could see the mass of saplings on the opposite river bank and the hockey rink and park beyond them. Patsy was looking out with her binoculars.

'There they are again. Monday must be their day.'

'Who?'

'The teenagers. Same grey blanket. Same couple. Take a look.'

Even with the binoculars, it was hard to make out the details. A boy and a girl lay on a blanket, and the upper part of the boy's body was bent over the girl. Her arms were wrapped around his neck and shoulders.

'Can you see them?' Patsy's voice came from close beside me. It seemed hoarse.

'Yeah. No rats, though.'

'What are they doing?'

'The same thing. Necking, I guess. It's sick.'

'Why?'

'Huh?'

'Why is it sick? You see it in the movies all the time.'

I pulled away the binoculars to tell her that we did not see many movies. Her face was very close to mine and it looked from her eyes as if she was starting to fall asleep. I made no conscious decision. Something in my blood told me what I had to do, and I brought my lips close to hers. As soon as they touched, I felt panic. What came next?

She seemed to know. She kissed me twice, parting her lips slightly at the end of each kiss. Then she lightly kissed my upper lip and the lower one before she pulled away.

'We have to practise,' she said.

'What for?'

'For when we get older. Put your arms around my neck.'

I did as I was told. She wet her lips slightly and then kissed me again.

'We can't make babies yet because we're too young,' she said.

I didn't know what she was talking about, but I was willing to sit close beside her and listen to anything that she said. My heart was beating fast and I was finding it hard not to pant.

'Let's see what they're doing now.'

Patsy took the binoculars from the floor where I had left them.

'Just the same old thing,' she said. 'I guess they're still too young too.'

We practised twice more before I saw it was late and I had to go home for supper.

'Who's coming tomorrow?' she asked.

'Gerry has football practice.'

'I'll see you.'

She had given no word of preference between Gerry and me, and I was in turmoil all the way home.

I was late. I blamed it on my foot, which really was aching badly, but my father was still unconvinced. I would have to come straight back home after school each day for the rest of the week.

'Did she ask about me?' Gerry asked from the other side of the table where we were both doing our homework after supper.

'Yeah.'

'What did you tell her?'

'You had football practice.'

Gerry was silent. I looked at him surreptitiously above my notebooks and wondered at what he had not told me. He could have her whole garage full of games, as long as she practised kissing with no one except me.

On Thursday after school, I was home playing with Tom and his building blocks when somebody knocked on the door. My mother was getting supper ready in the kitchen. Tom started to whine as soon as I stood up, so I took his hand and we went to answer the door together.

Patsy was standing outside with a baseball bat over her shoulder and three gloves hanging from it. She was tossing a softball up and down in her other hand.

'Don't you like me any more?' she asked when I opened up the screen door.

'How did you find this place?'

'I looked it up in the phone book, stupid. Where's Gerry?'

I couldn't answer her. At any minute my mother would come to the door. My father would be home soon and then everyone would know about her. And she had asked for Gerry first!

Before I could think of anything to say, Tom had his hands out for the softball. Patsy crouched down to give him the ball just as my mother showed up behind me. Patsy stood up, and when I still didn't say anything, she told my mother her name and stuck out her hand. Patsy looked at her legs. No braces.

'Very nice to meet you, my dear,' my mother said, and then to me, 'I'm making supper right now. Why don't you go out in the back yard? Gerry and your father will be home soon.'

The last thing I wanted was to have her there when Gerry and my father arrived. I wanted her away, quickly, but I could think of nothing to do, so we went around to the back.

'So how come you've been avoiding me?' Patsy asked out back.

'I got grounded because I came home late.'

'Why didn't you phone?'

'We just got the phone in a little while ago. I guess I'm not used to it.'

'Well, get used to it. You could have phoned me when you were grounded, couldn't you?'

'The phone's in the living room. Everybody can hear.'

'So what? No big secret.'

'What about practising?'

She smiled sweetly. 'No need to talk about that. Come on, let's play catch.'

Tom didn't want to be left out, and she had to roll the ball to him every second throw. My mother could see us out in the yard from the kitchen window and I feared she might see right through me to my heart.

'Hi, Patsy. Toss me a glove.'

Gerry dropped the satchel with his books and we formed a triangle. I was glad that she threw to me, and I caught each throw lovingly. But I hated it that Gerry was throwing to her. He got a wicked smile on his face after a while, and started to drill the ball right at her face, but Patsy just reached up without flinching and snatched the ball from the air. She was just as good with grounders and fly balls.

I heard my father come around the corner of the house, home from work. He carried the two heavy wooden boxes of tools in his hands, and he wore the baggy grey trousers patched at the knee, a wool jacket buttoned at the throat, and a cap with a brim and the earflaps down. Smoke billowed from his pipe and even from a distance I could see the thin cloud of sawdust that followed him whenever he wore his work clothes.

'What is this?' he shouted. 'I have a daughter? All these years and my wife never tell me? Come here, my daughter, and tell me your name.'

Patsy smiled as she walked up to him and she held out her hand and told him her name. My father put down his tool boxes and shook her hand.

'Good, strong grip!' he said. 'Good for making bread! Okay, Patsy. Do not let boys hurt you. Big one is rough.'

'I can handle them.'

My face was crimson, but Patsy went back to her spot in the triangle and continued to throw the ball. I loved her because she did not show on her face what a fool my father was, but I still hated him for coming home.

'Patsy!' my mother called through the window. 'Do you want to phone your parents and stay for supper?'

'Sure.'

My entire family was made up of enemies. Even Tom clung to her leg when she went inside to make the call.

'Father's going to say something stupid at the table,' I said to Gerry. 'He never closes his mouth when he's eating. She's going to get sick just looking at him.'

Gerry nodded. 'I hope there isn't any borscht tonight. That would scare her just to look at it. She'd run screaming through the door. Her father might call the cops.'

What bewildered me most of all was my parents. I had expected cool disapproval from my mother, and some kind of shouting from my father. We all sat at the table as if we were normal people. But how long could the act go on? I winced when my father slurped at his soup, but Patsy talked with him as if she didn't notice. Thank God, it was a barley soup, a pale glutinous mixture that even a Scot would recognize. When my mother put the pork chops on the table, Patsy asked for applesauce. I thought my father was going to fall off his chair with laughter.

'What, Patsy, you want dessert already? Is this how Canadians eat? First dessert, then meat?'

'We always put applesauce on pork chops,' said Patsy.

'Hoo hoo! Wait until I tell the men at work. You put pie in soup? Cake on potatoes? Hoo hoo!'

I was staring at my plate, mortified, but my mother had a jar of applesauce for Tom, and she put in on the table. My father reached into the jar with his soup spoon, and ladled a puddle of it on his chops.

'Not bad, Patsy! Maybe you teach us something!'

I had never seen my father be so friendly over such a long period of time. His bursts of good humour were usually limited to a few short minutes, but he talked to Patsy right through supper. Incredibly, she talked back to him as if he was normal.

After dinner, he pushed his chair from the table and lit his pipe. 'Patsy, now I walk you home.'

'It's all right. I know the way.'

'No, no. Is dark already. Your father, he worry.'

'Okay.'

'I'll go too,' I said quickly, hoping to beat Gerry.

'What, skip homework? Fail your school? Be a hobo? A bum? No! You stay and do work. I go home with Patsy.'

I thought I was going to die. Away from us, he would make more jokes. But there was no changing his mind. They walked down the street together.

'What a nice girl,' said my mother as she cleared the plates.

It took a long time for my father to return. I hoped Mr Lots did not offer him a drink. In my father's guide to good guestmanship, a bottle opened was a bottle finished. He might get drunk and begin to sing. But when he did return, there was no smell of alcohol on him.

'Thanks for taking her home,' said Gerry.

'No problem. Her father is an interesting man. He helped bomb Hamburg. If we'd been a little later on our way across Germany, or he'd bombed a little earlier, he might have killed us.' My father found this amusing, and he whistled to himself for the rest of the evening.

But my heart was bursting with perplexity. How could she have betrayed me by playing ball with Gerry after she had kissed me in the treehouse? How could she act as if she thought my father was normal when he was the tyrant who controlled my life? That night, I waited until Gerry's breathing fell into the even pattern of sleep, and then I imagined how easy it would be to slip across the floor and strangle him.

Gerry and I went over to Patsy's house on Saturday. Because she lived across the river, she went to another school, and some of her friends were over that day as well. They were all boys, but

Gerry managed to stay out of a fight. Her father's garage was like Sinbad's cave, filled with all the games and toys we had seen only on the backs of comic books. I tried the pogo stick, but never got more than three or four hops down the sidewalk before I lost my balance. When we were finished with darts and archery and the go-kart, Mr Lots let us go down into the basement and try his billiard table. But he wouldn't let us put any English on the ball because the table was new and he was afraid we might rip the felt.

In the midst of all these wonders, my heart was aching. I wanted to be alone with Patsy, but there were too many people around. As the others raced around the yard and street, I climbed up into the treehouse and looked out across the river. I thought very hard, so that she could read my mind and follow me up there. 'I'm calling you,' I whispered, and I pictured her face and lips, but I still heard the sounds of her playing out in the yard with the others. I waited a long time, but finally Mr Lots called us all into the yard for hamburgers he had cooked on the stone barbecue.

My father kept us home again for church and chores on Sunday, even though it rained all day, and each day of the week events conspired to keep me from going over to her house after school. In bed at night, after the lights were turned out, I practised kissing the air so I would be ready when I met her alone again.

'What the hell are you doing?' Gerry asked one night in the darkness.

'Nothing.'

'You sound like the Old Man slurping at his soup over there.'

I thought I should pray for her, but this felt wrong, somehow. She wasn't even a Catholic, and I was unclear if one could pray for a Protestant except for her conversion. By the middle of the week I was sick with pining for her. The nuns kept us in from recess during the week because it was raining so much, but I asked to be allowed to go to the church next door, and there, off at the side altar, I put three cents I had shaken out of Gerry's piggy bank into the slot and lit a candle, not for Patsy but for myself. I wasn't sure if this was allowed either. Worse, to pray for the opportunity for a kiss might be blasphemous, like praying for a successful bank heist, but my desire overcame my religious training.

On Friday at noon, the nun came for us.

'You boys need to go home. Your mother called. She's sick.'

'I hope she's not dying or anything,' Gerry said on the way home. It was hard to hear him because his face was deep inside the hood of his yellow rain slicker and my ears were covered as well. 'Could you imagine living with the Old Man?'

It was a punishment, I was sure, for my profane prayers.

Mrs Taylor was sitting in the living room with Tom when we got back.

'Boys, the doctor says your mother has appendicitis. There's nothing to be afraid of. Mr Taylor came home and drove her to the hospital. There's going to be an operation, but it's perfectly safe. Now we need to get in touch with your father, but no one seems to know where he's working. Do either of you know?'

We had heard him talk about Thistletown, but neither one of us knew anything more than that.

'There are sausages in a roasting pan in the oven. I'll turn them on now, and I'll be back to turn them off in an hour and a half. I'll call Mr Taylor from home and he can take a drive out to Thistletown and look around. Do you think you'll be all right until then?'

'We can take care of ourselves,' said Gerry. 'Dave'll watch Tom, and I'll go down to the hospital.'

'I don't think so. There's nothing you can do and she may already be in the operating room. You're the oldest one, so you should watch the others.'

Gerry liked that. He took charge. He made me peel potatoes and set the table, even though it was too early for supper.

'Why did you set a place for Mom?' he asked.

'Maybe she'll be back for supper. Do they feed you in hospitals?'

'You're so stupid. She might be in there for days. I'm going to pack her some clothes.'

'What's appendicitis?'

'It's this disease where part of your guts blow up inside, and if they don't clean it up fast, you get poisoned by the crap in your blood.'

In all the anxiety of waiting for my father and walking restlessly around the house as Gerry stuffed clothing into two pillowcases because he could not find a suitcase, I thought of nothing so much as Patsy. The roof on her treehouse was covered with shingles, and inside we could be dry, even in the rain.

I heard my father come in through the back door with his tools.

'Mom's in the hospital!' I called down to him, and when he did not answer, Gerry and I went down to the basement. He had his shirt off and he was washing himself in the laundry sink.

'I know, I know,' he said. 'Mr Taylor's waiting in his car outside. They let us off early anyway because of the rain.' He continued to wash his neck and under his arms. He looked big in the chest and arms without his shirt on. Not like a body-builder, but still big. It was disgusting. 'First I lose a week's pay to the bankruptcy. Then I keep getting rained out of work day after day. Now this.'

'But what about Mom?'

'I'll find out at the hospital. I may not be back tonight. Gerry, do you want Mrs Taylor to spend the night here?'

'I don't need her. I can take care of things.'

'Good boy. I'll change my clothes and get the chequebook, and then I have to go.'

'I put some clothes in a couple of pillowcases for her.'

'Smart move. At least someone around here can think.'

At the door, he puckered his lips and kissed each of us. He smelled of pipe tobacco.

'Okay,' said Gerry as soon as the door had closed. 'Everyone to the table for supper.'

'It's only three-thirty.'

'Yeah, well you can get an early start on your homework.'

'On Friday?'

'Look, I'm in charge. Keep your mouth shut and do what I say.'

It felt strange to sit down at the kitchen table with only three of us there. Tom had to have his food cut up into tiny bits. Halfway through the meal Gerry decided that we had to eat vegetables, so we had to stop and wait while he heated up a can of peas on the stove. By the time they were ready, the rest of our food was cold.

'I think I'll stop by Patsy's house tonight,' I said when we were done.

'Nope.'

'What?'

'What are you, deaf? I said no. You have to get your homework done in case there's a funeral or something.'

'Mom's not going to die. Mrs Taylor said she'd be fine.'

Tom started to ask for Mom, and when we told him she wasn't there, he asked for our father. Then he started to cry.

'Geez, you're an idiot,' said Gerry. 'Now the kid's all upset. I'm going to take him into the basement to play. You wash the dishes.'

I cleaned off the table, stacked the dishes in the sink and ran hot water over them. As the water ran over the dishes, I began to feel sick again, something like I had felt after I hurt my foot. I didn't know what to do. When I turned off the water, I had to sit down for a minute because I thought I was going to cry. Then I tiptoed over to the front door, slipped on my rubber boots and rain slicker, and closed the door behind me as softly as I could. Gerry might have heard me from the basement, so I ran down to the bottom of the street without looking back. The way to the hospital was left, but I turned right, towards Patsy's house.

The rain was coming down very hard, the way it sometimes did for a minute or two in a thunderstorm, but this kept up without stopping. I felt clammy inside the yellow rubber suit, and the rain came down so hard that it filled the pockets where I stuffed my hands, so I pulled them out and let the rain beat down on them. I passed our school and when I came to Weston Road, the street was a solid line of unmoving cars in both directions. People ran from one shop to the next with newspapers stretched over their heads. I thought of cutting down by the Humber for the footbridge, but the earth was so wet that I would only get mired in the muck, so I crossed at the big Lawrence Street bridge which had cars stopped on it in both directions. Down below, the river looked high, like it did in spring, except there were no ice floes on it. It was a fast-moving brown from all the earth that had washed into it. There seemed to be a lot of stuff floating in the river. As I looked down, a big branch of a tree rolled up slowly and then went down under again.

I cut down to Patsy's street and knocked at the front door. Mrs Lots answered it. I could smell the food cooking for dinner and Mr Lots stuck his head around the corner from the living room.

'My mother's in the hospital,' I said to Mrs Lots, and then I began to cry.

I felt like a kid no older than Tom, and I let her peel off the rain slicker and help me step out of my boots. Mrs Lots said words to me that had no meaning in my ears, but were as sweet as the cooing of a dove. She took off my wet clothes and put them in a dryer in the cellar, and then put Mr Lots' housecoat on me, rolled up the sleeves, folded up the long bottom and cinched it tight with the belt. She sat me down in the kitchen and made cocoa, and then when I was no longer blubbering, made me sit at their dinner table. Patsy looked at me coolly through the meal, and then by dessert I could finally make out what Mrs Lots was saying.

'Did they take your Mom to Humber Memorial, dear?'

'I think so.'

'I work in the maternity ward. I'll call up the girls on the next floor and they can tell me how your mother is doing.'

Mr Lots lit a cigarette while his wife phoned.

'Will you look at all that rain, Dave! It's going to flush out all the hobos along the construction sites. In a little while, we'll have hobos on rafts floating down the river like Huckleberry Finn!'

'Who's he?'

'A kid on a raft,' said Patsy.

Mrs Lots came back from the phone. 'You mother is fine, dear. She had the operation and they'll keep her in the hospital for a few days to give her a chance to rest. I told them to tell your father where you were.'

'My father?'

'He would have been worried, dear. On a night like this, with all the rain. Is your brother at home?'

'Yeah.'

'I think you ought to phone him.'

'What for?'

'So he doesn't worry.'

'Just you wait,' said Gerry when I had him on the line.

'What for?'

'The Old Man's going to kill you. He's going over to Patsy's house to pick you up after he leaves the hospital. Why didn't you wash the dishes?' My father phoned and refused the offer of a drive from Mr Lots. He said the streets were all snarled up with traffic because of the rain. He was coming to get me. Mrs Lots sent me and Patsy downstairs to play billiards while we waited.

'Remember, no English on the ball!' shouted Mr Lots.

Down in the cellar, Patsy set up the balls for snooker. I had a sense that my father was already outside the hospital. He would be coming for me through the rain. I was going to be grounded for the rest of my life.

I missed the entire triangle of red balls when Patsy asked me to break them. She did it for me on her shot.

'Patsy.'

'Yeah?'

'You want to practise?'

'Practise what?'

'You know.'

'Not now, you drip.'

We shot a few balls around the billiard table, but none of them fell into the pockets.

'My dad is going to be really mad at me. I might not be able to see you for a while.'

'I'll wait for you. Nobody gets grounded forever.'

We shot the balls around, but none of them went where we wanted them to go. That was the trouble with billiards. It looked so easy, but if none of the balls fell into the pockets, it became boring.

'I'll make you a bet,' I said.

'What is it?'

'If I sink the next ball, we practise.'

'And if you don't?'

'I don't know.'

'It's got to be worth something. Hold on.' she thought for a while. 'If you lose, you draw a big heart with our initials on it on the wall beside the front door to your school.'

'In chalk?'

'Uh-uh. Pastel.'

'Pastel doesn't come off.'

'That's the whole point.'

I prayed to the Virgin Mary and the Infant Jesus, sighted down the pool cue and sank a red ball. I looked up at her in triumph.

'Okay, I'm a good loser. You win.' She marched right up to me and stood a few inches away from my face. I could smell her hair and skin. She put her arms around my shoulders and began to tilt her head for the kiss when she looked over my shoulder. 'Will you look at that!'

I thought it was a cruel joke. I wanted to look at nothing. I wanted only the warm, sweet darkness of closed eyes and the touch of her lips on mine. But she pointed, and I looked behind me.

The cellar wall had started to cry. It was a white-painted mortar wall, but drops of water bulged out through the cracks and began to run in small streams down to the floor.

'I've got to tell my dad!'

She raced up the stairs and I was right behind her. Mr Lots came down to turn on his sump pump, but there was already a puddle at the foot of the wall. Mr Lots lifted the drain cover under the billiard table in the middle of the floor. The water touched the tip of his finger when he stuck it down there.

'God protect my billiard table,' he said.

Mrs Lots got my clothes out of the dryer, and then we were all mobilized to bring movable things upstairs and to help Mr Lots put blocks under the appliances in the basement so they would not get soaked if the basement flooded.

The doorbell rang. My father stepped in wearing his cloth raincoat, but it had not done him any good. He was soaked right through.

'Is your wife all right?' Mrs Lots asked.

'Fine. Sleeping. I take Dave home now.'

'I'd give you a ride, but my basement's flooding,' said Mr Lots.

'Rain is very bad. Footbridge over Humber under water. Floating trees backed up there. Soon it will break. Police stopping cars on big Lawrence bridge too. Maybe you all come to my house.'

Mr Lots smiled. 'Thank you, sir, but I have to be here to bail out the basement. I've lived here through forty-three years of spring floods. This couldn't be any worse.'

'You get wet here. My house on hill.'

Mr Lots looked at his wife.

'I don't know dear, what do you think? Do you and Patsy want to go over there for the night?'

'If we can't take the car across the bridge, we'll have to go on foot and we'll get soaked. That's not for me. Do you want to go, Patsy?' I looked at her imploringly.

'It's freezing out there.'

'We must hurry,' my father said. 'You come or you stay?'

'I guess we'd better stay.'

'Good night. Thank you for watch Dave.'

Mrs Lots helped me with my raincoat and boots. My heart was already aching again because Patsy was not coming to our house. Not that we could practise there. That would have been too dangerous.

Mr Lots came outside with his flashlight to look over the slope at the back of his yard and see how high the river was.

'Want to take a look?' he shouted to my father.

'No time. Goodbye.'

My father took my hand in his and began to walk up the street in long strides. It was hard to keep up with him. There were some people out with flashlights, and someone had driven his car to the end of his driveway to shine the headlights over the river. We were too far up the road for me to see what was visible. I had expected my father to stop once we were out of earshot and to give me a few words, but he held tightly onto my hand, strode up to Scarlett

Road and over to Lawrence Avenue and started to head down to the bridge. Cars were stopped on the road and some jockeyed to find enough room to turn around.

'They have stopped the traffic,' my father shouted above the rain.

We walked down to where a police car was parked across the road.

'You can't cross the bridge!' the policeman shouted at us.

'We live on other side. We go fast.'

'It's not going to hold up. Look down there!'

He shone a long-handled flashlight over the side of the bridge. It should have been a drop of thirty or more feet down below, but we could see the water just half a dozen feet below the span.

'A tree or something is going to get jammed in there, and then the force of the water is going to take down the bridge.'

Even as he spoke, something heavy hit the bridge and the earth beneath us seemed to shudder.

My father followed a road north, parallel to the river, but we could see nothing of the high water because of the houses between us and the river. The street lights flickered and went out, as did the lights in all the houses. My father picked up the pace. I was almost trotting beside him by this point, and I had a stitch in my side, but I just squeezed it with my free hand and kept on going.

My father passed the Saint Philips bridge and took a road that led back towards the Humber. The rain kept pouring down, and in the dark I was not sure where we were going. Until we came to the railroad tracks. He bent towards me so I could hear what he said.

'Listen to me. We could have tried the Saint Philips bridge, but it is probably going to come down too. We cannot be caught on this side of the river because Gerry and Tom are alone at home and your mother might need us tomorrow. I don't think the trains will be running because of the danger. We're going to start on dry land so you feel the space of the ties under your feet. Then we walk across. Keep away from the sides because it is going to be slippery and dark. Hold onto my hand. If a train does come, I'll pull you one way or the other, depending which way is the shortest. Do you understand?'

I nodded at him.

'Do you understand?' he repeated. It was too dark and wet for him to have seen my nod.

'I do!' I shouted.

His grip tightened on mine until my hand hurt. We started to walk along the ties. At first I missed them, but then I got used to the regular spacing and stepped solidly on the wood.

Then we got to the trestle. The wind was high down the river valley, and I could tell when we were over the water. It was roaring somewhere beneath us and I could feel the trestle tremble whenever something heavy hit one of the pillars. It was too dark to tell what might be floating down the river. My father stopped.

'You're pushing me over too far. I won't let go of your hand. Don't be afraid.'

We continued. Strange sounds came out of the darkness below us, shrieks of wood against concrete and a pinging noise as if a metal cable was flapping in the wind. At times I thought I could hear voices. In the distance there were lights flashing at the Saint Philips bridge. I tried to concentrate to keep my steps the right distance, but the more I thought about it, the more difficult it became, and I began to miss some of the steps and stumble.

'Steady on your feet,' my father shouted. 'Think of your mother.'

But all I could think of was Patsy.

I knew we had crossed over when I could feel bits of gravel on the ties. My father did not stop, but continued on the rail bed until we reached a short bridge that came over Weston Road. We came down the embankment, and my father went under the bridge. Two feet of water and a stalled car were already there.

'Come on, we're soaked already. At least it won't be coming down on our heads.'

We waded under the bridge and I slipped off my hood. The rain was still pouring down on both sides of the bridge. My father reached inside his breast pocket and pulled out his foil package of pipe tobacco. We were standing in water up to my knees, but he took his pipe and two matches from inside the pouch, stuffed the pipe and lit the matches by striking one head against the other.

'Always keep your powder dry, eh, Dave?'

I did not know the man who stood beside me. If he had shouted or swung at me, I would have felt that I was in the comfort of normality, but instead I seemed to be with some kind of Englishman with a stiff upper lip. Once he had the pipe going well, we came out from under the bridge, emptied our boots of water, and continued the rest of the way home. My father no longer held my hand. Instead, he kept one hand cupped over the pipe so the rain would not put it out.

'I thought you were both dead,' Gerry said when we came into the house. 'The radio is talking about a hurricane out there. Cars are getting washed away and fire trucks are screaming all over the place. I thought I was going to have to take care of Tom for the rest of my life. What do I look like, some kind of nanny?'

'Put on some tea,' my father said. 'Dave, come downstairs and take off your clothes. Hang them on a line in the cellar to dry.'

By the time I had changed out of my wet clothes, put on dry ones and returned to the kitchen, my father was sitting there with half a mickey of rye at his elbow. We all drank tea and my father took shots of rye as we listened to the radio. We still had electricity on our side of the river. Bridges were out all along the Humber, at the Etobicoke Creek, and up in the Holland Marsh. My father's hand began to shake. When he lifted a shot of whisky to his mouth, half the glass spilled out on the table.

'Now go to bed,' he said when we had finished our tea.

We lay there for a while, but we could hear him still moving about, starting to bump into the table and chairs. He was muttering to himself as he did whenever he drank alone. We heard him walk up to our door and listen to make sure we weren't talking.

'Almost shit my pants,' he muttered before he went on to his own room.

'Let me see your scar,' Gerry said to my mother.

'It's all covered up, dear. You can see it when the bandage comes off.'

Tom kept trying to climb onto the hospital bed to get on top of my mother, and Gerry kept pulling him down. The ward was full of women, mostly old and with tubes stuck in them. Some were wrapped in bandages. The place was packed with women hurt in the flood. After we had kissed my mother and she had given detailed instructions on the laundry and the meals, we left the hospital.

'Let's go take a look,' my father said, and we walked over to Lawrence Avenue. Tom soon got tired and my father had to carry him on his back. Up by Weston Road, there were knots of people talking at the street corners. Fire trucks were parked on Lawrence Avenue, up from where the bridge used to be.

They would not let us get close, but from the rise where we stood we could see that the entire valley was full of water. Whole trees floated by. I could not get close enough to see downstream to the curving bank where the Lotses had their house.

My father took us to a restaurant for the first time in my life. He ordered coffee for himself and soda floats for each of us, and he bought himself a newspaper. His lips moved as he mouthed the English words. Gerry looked over his shoulder, but I could not bear to look at the words on the paper. There was already too much talk around us.

'Any more survivors?' someone asked above the hubbub.

'Nope. Now they're just looking for bodies.'

On the way back home, I asked my father what happened to Protestants when they died.

'They go to limbo,' said Gerry.

I looked up the phone number for the Lotses and dialled it, but all I got was a repeated ringing that no one answered.

'Why don't you just look in the paper?' Gerry asked. 'See if their name is listed.'

Missing. Half of their street had been washed away in the night.

In the days that followed, I went down to the river to look over from our side. All the bridges were down, so there was no way to get across. Day after day, I phoned the number, but no one answered it. Gerry read the papers.

'Still missing.'

It was all the papers wrote about for days. Houses were washed away. Five firemen died when their truck got swamped. Some people clung to trees for the whole night before they were rescued in the morning.

Then the talk stopped. People were tired of it. The Lotses were still missing.

The water dropped pretty low again before the winter freeze-up in December. The river was full of junk, mostly concrete blocks and twisted pieces of iron reinforcing rods. From our side of the river, I thought I could see the chimney of the Lotses' stone barbecue sticking up from the shallow water on the other side, but I couldn't be sure.

I kept phoning their number. One day between Christmas and New Year's, someone finally picked up the phone.

'Can I speak to Patsy?' I asked.

'I'm sorry, I don't know anyone by that name,' a woman's voice answered.

'You're a liar!' I shouted, and I slammed down the phone.

My mother and father whispered together a great deal. That night at supper, my father would not let us get up from the table when we were finished.

'I have something to say to you.'

He filled his pipe with great ceremony, and then lit it and filled the room with smoke. He leaned forward towards me.

'Listen. My father was shot,' he said to me with no other explanation. 'The farm where I grew up was burned down. Half my brothers are in Siberia. One of my sisters is dead. This is how life is. Get used to it.'

He leaned back again as if he had just finished a long speech.

'That's supposed to make him feel better?' my mother asked.

'Who said anything about feeling better? It's just the way things are.'

All that winter I hid my thoughts from them. I played hockey with Gerry, and then moved on to baseball well before the winter had ended. When the weather warmed up in May, I started to go down to the river again. It was hard to get away from Gerry. I crossed over the new bridge and went down by the banks where their house used to be. Patsy still owed me a kiss. I needed to find them. Somewhere under the mud and the silt they were still to be found. I took a stick with me and dug through the pieces of shale, turning over each piece so I didn't miss anything. I was studying a piece one day when I heard a voice.

'What are you doing?'

It was a man in dirty clothes and a walking stick. A hobo. Not the same one we had met the year before.

'I'm looking for fossils,' I said.

Smoke

A BLOND WOMAN ABOUT MY MOTHER'S AGE WAS LEANING against the concrete front porch when Gerry and I got home from school. She was lighting another Du Maurier off the end of her first cigarette. Her cloth raincoat lay across the top of two suitcases on the scrub lawn at her feet. As soon as she looked up, she smiled and flicked the butt of her first smoke halfway across the yard where it landed in a heap of construction debris.

'Must be a lost dame,' Gerry whispered to me.

'Hello, boys,' she said when we were up close. 'Come on and give me a kiss. Keep it on the cheek. I just put on my lipstick.'

Gerry and I looked at each other, but we didn't move.

'Come on, I'm your Aunt Ramona. Let's get off to a good start.'

Gerry kissed her on one cheek, and I followed suit. Then we just stood there with our lunch pails in our hands.

'I think I've got some chewing gum around here,' she said, and she dug around in a deep rose purse that matched her shoes and nail polish. 'I've got some other things for you too, but they're in my suitcase. Here, hang on to my cigarette, will you?' and she passed it to Gerry. He handled it like a pro, and took a quick puff. 'Don't get the filter wet — I hate a soggy cigarette,' she said distractedly, and then came up with an opened package of Beech-Nut gum. 'This'll have to do for now.'

Gerry took the pack, slipped out pieces of gum for each of us, and then put the rest into his pocket.

'Do you live in the States?' Gerry asked.

'Oh, I've been all over. Let's get off the street, boys. Maybe your mother will have an extra pair of nylons around somewhere. I've ripped a hole the size of a softball.'

The house was quiet when we got inside.

'Not a bad little place,' she said as she looked around the living room. She went over to the TV and turned it on.

'I always like a little noise in the background. It keeps me from getting blue.'

I got nervous with her up so close to us inside the living room. Aunt Ramona seemed to fill the whole place up. She didn't look like my mother or my father, but she acted like she belonged. She went straight into my parents' bedroom and found a package of nylons.

'Now wait for me in the next room. I want to get these on before your parents come home. Too bad your Mom doesn't have the right shade.'

'What if she steals Mom's jewellery?' I whispered furiously to Gerry.

'Come on. Relatives don't steal.'

'If she's our aunt, how come we never heard of her?'

'Beats me. Maybe she just got over from Europe.'

'Nobody gets over from that part of Europe. You know that.'

'She could get out of anywhere. Anyway, she had a pack of Beech-Nut. She's from the States.'

'But look at her. She doesn't belong here.'

'She said she had some stuff for us, didn't she?'

That was true. It was worth waiting to find out what she had before we called the police.

I could hear keys jangling outside the front door. It was my father. The sickening twinge in my gut just before he appeared was a sure sign. But what was he doing using the front door instead of the back? He came in wearing his work clothes with the pants patched at the knees, and a swirl of sawdust came in behind him. He strode straight across the room to take Gerry by the ear.

'So now it's smoking! At your age! I should send you straight to the reformatory.'

It was terrifying how he knew everything about us.

The door to the bedroom swung open. My father looked at the blond. I still didn't think of her as our aunt. He did not let go of Gerry's ear even though Gerry was whining.

'Hush,' he finally said, but he didn't let go.

'Happy to see me?' the blond said.

'I should have known it was you as soon as I saw the fire burning on the front yard. I'll get you a bucket. Go and put it out.'

'Give me a hand, boys?'

'They have homework. Lots of it.'

My father pushed us into our room without even letting us take off our jackets.

'Is she our aunt or what?' Gerry asked.

'Be quiet. Stay in here and don't move until I tell you to.'

'But is she our aunt?'

Gerry never let up. Sometimes it worked.

'Yes, she's your aunt, but she's come back from the dead. Maybe I should call a priest for an exorcism.'

'Whose sister — yours or Mom's?'

'Mine,' and he walked out and shut the door behind him.

'I guess I kissed a ghost,' I said.

'It was a metaphor. Don't you ever listen in school?'

'I always thought his sisters would wear headscarves.'

'Huh?'

'You know, heavy raincoats and scarves tied over their heads and under their chins.'

'You're thinking of that picture of our grandmother.'

'Everybody looks like that over there.'

If my father told us to stay in our rooms, it meant not to go out unless there was a fire. Gerry and I did our homework, and didn't dare open the door even when we heard our mother come home. Her voice on the other side of the door brought hope of rescue, but she didn't let us out for a long time. When she did, my father and Aunt Ramona were already sitting at the kitchen table. Our little brother, Tom, was wearing blue suspenders and a matching bow tie and beaming at us like he was getting married. Aunt Ramona and my mother and father had cocktail glasses by their plates, and an opened bottle of Canadian Club was by my father's elbow. She'd even remembered the mix. Matching grenades were set at my place and Gerry's.

'I wasn't so sure about the grenades,' my mother said, 'but I guess you can have them.'

'They're defused anyway,' my father said. 'Just toys.'

Aunt Ramona smiled at us and lit another cigarette. She knew our hearts were easy to buy.

The whole family walked into the church together, and our little brother Tom began to snivel as soon as we walked down the centre aisle of the church.

'What's the matter?' my mother hissed at him.

'The big candles are lit. We're going to be here all day.'

If I'd been any younger, I would have snivelled too. Tall candles meant a high mass, and on the worst day of the year, Palm Sunday, when the reading of the passion and death of Jesus went on long enough for the squeaky Sunday shoes to pinch our feet in a dozen places as we stood and listened to the same old story.

It wasn't supposed to turn out that way. Gerry and I talked hard to get our father to go to the ten o'clock service because it was Palm Sunday. At least at ten it was a low mass, and the priests hurried because there was another service coming up. At eleven-fifteen, the choir sang and they let the old, long-winded priest give the sermon. He could easily talk for an hour. What was there for boys to do on a Sunday afternoon anyway?

We could still smell the incense from the service before, like the smell of blood from others who had been tortured before us.

'I can't put on my coat. My nail polish hasn't dried yet,' my Aunt Ramona had said that morning when my father was trying to get us into the car to make it on time for the ten o'clock mass.

'So put on some gloves.'

'It'll ruin the gloves and the polish as well.'

'I'm not going to march in late to mass with the whole church looking at us. You get in the car right now, or we're going to the later service.'

'Why can't we go to the local church? It'll be faster.'

'On Palm Sunday, we go to *our* church. You want everyone we know to think we're atheists?'

'Well, I have to wait a couple more minutes.'

'No. We go now, or we go to the next mass.'

'I can't go now.'

'Then it's settled.'

Aunt Ramona flashed a look of regret at Gerry and me.

'Remember, I don't want any men looking at you,' my father said to Aunt Ramona as we finally climbed up the steps to the church.

'As if I could stop them.'

'Don't play up to it. Don't bat your eyelashes. You're a married woman.'

'I told you. He's dead.'

'You don't know that.'

It was hopeless. Wherever my Aunt Ramona went, men's heads turned. I could see them down at the far end of the pew where we sat, glancing sideways over hands clenched in prayer. When the priest made the rounds with the holy water, he sprayed us thick and heavy, and when Aunt Ramona put her tongue to her lip where a drop of holy water had landed, I heard a man gasp lightly.

The cigarette smoke in the church basement was so thick, it stung my eyes. Big round tables were set up in one room where the church ladies served coffee, and in the adjoining gym, men in shirt sleeves were setting out spectators' chairs for the basketball games that happened every Sunday. It was a special league, for basketball players from countries that didn't exist any more. Sometimes I whirled the globe at school, but I could never find Estonia or Ukraine or any other of the funny names of countries that were printed on the back of the basketball players' shirts. Including the name of the country we came from. It didn't really bother me that it could never be found on the map. It just bothered me that we were from there in the first place.

The church basement was the payoff for Gerry, Tom, and me. My aunt bought us chips and pop, and we could hang out with the kids of our parents' friends. The altar boys brought down leftover communion wine, which we shared in the back parking lot, and sometimes a few hosts that hadn't been consecrated yet.

'It's not a sin if it hasn't been consecrated,' Gerry said when I balked.

'How do you know that for sure?'

'No altar boy is going to get his hands on one of those. They're locked up in the tabernacle. Besides, if you tried to touch a consecrated host, it would burn your hands.'

'That's not true. It doesn't burn your tongue.'

'What do you think the priest puts it there for, stupid? It's the only part of your body that can take a host without burning. And if you're scared because you missed confession, and say your tongue dries out because of the fear, it'll burn that too.'

'You've skipped confession before.'

'Yeah, but I'm too cool to panic. I roll my tongue around in my mouth, just to make sure it's good and wet.'

The back door opened up, and our Aunt Ramona came outside.

'Oh, there you are, boys. Tell your father I'm going over to Maggie's house for the afternoon. Here's a dollar. Buy yourselves something,' and she walked to the end of the parking lot and turned around the corner of the church.

'That aunt of yours is really something,' said one of the altar boys. He kept wiping his nose and looking the way she had gone.

We were halfway home in the car before my father spoke up from the driver's seat. He had been sucking hard on the empty pipe all the way.

'I knew it would come to this.'

'What?' my mother asked.

'She's starting to upset things already. You never should have let her stay.'

'What has she upset?'

'Palm Sunday. An honest woman doesn't take off on Palm Sunday. She'll be carousing with that Maggie again. Men guests. There'll be a lot of those. On Palm Sunday. I could die of shame.'

'She's young. She doesn't have a family. Let her have some fun.'

'What do you mean by young? She's your age.'

My mother let that pass.

'I just wish she had a death certificate,' my father went on. 'Then we could be sure.'

My mother laughed.

'She's lucky she got out alive. Don't expect her to have a pile of documents.'

'It's not just the documents. It's the years between. What took her so long to get here?'

'Sometimes I wish we could just forget the past,' my mother said. She traced a pattern on the window at her side with her gloved hand. White gloves, even though it wasn't quite Easter yet. 'I'm beginning to forget what my sisters looked like. Funny, isn't it? If we went back now, I wouldn't recognize them in a crowd.'

'We're not going back soon. Not unless the Americans bomb the Russians, and they're too scared to do that. No need to worry about it.'

'I know that. World without end, amen.'

Aunt Ramona slept in the basement on a fold-out couch. She had a wardrobe and a chest, and she even bought a coffee table and two chairs. Her world started partway down the steps to the basement, where we left the smell of my father's pipe and walked into the smell of her Du Mauriers. She bought the first record player in our house, and when the radio wasn't on, she stacked up the forty-five rpm discs six at a time. The last couple of songs sounded strange because the records below them slipped on the turntable and Sinatra's voice wobbled like a drunk's. She also played Edith Piaf.

'How come you play Frog songs?' Gerry asked.

'You mustn't call them that.'

Gerry didn't sneer at Aunt Ramona. He just waited for her to tell him why not.

'The culture of France is magnificent. You can drink wine at tables out on the street and they have thousands of artists.'

'Did you live there?'

'For a while. I was a model.'

'No kidding! Did you ever make it into the Eaton's catalogue?'

'I wasn't there for long. I was going to marry a man in the Legion, so I went down to Algiers.'

Gerry shifted his weight from one foot to another, and I looked away. The love business kept creeping into the conversations we had with adults. It was embarrassing.

'Where's Algiers?'

'In Africa.'

'The Legion? You mean the French Foreign Legion?'

'Sure.'

'Did he kill a lot of Arabs?'

'No. They killed him.'

Not only did the adults always end up talking about love, they didn't even know how a story was supposed to end.

'Did they torture him?' Gerry asked.

'I don't think so.'

'Was his fort overrun?'

'He got into a fight in a bar and somebody stuck a knife in him.' Aunt Ramona lit another cigarette and thought for a while. The last record on the stack was a piece of French accordion music, but it was slipping so badly it sounded like a cat wailing.

'I don't think you should tell your parents about that.'

She knew better than anyone how to make us love her.

The men had started to appear with the fine weather. Ramona had so many callers, my mother had to buy extra ashtrays. Some of them were too shy to come alone, and they arrived in twos and threes, and sometimes there was more than one group at a time.

'The neighbours will think I'm running a brothel!' my father said.

'What kind of language is that to use in front of the children?' my mother asked. I made a mental note to look the word up in the dictionary.

'If you don't want the visitors around in the living room, they can come downstairs.'

'Not on your life. I want them up here, where I can see what they're up to.'

As far as Gerry and I could tell, they were mostly up to making big round eyes that looked stupid on the faces of adult men. Most were our people, ones we had seen at the church, or ones that had heard about her from as far away as Tillsonburg, a hundred miles down the road, but some Canadians got into the act as well. There was a tall, skinny man who worked shifts at the CCM bicycle plant, and he was around our street all summer at the strangest times of the day. He had a grumpy German shepherd that he walked around the neighbourhood, and every time he ran into Gerry or me, he kept asking about our aunt. The dog would snap at us if we got too close. I didn't even know his name. He was just the man with the short pants, skinny, hairy legs, dog and a leather bag. It wasn't exactly a briefcase, more like a small duffel with handles, but he carried it around with him all that summer.

My father liked the jeweller from Cleveland. I could hardly believe that one of our people could be a jeweller. The men tended to work in factories and a few were doctors or engineers. The jeweller came up to Toronto in a pink Lincoln Continental and he wore a Stetson and a string tie. I liked the Stetson, but it seemed strange on the head of a man whose English was heavily accented. He came every weekend from the middle of July, thick gold rings on his fingers and the trunk full of gifts. Melted chocolate cherries for my mother, a bottle of sweet wine for the women, and Canadian Club for my father.

The man we liked best was Frank the plumber. He visited her every Friday night, and his bottles of Five Star whisky and Canadian champagne were pitiful by comparison. One time Gerry and I found him crying outside by his panel van.

'How can a plumber compete with a jeweller?' he sobbed, and he laid his head against the 'Frank's Plumbing' lettering on the side of the van, and the tears fell in big fat drops onto the gravel driveway. It made me sick to see adult tears, but at least he let us keep the change whenever he sent us out to buy a package of cigarettes.

I wasn't sure if the jeweller was an idiot or if I loved him. He brought things for us too. With every appearance, he added a new item to our Western outfits. Gerry and Tom and I already had matching six-guns in double holsters, cowboy hats and plastic Western boot tops that fitted over our shoes and the ends of our pant legs. All we still needed were Western chaps. Aunt Ramona got dresses and jewellery and a box for the rings and brooches. The box played 'Autumn Leaves' whenever she opened it.

'At least Frank is solid,' my mother said.

'Are you crazy?' my father objected. 'All day long he runs wire snakes through plugged toilets. Think of what gets on his hands. If she married the jeweller, we'd finally have some money in this family again.'

'Feh! He's like Liberace, that one.'

'I wouldn't care if he wore dresses. He's got money, and somebody has to get her off our hands.'

'You're the one who was so worried about her husband.'

'It wasn't even a proper wedding. It doesn't count.'

'Because he was a Jew?'

'Be quiet. The kids will hear you.'

'So she married a Jew. She was still married.'

'By a rabbi.'

'Did she convert?'

'No. Neither one wanted to convert. They found some renegade socialist rabbi who felt sorry for them. But the point is, I don't think there was ever a civil record. The Nazis came in right after, and then *bang*. The Jews, the synagogues, the records — all up in flames.'

'You should be ashamed of yourself.'

'As if it was my fault.'

'You kept telling her she was married, and now you say she isn't.'

'She was married until someone better came along. This is it.'

'So what if someone better came along for me?'

'Don't be ridiculous.'

I came home from the park one day to find Aunt Ramona hiding behind the curtains in the living room, and peering out at the street.

'Did you see the man with the German shepherd?' she asked.

'Nope. Is he bugging you or something?'

'He's over in the Taylors' lilac bushes changing his pants.'

'Did he wet them?'

'He doesn't like me to see him in his shorts. He changes into long pants when he gets near the house, and then he walks by and looks in our windows.'

'Why doesn't he just wear long pants all the time?'

'I don't know.'

'Why doesn't he knock on our door if he wants to talk to you?'

'I'd laugh in his face.'

It was hard to tell what Aunt Ramona thought of the jeweller. She made him sleep in a cot in the garage, even though my mother was willing to put him on the living room couch over the weekend.

'Is he dangerous?' my mother asked.

'I just don't want to be under the same roof with him at night.'

'Oh, Ramona, that's not a very good sign. Maybe you should tell him to stop coming. Think of all the miles he's putting on that car of his.'

'Who told him to come here in the first place? It's not as if I'm encouraging him.'

'You have to make it plain to men. They don't understand anything less.'

'I told him a pink car was ridiculous.'

'What did he say?'

'That he'd paint it any colour I wanted. I told him I liked chartreuse.'

My mother began to laugh, but Aunt Ramona didn't get the joke.

'We're going to a dance at the ballroom on Saturday. I bought a new chartreuse dress and matching bag and shoes.'

We were sitting at supper when someone knocked at the door.

'This place is turning into a train station,' my father said as he slammed down his spoon and wiped his mouth with the back of his hand.

'Use the napkin,' my mother said.

Whoever it was knocked again. It was not a friendly knock.

'I'll get this,' my father said. 'If it's one of the children's friends, I'll give them a lecture. But if it's one of your men friends, Ramona, I swear I'm going to give him a number and tell him to wait in line.'

'If it's for me, I'm not at home,' said Aunt Ramona.

My father had stood up, but now he sat back down. 'What am I? Your butler? Gerry, you go answer the door.'

The knock came again. Three sharp raps. Gerry got up, and the rest of us waited in silence. It was hard to tell what was being said at the door, but it went on a long time.

'Jehovah's Witness,' said Gerry when he came back.

'Honestly,' my mother said. 'They always come at dinner time or Sunday morning.'

I was going downstairs to Aunt Ramona's, but I stopped partway down the steps. I could hear her talking with Gerry.

'He said you owe him thirty-three dollars. You're behind on payments. He said he'd be back.'

'The man's a real thief. The first payment on the chartreuse outfit isn't due until next Friday. He must have gotten mixed up. Don't tell your father. He always takes the other side when this kind of thing happens.'

'I won't. But he was mean-looking. He'll be back.'

'They all say that. And hold the cigarette with the outside of your lips. If you stick it that far in, it gets sloppy. Not like that either. If it falls out and burns your shirt, I'll have your mother after me as well.'

'And another thing.'

'What?'

'The guy with the German shepherd was in the Taylors' bushes again. I think he must be nuts or something.'

'I'll say. You listen to me, Gerry. If there's one thing a woman can't abide, it's a fool. I never want to see you acting like a fool around women.'

Gerry and Tom and I were waiting for the jeweller to arrive after lunch on Saturday. We were on the front porch in our twin six-guns and double holsters, cowboy hats and vests and boot-tops. Tom was still so small that we'd had to punch holes in his gun-belts to make them cinch tightly enough, and the ends of the belts hung floppily at his sides. His six-guns reached all the way to his knees. Our mother came out to snap a picture with the Brownie.

'I'm not so sure it's a good idea to wait for him like this. He'll think you just want more gifts.'

'Schnapps!' said Tom. 'He promised to bring us some schnapps.'

'Chaps, you idiot,' said Gerry. 'Look, Mom, we're just showing our appreciation. He bought us this stuff to make us look good, so now we do.'

She was too busy with cleaning the house to argue much. Gerry took us through our moves, but when the car finally came up the street, we didn't recognize it.

'Holy smokes, it's him! Let's go!' said Gerry.

As the chartreuse Lincoln Continental pulled into the driveway, the three of us stood in a line on the porch, pulled out our double six-guns, and fired madly until we stood in a cloud of smoke from the rolls of caps we had fired off.

'Boys, that was great!' said the jeweller when he stepped out. 'How do you like the car?' He didn't even wait for an answer, but went around to the trunk and pulled out a pile of boxes like he did every week.

'Too bad I didn't tell him to do something about the interior,' said Aunt Ramona. She was on the porch beside us, and she turned her cheek to let him kiss it as he came up the steps.

'Well, Ramona, what do you think?'

'Amazing. You matched the shade of my dress perfectly.'

'The body shop had to put on three coats. The pink kept on showing up from underneath.'

We went inside for the weekly ritual. My father poured drinks from the bottle the jeweller had brought, and Aunt Ramona opened the boxes. There was a lot of woman stuff, like gloves and figurines and even a new raincoat. No sign of the chaps.

'Don't worry, boys. I haven't forgotten you. I ordered the chaps from a special Western store. They're being cut to size this week, and I'll have them for you next Saturday.'

It was some consolation, but he didn't even bring us anything to tide us over.

When the room was already full of ripped wrapping paper, he pulled a small box from his coat pocket.

'The best for last,' he said.

Aunt Ramona opened up the box, flipped the lid, and looked at the diamond ring for hardly a second before she slipped it on her finger and held it up to the light. My mother immediately reached for her hand and looked at the stone.

'The size of the Matterhorn,' she said.

The jeweller cleared his throat a couple of times and went red in the face.

'I guess you know what this means,' he said.

'I accept,' Aunt Ramona said. She kept holding the ring up to the light as the jeweller tried to manoeuvre closer to her to give her a kiss. She finally saw what he was up to, and offered him her cheek again.

'I've got a bottle of champagne in the trunk.'

'Skip it. Champagne gives me a headache.'

It seemed to be a big deal to the rest of them, but it didn't make much of a difference to us. Gerry took off his Western outfit before we went down the street to play with other kids.

'I'm too old for this stuff anyway,' he said. 'Unless you've got the chaps, you look like an idiot in the outfit. I'd kind of like a pilot's jumpsuit instead. Maybe even a parachute.'

Dinner seemed to go on forever. The jeweller kept talking about the better parts of Cleveland where he planned to buy them a new house. My father was busy eating and drinking, and he didn't say much. Aunt Ramona just smoked throughout the meal and sipped on her highball. My mother kept asking him questions and he answered them all, but he only had eyes for Ramona. After dinner, she went downstairs to change into her chartreuse outfit, and when she came back up, even I was impressed. The shoes and bag and dress were all of a shiny material, almost metallic, and she had a band of sequins along the neckline.

'If the car breaks down, just make her stand at the curb and the police will be there in no time,' my father said.

Aunt Ramona was above making any answer. All of us went out onto the porch to see them off. First my mother made them stand by the car so she could snap another picture with the Brownie.

'I wish I could get this in colour,' she said.

The jeweller opened the door for Aunt Ramona, and she reached in and brushed off the seat of the car before she got in. He closed the door and started up the engine, but just after he put the Lincoln into gear, a black Ford pulled up to the end of the driveway and blocked the way out. A small man in a suit got out of the Ford. He held some kind of papers in his hand, and he walked right over to where Aunt Ramona was sitting and he tapped on the window.

'I'm glad I caught you. I've come for the money for that dress.'

Aunt Ramona slowly rolled the window down part way.

'I'll see you on Monday.'

'No, I'm afraid not. You must either pay me for that outfit now, or return it to me. I've had enough of chasing after you.'

'You men make me so tired sometimes.'

I could see the jeweller was talking furiously, and reaching for his wallet in the breast pocket of his coat. The rest of us stood on the porch as Aunt Ramona opened the car door and got out. She emptied her purse on the hood of the car and tossed it onto the scrub yard. Then she stepped out of her shoes and tossed them as well. She turned her back to the small man.

'Undo the clip at the top. I'll have this off for you in a second.'

'Ramona!' the jeweller pleaded. He was out of the car now, coming around the hood with his wallet out. 'There's no need!'

The man had his mouth open. Maybe because we didn't have much of a lawn yet, and she'd thrown the bag and shoes into the dirt.

That was when the police cruiser pulled up on the other side of the street. My mother put her hand on her mouth. I couldn't figure out how they had reached our place so fast. The two big cops who got out of the car didn't even close the doors behind them. They raced straight for the bushes on the edge of the Taylors' property. Everyone at our place froze at the sound of barking and shouting and swearing. The bushes at the Taylors' place shook and swayed and the noise was very loud. Then there was a single gunshot and a loud wail.

'My dog! You went and shot my dog!'

By this time, Mr and Mrs Taylor were outside as well, and they watched while the two policemen brought out the skinny man with hairy legs. They had him handcuffed, but at first I couldn't tell because it looked like his hands were down to cover his private parts. He was wearing boxer shorts.

'They shot my dog!' he shouted across the street to us. 'Ramona, I was doing it for you!'

His legs looked darker and hairier than usual against the white of his boxer shorts.

Everyone turned to look at my Aunt Ramona, whose shoes and bag were lying in the dust. She stood in her nylons on the gravel driveway, her back still turned to the man from the dress store.

'Somebody give me a cigarette,' she said.

They never made it to the dance. One of the policemen came over to talk to us after they had the man in the back of their car. Then my father had to go over to talk to the Taylors, and the jeweller took the dress store man aside and slipped him some bills to make him go away. Aunt Ramona went downstairs to change.

Back inside the house, the jeweller was pale and drinking his highballs as fast as my mother could make them.

'You know,' my father said, 'Christianity is a wonderful thing.'

The jeweller looked at my father as if he had gone out of his mind.

'I mean, it teaches forgiveness. If somebody punches you in the eye, it's natural to want to punch him back. My fingers twitch at the thought of somebody hitting me, but the Bible taught us there is a better way. Forgive your enemy, and you earn the kingdom of heaven. Now, the Bible never tells us to be fools. No use putting yourself in harm's way intentionally, but on the other hand, you have to learn to overlook some things.'

'If you're talking about that fool the police took away, I don't care about him.'

'That's not what I was talking about. I was talking about women.'

'What about them?'

'Have you been listening? God put them on this earth to give us a chance to practise forgiveness.'

'Maybe you might want to explain that a little,' my mother said as she came into the living room with another pair of highballs for the men.

'It's what marriage is all about. Women are like children. They make mistakes and they have to be instructed, and some learn better than others. Think of yourself as a teacher. Now occasionally each of us comes up against a dunce, but God told us to love everyone. Think of Mary Magdalene.'

'Remember you're talking about your sister,' my mother said bitterly.

'Who said anything about her? I was talking about women in general.'

'And does that include your wife?'

'Aren't you a woman? Haven't you been listening?'

A sofa cushion flew across the room and hit my father in the face. Luckily, he wasn't holding his highball at the time, but it did knock the pipe out of his mouth.

My father took a moment to gather his wits as my mother stormed out.

'You see? Life is a trial and women are the biggest one of all.'

We waited a long time before my mother finally went downstairs to see what had happened to my Aunt Ramona. My mother came back quickly.

'She's gone.'

My mother wanted the police to look for Ramona because she had left without taking anything more than her wallet, raincoat, and a small bag.

'And the ring,' my father said. 'She's so stupid, but she's not that stupid.'

'She could be in trouble somewhere.'

'She's trouble anywhere she goes.'

My mother was making up boxes to send to Cleveland. Gerry was furious when she included all the Western outfits along with the gifts that the jeweller had given Aunt Ramona.

'It's not fair. He gave them to us.'

'And if they'd gotten married, you could've kept them too.'

'No schnapps,' said Tom, and he started to cry.

We'd managed to save the rolls of caps from the six-guns, and sometimes we would take them outside and snap them between rocks in the back yard. I thought we'd used them all up, but we found one more roll under Tom's bed late that fall, and the three of us were in the yard making little puffs of smoke. My father was digging up the remains of the garden for the winter when my mother came out from the house with a letter in her hand.

'Don't tell me,' my father said. 'I can guess.'

'She found her husband. And he's rich! He owns a car wash in Melbourne!'

'Where's that?' I asked.

'In Australia.'

My father took out his pipe and spat onto the freshly turned earth. 'Still too close for comfort.'

I thought I caught the whiff of cigarette smoke, but it was just the smell from the little puffs that came up from our caps.

The Crystal Palace

No more hamburgers. Now it was roast pork. Almost every night was a roast pork night. Sometimes, for variety, we had pork chops, and on every second weekend a big ham that lasted all the way to Thursday's sandwiches. My father refused to eat casseroles or spaghetti. He said fish was all right for Fridays, but chicken was for women and invalids, beef was too tough, and lamb smelled bad — it reminded him of the mutton fat candles his mother used to make when he was a child.

'Birthday candles?' asked Tom. He had this wide-eyed little kid look on him. It drove me crazy. Tom was so small that he still looked up to the Old Man.

'We used candles for light. Every night we lit up a couple of mutton tallow candles, and the whole place stank like wet wool. It was really bad in the winter when it got dark at four in the afternoon and it was too cold to open the door to let in some air.'

'Why didn't you use oil lamps?'

'Kerosene cost money. Mutton fat didn't.'

'You must have been really poor.'

'Nah. The poor people used reed torches.'

'Dad, do me a favour,' said Gerry. 'Don't tell this story to any of my friends, okay? They'll think you were a caveman or something.'

'My mother spun her own wool and flax too.'

'Yeah, yeah,' said Gerry, 'and you used flint to start fires.'

'You needed a licence to own a lighter. Matches were a state monopoly.'

Gerry rolled his eyes.

My father kept explaining to us how lucky we were to get roast pork.

'When I was a kid, we ate potatoes and carrots and cabbage, with a little melted pork fat for flavour. No eggs either. We sold those in the city for cash. As a child, the only time I ate roast pork was at weddings and funerals.'

He always ate with gusto, cutting off huge slabs of meat at a time. I couldn't understand how he could be excited about the same dish day after day.

That night it was barley soup first, made with the bone from last week's ham. My father used a spoon as deep as a ladle.

My mother waited until he had swallowed about a quart of soup off his spoon before she asked him a question. She had to time it right when she asked him things at the dinner table, because he would answer right away, even if his mouth was full of food. Gerry and I tried not to look at him during meals.

'So what do you think about my new job offer?' my mother asked.

'If he's willing to pay fifteen dollars a week more than you earn now, he must have money to burn.'

'It's a big operation. He has thirty people working in the warehouse alone. I never thought so many people bought crystal.'

'So what would you do there?'

'Deal with the imports from Germany and Czechoslovakia. Write letters, make some phone calls.'

'He phones Germany? Do you know how much that costs?'

'Usually he sends telexes.'

'What's he like?'

'Very cultured. We talked about Rilke, and then he offered me the job.'

'Why not?' my father said. 'We can always use the extra money.'

He began the long slurp from the edge of his big spoon, and I could see the barley bits flying into his mouth.

'There's only one catch,' my mother said. 'I didn't tell him about the children.'

My father sucked back the last of the soup.

'What's to tell? Does he want to check their fingernails?'

'He doesn't know they have fingernails.'

Even Tom was interested in this one.

'Does he think we have claws?'

My mother was not a secretive person, so she was going to tell us sooner or later, but first she had to go through a few shades of colour, starting at pale and moving up to a high-blood-pressure deep pink. She looked up at us, then down at her plate, and started and stopped a couple of times before she got it out.

'He thinks women with children should stay at home.'

'Hmph. Caveman,' said my father.

'I think Mom should stay home too,' said Gerry. 'Then we could have hot lunches.'

My mother looked at Gerry with her eyebrows arched in concern. He had hit her tender spot. Breakfasts in our house were three or four courses laid out in a warm oven before my mother went to work: grilled cheese, fried bacon, scrambled eggs, oatmeal, and half a grapefruit made her feel a little less bad about leaving us to go out to work each day. But our cold lunches bothered her. Somehow, sandwiches didn't seem right. Mothers were supposed to stay home and make hot lunches for their children. If she was feeling particularly guilty, she would leave Gerry and me fifty cents each, and we went up to the fish-and-chip shop at lunch. We'd skip the fish and order a double order of fries, and then spend the rest of the money on candy.

'You told him you didn't have any children?' my father asked.

My mother's face had gone beet red, and she was twisting the napkin in her hand.

'No. He didn't ask and I didn't tell him.'

'Hah! So he'll never be able to say you lied to him. Take the job, take the money, and worry later.'

She did take the job, but she could not put off the worrying.

My mother had changed jobs before, but there was something different about it this time. Her clothes changed too. She went from dresses to business suits in muted 'feminine' colours. My father often picked her up at the bus stop after work. The Strato Chief he drove was splattered with mud from the construction sites, and his wooden tool box was too big to fit in the trunk, so he kept it on a rug on the back seat. He wore a green working man's hat with the earflaps down from September to May, and beneath that a checked Hudson's Bay lumberjack coat and old baggy woollen pants with patches on the knees. When he and my mother stepped out of the car, she looked like she was getting a ride from her gardener.

In the old days, when she came back from work, she went straight to the oven in her coat to start the vegetables and make the gravy for the pork roast. After a few weeks at the new job, she kissed each one of us when she came in and went into her room to change before going to the kitchen. Worse, she wrote out a list of chores for each of us, and now Gerry and I had to wash the dishes on alternate days after she banned my father from the sink.

'No more dishwashing for you,' my mother said calmly.

Gerry and I were horrified. It was one fight we hoped that my father would win. 'You leave invisible bumps on the dishes you wash,' she added.

'Invisible bumps? What do you think I am, a magician?'

'You do not run your hands over the plates when you wash them, and you leave small bits of food that turn hard. Also, you do not use enough detergent.'

'My mother never even heard of detergent! That's just some crazy new product the marketing people dreamed up. Hot water is all you need.'

'I also want you to put up a paper towel rack for me.'

'Absolutely not. I draw the line at paper towels. What's wrong with rags?'

'Rags are unhygienic.'

My father raged, but I could see that he liked the way things were going. The household was beginning to tick to a schedule. We were allowed an hour of sports on the street outside when we finished the dishes, and then television only if all our homework was done.

'It's like living in a bloody boot camp,' said Gerry.

A boot camp with music. She made us bring Aunt Ramona's old record player up from the basement and into the living room. She started to buy records, which seemed strange to us. Records were for teenagers, not adults. Some of our friends' parents bought records, it was true, but they bought singers like Frank Sinatra or Doris Day. My mother bought opera sets, and Strauss and Chopin and Schumann. Even worse, she would play this music in the living room where we were forbidden to turn it off even if a hockey game was about to begin on TV.

'Mom,' said Gerry, 'you can put the record back on later. This hockey game will never happen again.'

'Music is superior to hockey, so hockey will have to wait its turn.'

This was outlandish. But even our father, the big hockey fan who knew all the players for the Leafs and some of the Canadiens, did not stand up for us.

'It makes her happy. Let her listen.'

It made her happy all right, but what about us? Even worse, the little traitor Tom would sometimes sit in the room with her and just listen. He didn't even read while he listened.

This was an attack from a quarter we had never expected. Usually it was our father who ruined our lives. Who knew where things would stop now that our mother was trying to tame us? Next, she might ask us to help vacuum on Saturdays, or do the laundry — even insist that we sew on our own buttons! We were on a slippery slope that might end with piano lessons. We might be forced to go to the ballet. It was intolerable.

'She must be in love,' said Gerry.

The thought of my mother in love horrified me. Mothers weren't supposed to be in love with anyone, not even their husbands.

'Maybe,' said Tom, who was playing on the floor with his Dinky toys. 'She bought Dad a new tie, and it's not even his birthday or anything.'

'Not with the Old Man, you little jerk,' said Gerry. 'She's probably in love with the Czech she works for.'

A sickening silence came down on the three of us. Tom took a Dinky toy in each hand, set them on the floor and then smashed them together.

'We just have to make sure she loves Dad,' said Tom.

Gerry considered what Tom had said.

'The kid's got some brains. If we make her feel wanted, she'll leave us alone.'

My father was at home for a couple of days between jobs, and Gerry and I spoke to him when we came home for lunch.

'You want to bake a cake? What for?'

'Just to make Mom feel good. You know, she's been working so hard and stuff.'

'You want to bake a cake after school, go right ahead. I'm not stopping you.'

'Yeah, well there's a couple of other ideas we had as well. Like you could buy her some flowers.'

'Flowers?'

'Yeah, go out to Weston and pick her up some roses or something.'

'Do you know what roses cost?'

'Then carnations. Jeez, this is no time to be cheap. And put on some nice clothes too. We want to make her feel good when she gets home.'

Gerry and I checked her cookbook, and picked a yellow cake that didn't look too hard to make. We dug out the ingredients so they'd be ready by the time we got home after school.

When we came in that afternoon, my father had already set the table with the good plates and crystal glasses my mother had bought at work. Right in the middle of the table, set on a wooden cutting board, was a rose bush he'd picked up at the nursery, with the stems clipped short for planting in the spring and the bottom wrapped up tight in waxed paper.

'Jeez, I meant cut flowers, not a bush you have to plant.'

My father did not seem to be around. When we pushed open the bedroom door, he was lying on top of the sheets in his Sunday suit. His eyes were open and he was staring at the ceiling. His shoes were freshly shined and set on the floor at the foot of the bed.

'What's the suit for?' Gerry asked.

'You asked me to dress up nice.'

'I meant a sweater or something. You look like you're going to a funeral.'

'This will be fine. Wake me when it's time to pick her up at the bus stop. I'm just going to take a little rest.'

There was no time to argue with him because we had to get the cake baked. Searching for the vanilla, I found my father's mickey. It was Five Star whisky, his favourite brand. He'd finished half of it.

'Think he'll sober up by the time she gets home?' I asked.

'Depends. He's always in a bad mood when he's hung over, so maybe it's better if he's a little looped.'

We mixed sugar and butter and beat eggs as well as we could, but the cake rose unevenly in the oven. It sloped gently to one side, like the roof of the old outhouse that had once stood outside in the back yard. Then we realized we didn't have any icing sugar.

'We'll just beat together some regular sugar and butter, and then spread it on top,' said Gerry. We didn't like the colour much. The yellow mixture wasn't festive enough. We added a little red from the Easter egg dyes and came up with a pale pink. It tasted all right, but we didn't know that cakes had to be cold when they were iced, and we were only halfway through when the butter icing started to melt and run down the slope of our cake.

'Just glop it all on, and maybe it'll melt evenly. We can whip it into the fridge and it'll turn into an even glaze,' I said. Gerry scooped all of the icing out of the mixing bowl with a spoon and set it on the cake, and then we put the whole thing into the freezer. That was when my mother called.

'Tell your father I have to work late tonight. Have dinner without me and pick me up at the bus stop at eight.'

'Jeez, Mom. We fixed a special dinner tonight.'

'That's very nice, but there's nothing I can do about it. Save me some leftovers, do your homework, and I'll see you tonight.'

'I don't feel well,' my father said from the bed when we told him. 'I think I'll pour myself a little drink to take away this headache.' He went and got the mickey, and took two quick shots.

'Have dinner without me, and let me know when it's time to pick up your mother.'

When we took the cake out of the freezer a half hour later, a pink lump of sugar butter the size of a golf ball had frozen on top. We decided to leave the cake on the table and just let it melt down naturally. Then Tom came downstairs from the Macvittys' for dinner.

'Where's Mom?'

'She's working late.'

'Where's Dad?'

'He's lying down in the bedroom.'

Tom trotted down to the bedroom to look in on our father. It annoyed us, this concern he had for our father. We figured the Old Man was as solid as Gibraltar, a rock that repeatedly sank our ships of dreams.

'I think he's dead,' said Tom when he came back.

'Nah, he's just drunk,' said Gerry.

'His eyes are open, but he didn't say anything when I called him.'

The three of us went to the bedroom.

'He's sleeping with his eyes open,' said Gerry. My father's eyes were indeed half open, like those of a guard dog dozing on the job, but his breath came in a wheezing, rasping sound, like a locomotive starting up, and that meant he had to be asleep.

'He's dead,' said Tom, and he started to cry.

'He's not dead, you idiot,' said Gerry. 'Shut up, or you'll wake him.'

But there was no stopping Tom. I guess he figured he was going to be an orphan, and he'd have to grow up with us taking care of him. When he started to wail, the Old Man blinked a few times and then sat up in bed. You'd think this would have calmed down Tom, but the Old Man waking up from sleep after a few drinks was enough to scare anybody. His face was pale and his eyes started to water and you could barely understand him until he cleared his throat a few times.

'What's going on?' my father asked.

'I want Mom,' Tom started to shout, and he went tearing out of the room when my father reached for him. He only made it halfway down the hall before he slipped on the floor and flew into an open door. His forehead banged against the edge with a thump, and his volume went up a few decibels.

My father staggered into the hallway, picked him up, and carried him into the kitchen where the light was better. Tom had only scraped his head, but he was bleeding hard above his right eye.

'Get me a towel,' said my father. He held it in place for a while, and then put some gauze on the cut and tied another tea towel over Tom's head to keep the gauze in place. Tom was down to whimpering at this point, but he kept on asking for Mom.

'Boys,' said our father, 'we are going to get your mother.'

'It's too early,' said Gerry. 'She won't be at the bus stop for another hour.'

'Then we'll go to the crystal warehouse and pick her up. Get your coats on.'

'Her boss doesn't know about us,' said Gerry. 'We're not supposed to go there.'

'So we'll wait outside and surprise her. Come on.'

Tom and I sat in the back of the Strato Chief and Gerry sat in the front with a map.

We drove to a new industrial park that was mostly vacant lots and torn-up earth, but the crystal warehouse was a neat building of concrete blocks surrounded by a well-kept lawn. There was a parking lot in front of the office and a driveway down the side to the loading docks behind. My father parked the car by the ditch a little way down from the building.

'What time is it?' Gerry asked.

'Seven.'

'We've still got a half hour before she gets out. Too bad you didn't get a radio in the car.' My father did not answer. Whatever energy he had mustered to get us into the car had been burned away in the drive to my mother's work place. The sun coming in through the windshield was very warm, and he laid his head against the side window and was snoring within seconds.

'Why can't we go in and get her?' Tom asked. The tea towel my father had wrapped around Tom's head was slipping, and he looked like a kid in a Halloween pirate costume.

'We've got to wait until she's finished work.'

'I don't want to wait. I want to get her now.'

'Don't be a dope,' said Gerry. 'It's like school — you can't just go in and pull somebody out of class whenever you want. You have to wait until the bell rings.'

'I have to go to the bathroom.'

'There's no place to go around here,' I said. 'Just hold it.'

'I can't hold it.'

Whatever trees had once stood on the land were long gone. The wild grass that grew in thick tufts was not tall enough to hide him.

'I could go behind that house,' said Tom.

'That's where Mom works, you dope,' said Gerry. 'We're supposed to stay away from there.'

But we had to do something, so all three of us got quietly out of the car to keep from waking our father and then walked into the vacant lot beside the warehouse. Once we were out of sight of the windows at the front, we looped up behind the building.

'One of the bays is open,' I said when Tom had zipped up his fly.

We were drawn to it as if it were Ali Baba's cave. There were a couple of cars parked around the back, but we could not see any people. We edged up to the open bay and looked inside. It was a big warehouse, with aisle upon aisle of steel shelves. The shelves were filled with crates and boxes, and straw packing lay in heaps on the floor, but there were no people around.

'This guy could get robbed blind,' said Gerry.

I held on to Tom's hand, and we walked quietly among the shelves towards the front of the building, dangerously close to where our mother worked. We came up to the front wall of the warehouse without seeing anyone. There was no farther to go unless we went through a single door. Gerry looked through the small window.

'Holy cow.'

'I want to see. Lift me up.'

I lifted Tom and we all looked through. The showroom was lit by two great chandeliers, and all shapes of vases and bowls and glasses stood on the shelves, backlit so the light broke as it passed through the crystal and all the surfaces shimmered with specks of bright colour. With the slightest movement of my head, the light on the crystal shifted and new constellations of colours came out of the glass.

'It's beautiful in there,' said Tom. 'I want to go inside.'

'We're not even supposed to be in here,' Gerry said. 'This is nuts. We've got to get out before anybody sees us.'

'Come on, gutless,' I said. 'We'll be in and out of there in two minutes. If they're so busy working up in the office, nobody's going to come back here anyway.'

We opened the door and walked in. The floor underfoot was soft with new broadloom. I was tempted to slip off my shoes. Low music was coming out of invisible speakers.

'That's the same music Mom's got at home,' Tom whispered. The tea towel over his forehead had slipped right down and covered one eye completely. 'It's Chopin. A mazurka, I think.'

'Shut up,' Gerry hissed. 'We've got to be quiet.' There was a shiny wood table in the middle of the room, with a crystal vase and glass fruit inside. I sidled up to the only other door and looked through the small window.

'They're in there all right. The Czech's at his desk. Mom's talking on the phone.'

We walked around the shelves and looked at the colours sparkling off the cut glass. I almost wished I'd had my church clothes on; it was blasphemous to be there in sneakers. We worked our way around the shelves until we came to a corner where there were figurines. Most were little crystal things, but there were a few of coloured, blown glass.

'That blue deer is really cute,' said Tom. 'I wish I had one like that. Do you think I could touch it?'

Tom was already reaching for it.

'No,' Gerry and I hissed, but he was halfway across the room. My hand flew up to Tom's. Then we heard the door from the office swing open behind us. We swung around too to see who it was.

'What's this?'

He was a man in a brown, three-piece suit with a pocket watch chain strung across his vest. I had never seen a watch chain in real life before. His body was not particularly thin, but his nose was. It was the kind of nose that you knew picked up offensive smells easily. He had a forehead that sloped back gently, and it looked twice as high because his curly hair was receding a couple of inches off the front.

'What exactly are you doing here?' he asked.

'We're looking,' said Gerry. 'The back door was open.'

'It's really beautiful,' said Tom.

'Three pirates,' said the Czech. He smiled, a tyrant in a generous mood. 'Do you have cutlasses too?'

'I've got a wooden one at home,' said Tom.

'Well, if you were only looking, then there is no harm done, but you should have come through the front and asked. I might have thought you were thieves. And you, little pirate. What do you have in your hand?'

Tom's lower lip started to quiver.

'I was just looking.'

'Yes. One looks with the eyes and not with the hands. Open yours, please.'

Tom opened his closed fist. He had the little blue glass deer in there, and one leg had broken off.

'I see. I am afraid, boys, that this is no longer just looking. You have slipped into villainy. This is theft.' He walked over calmly to the back door we had come through, took a key from his pocket and locked it. 'I will lock the front door on my way out, and then I will phone the police. You will wait here, and do no damage to the pieces on display or the police will be even harsher. You, the little one, give me the broken piece, please.'

Tom was crying a steady stream of quiet tears by that point, but he opened his hand and held out the broken glass deer. The man plucked the two pieces from his hand.

'I will give this to the police as evidence. You have broken the law.'

I was feeling sick, but even so, the strange precision in his voice fascinated me. I was used to fists being waved wildly in the air, accompanied by shouts, but his voice sounded like that of our school principal, Mother Leone, at her worst. But Mother Leone was a nun. She knew about forgiveness.

My mother walked through the door with a stack of bills of lading in her hand. She could tell what had happened. Mothers knew things in mysterious ways. But I could see a moment of doubt in her face, a moment of coolness, as if she were thinking whether or not to admit she knew us. For a second, I knew what it would be like to be an orphan.

Tom threw his arms open and charged to her, and then she was our mother again. But the instant of doubt had been there.

'Tom, what's happened to you?' The kid let out all the stops and he started to wail between gulps of air. He threw his arms over her shoulders when she crouched down, and I could see the snot and tears staining the shoulders of my mother's powder-blue business suit.

'Agata,' said the Czech, 'who are these children?'

'Just a moment, Mr Schuller,' she said, and she took out a handkerchief and cleaned off Tom's face and made him blow his nose.

'What happened to your head?' she said, peeling back the tea towel to look at the skin above Tom's eye.

'He was looking for you, Mom,' said Gerry. 'He got kind of crazy at home, and he whipped into a door.'

'I see. Well, I'm here now.'

Her English sounded strange, as if she had picked up the same accent as Mr Schuller, who spoke in words as hard and precise as cut glass.

'Agata, we have something to discuss,' said Mr Schuller. 'I'm very disappointed in you. I have put you in a position of trust, and I expected you to be forthright with me.'

My mother did not hurry to respond. She looked around at the shelves of crystal as if she was having one last look at the promised land before she went out into the wilderness.

'You have my immediate resignation.'

'Of course, but that is not enough. I want an explanation as well.'

'If you had looked at my application form, you would have seen that I am married and have three children. Here they are. They have come looking for their mother.'

She was so calm in her powder-blue suit, so not like a DP that I looked at her in awe. I studied her face, but it was stern and impassive.

'I have made a great mistake,' she said, but her face didn't look like she meant it.

Mr Schuller jumped into the opening.

'Yes, of course you have made a mistake. You will now stay home with them as a mother should.'

'I will find another job, Mr Schuller. It may not be this one, but I will have to work elsewhere.'

'That is not for me to determine. I can only act as my conscience dictates, and it says that no married woman with children in her home will ever work for me.'

The Czech broke into what I guess was German, and my mother spoke it right back to him. It was strange to hear those foreign words coming out of her mouth, but it was stranger still to see the way they argued. It was like the debating society at school, where they made us argue stuff we didn't care about, like whether meatless Fridays should be expanded to Thursdays as well. It was as if the music and the carpet and the beautiful glass made them into different people. My mother could blast me and Gerry or my father so badly that we went tearing out of the house with welts on our hearts. But here she was, like a diplomat or something, explaining herself in the German language.

They stopped talking. My mother looked at us.

'Kommt!' she said. We just stared and Tom looked like he was going to start crying again. She shook her head at herself. 'Come along, children,' she said in our language, but there were still traces of the cold German in her voice.

Mr Schuller stood with us as she took a compact from her desk and a cup from a filing cabinet and put them into her purse. Then she began to leaf through a stack of bills of lading until she found what she was looking for.

'The cost of the deer is twenty-seven cents,' she read. 'Shipping and brokerage fees add eleven cents for a total of thirty-eight. The wholesale price charged to retailers is ninety-three cents. I believe I have the right change.'

'That is not necessary,' Mr Schuller said. 'Cost plus shipping and brokerage will be sufficient.'

'That would not be correct. It is a popular item.'

Mr Schuller agreed with a small nod of his head and my mother counted out the money and passed it to him.

'I have bought the goods and I will take them,' my mother said. She held out her hand and Mr Schuller passed over the deer along with the broken leg. I could see the shine on the pieces that came from the sweat of his hands.

'Children,' she said in English, and we began to follow her out the door.

'Agata.'

My mother stopped, but she did not turn around.

'This is as painful for me as it is for you, but I have certain rules that I live by.'

He was not finished, but my mother did not turn around or answer him. We walked outside.

My father awoke as soon as we opened the doors to the car. His hair was bunched up where his head had pressed against the car window, and his eyebrows were mussed. He was the only person I knew who needed to comb his eyebrows. His eyes were watery too, and it looked like he could use a couple more hours of sleep.

'All finished?' he asked. My mother nodded.

Halfway home she started to cry, but she did it quietly. I only saw because I could see her face reflected through the sideview mirror.

'Can I have the deer?' Tom finally asked. My mother did not say anything. I guess she was afraid to speak. Gerry told my father what had happened.

'The moment I close my eyes, the three of you are running off like young colts! You'll all be in jail before you reach twenty! If I had any brains, I'd hobble your legs every time my back was turned. The car insurance is coming due next week. Just my luck.'

The pork roast had collapsed on itself from all the hours in the warm oven. It lay on our plates like strings of boiled meat, but my father ate with his usual gusto. All of us kept looking at my mother, but her face was now impassive.

'Why are you wearing a suit?' she finally asked my father at the end of the meal. She had not even noticed the rose bush on the table. She had just set that aside.

'The boys wanted to do something special for you.'

'We even baked you a cake,' said Gerry, and he went to the fridge to get it. The knob of pink icing on top had broken away and rolled to the edge of the plate. Tom reached towards it, but Gerry slapped away his hand.

'Do you like it, Mom?' Gerry asked.

My mother took the napkin from its place beside her plate. Cloth napkins were an innovation that came in the same time as the classical music. She wiped her mouth carefully, set the napkin down, and rose from the table. Without a word, she went to her bedroom and closed the door.

Gerry looked like he had been stabbed through the heart. My father helped himself to some more roast pork.

'Eat up, boys,' he said, 'tomorrow we go back to hamburgers. As for your mother, don't worry. She'll get over it. Women are fifty percent nerves and fifty percent hysteria. They can't help it.'

After supper, I went down to the basement to do my homework.

Usually I did that when it was too noisy upstairs, but this time it was too quiet. I'd been working there for a while when I heard light footsteps coming down. I didn't turn around when I heard him open the door.

'I know what you did,' said Tom.

'You're a little kid. You don't know anything.'

'I wasn't pressing on the deer. You squeezed my hand and broke it.'

'I was just trying to get it away from you.'

Tom kept standing there. I still didn't turn around to look at him.

'I won't tell anyone,' he said. I kept my back to him and eventually he went upstairs again.

Tom asked my mother for the broken deer, and eventually my mother gave it to him. My father tried to glue the broken leg back on, but it would never hold for any length of time. We'd go to bed with the blue deer set up on the windowsill, but each time, when we awoke in the morning, it lay with its leg broken again. One morning I hid the broken piece in my pocket, and the others thought it had gotten lost on the floor. The crippled figurine lay on its side for a few weeks, and then it disappeared.

All Boys in Canada Play Hockey

When the whole family watched *Hockey Night in Canada*, even the Old Man was bearable. My mother pushed back the dining room table and set up her ironing board so she could do her cuffs and collars and see the TV at the same time. Gerry and I lay on the floor to stay closer to the action. Even though we lived on the fringe of Toronto, the signal was unreliable, or maybe one of the vacuum tubes in the set was beginning to give out, because often the players were followed by ghosts that blended into their man when he stood still, but fell slightly behind when he was on a breakaway.

'Their souls can't keep up,' said Tom from his place up on the couch. He was in grade three and already singing in the church choir. Not because he had to.

'Souls don't get separated until you die,' Gerry corrected him. 'Those are guardian angels.'

Tom nodded at this, and Gerry gave me a quick smirk.

The Old Man spewed tobacco smoke in unending clouds, and his teeth clicked on the pipe stem whenever he got excited. 'Shoot!' he would shout in English from the corner of his mouth, and if the Leafs missed, he would settle back in his chair and mutter Russian swear words that brought down the wrath of my mother.

'Such filth coming out of your mouth,' she said.

'The children don't even know what it means.'

'It doesn't matter. You're poisoning the air.'

If my father got really excited, he might dig around in his smoker's box and pull out a cigar butt he had saved, and then stuff his pipe with the stub and smoke that. My mother hated the smell of cigars, and scolded him mercilessly from behind the ironing board, but he ignored her complaints. My father was inseparable from the smell of tobacco for me, and the smell of cigar smoke meant Saturday nights in front of the TV.

The smells of Saturday night were his cigars, and in the background, my mother's spray starch, and Tom's popcorn and melted butter. When Tom made popcorn, the Old Man set down his pipe and ate from his own bowl, one piece at a time. He was such a DP that he didn't even know you were supposed to stuff your mouth with popcorn until you emptied the bowl, and after that you ate the pieces that had fallen down on your lap or in the space between the cushion and the chair. During *Hockey Night in Canada*, the Old Man was tame. It was one of the few times we could be sure he wouldn't bite.

Tom had finished his popcorn and was looking at the colour comics from the Saturday paper as the rest of us watched the game. He liked comics, and our parents even let him buy some as long as they were Disney. Gerry and I were pretty much past comics, but it still rankled that Tom was allowed to buy any at all. For us they had been forbidden, but not for the golden boy.

Tom rattled the pages every time he turned them.

'Will you stop making all that noise!' Gerry said without taking his face away from the screen.

Tom looked up, wide-eyed. It's not that he was surprised or anything. It was just that his eyes were always opened really wide, like he was seeing everything for the first time. He turned another page of the colour comics.

'I told you to keep it down!'

'I'm just looking at the comics.'

'And I'm watching the game. Why can't you do the same?'

'Because it's not interesting.'

Gerry turned his face from the screen. 'You're eight years old now — no more little kid. What are you going to talk about at school if you don't watch the game?'

Tom shrugged.

'Don't you like hockey?' my father asked.

'It's okay.'

It all might have ended there if the second period hadn't finished. Even Gerry didn't watch the between period interviews with the sweaty French players whose English didn't seem much better than my father's.

'I think there's something wrong with him,' Gerry said to my father.

'The boy just isn't a hockey fan,' my mother said from behind the ironing board.

'No, it's more than that.'

Our parents paid attention to what Gerry said, especially my father. He was the one who brought home the news from school of the head-lice infestation, and all of us had to wash our hair with kerosene that night just to be on the safe side. We even got shampoo for the first time to wash the kerosene smell out of our hair. Before that, it had always been hand soap. Gerry was the one who explained to my father that because of the polio vaccine, he didn't have to worry about muddy puddles any more.

'I think Tom might have Lou Gehrig's disease,' said Gerry.

My mother put down the iron and my father set aside his pipe.

'I saw a show about it on TV. If you get it, you just waste away.'

My mother looked anxiously at my father.

'You only get that when you're grown up,' I said.

'Kids can get it too,' Gerry said hotly. 'If they're skinny and don't get any exercise, they kind of waste away. Tom's just reading or watching TV all the time. Look at him. He's got to get interested in sports or else he'll grow up sickly, if he grows up at all.'

'Like consumption,' my mother said.

'Nobody's got that since the war,' my father answered. 'It's more like leukemia.'

'Look at this,' said Gerry. He pushed back the coffee table and fell into push-up position.

'One, two, three.'

Gerry started to pump away at his push-ups, his back straight as a soldier's. He finally collapsed on thirty-eight. Then it was my turn. I made it as far as twenty-four.

When it was Tom's turn to do push-ups, he went along with the game, but he didn't get into the spirit of things. He seemed to have no sense of the family watching him. When he stretched out in position, his back bowed so much that his abdomen almost touched the ground. Gerry straightened him out and told him what to do, but Tom just collapsed when he tried to raise himself up.

'You're not trying,' my father said. 'Show me you can do five push-ups, and I'll buy you a bag of chips.'

The incentive was there, but Tom could not raise himself up by the strength of his arms even once. The skin on his arms trembled, and it looked as if there was no muscle under it. My mother and father exchanged glances.

'Don't you worry, Tom,' said Gerry.

'I'm not worried.'

'We'll make you into a sportsman yet. But the first thing you have to do is pay attention to the hockey game. You've got to get committed and then stay committed.'

'What does committed mean?'

'It means you have to want to get better.'

'I'm fine. I don't want to get anything.'

'Shut up, will you? The third period's starting.'

Tom was taken to bed before the period ended, and when my mother came back, she spoke to my father.

'Gerry may have a point. I felt his arms as I was putting him to bed. They were thin as sticks — no better than twigs. I don't think he's eating enough.'

My mother had begun to read about healthy food in the women's magazines. She never dropped anything from the breakfast menu, but she started adding extra dishes as the years went by. We'd always had ham and eggs, but around the middle of the fifties she had added oatmeal or cream of wheat. By the end of the fifties, we wanted cold cereal. We were allowed to have that if we ate everything else first. Now that the sixties had begun, she added half a grapefruit as well. Since she had to leave for work before we ate breakfast, the hot food was left waiting for us in a warm oven. But with our parents gone, we were free at breakfast, so we threw anything we didn't want into the garbage and covered it with a piece of newspaper. Gerry had never eaten a grapefruit in his life.

'Today's the first day of your training,' said Gerry to Tom. 'Today you eat everything for breakfast.'

'Not eggs.'

Tom had a delicate stomach, and there were some things he was allowed not to eat. Eggs were one dish. Potato pancakes were another.

'Yes, eggs. We've got to get some bulk on you.'

'I don't like eggs. They make me sick.'

'You'll get used to them.'

Gerry put his own eggs in front of Tom. It could have been worse. My mother cooked them sunny side up, and even my stomach turned if there was any clear white up by the yolk. But because she was always so busy in the morning, she cooked the eggs early, and they hardened as they sat in the warm oven. By the time we came to them, we could lift them off the plate like a piece of toast.

'I don't like the smell,' said Tom.

'Just hold your breath, take a bite, and swallow.'

Tom tried to follow Gerry's advice, but he had to chew first, and while he was chewing he ran out of air and had to breathe.

'I think I'm going to be sick.'

'No, you won't. Just concentrate.'

But Tom wasn't sure of the meaning of concentrate, and before Gerry could explain it, the oatmeal, bacon, and grapefruit came back up.

'It's okay, kid,' he said. 'Training takes time. Dave, you clean up the kitchen and I'll change his clothes.'

After dinner that night, Gerry and I took Tom down to the rink with one of my old sticks that we cut down. Some of Tom's friends were down there with their fathers, but Gerry wouldn't let him go to the recreational rink where the little kids played tag and crack the whip. Gerry even put on Tom's skates for him and tied the laces in his secret knot that kept them from getting loose during play.

Our old boarder, Mr Macvitty, who had moved out two years before and bought a house, was down there with his son as well.

'Getting him started on hockey?' Mr Macvitty asked.

'Yup.'

'You might be a bit late. I've been sending Ronny to hockey camp in the summer since he was six.'

'Did it help?'

'He can punch out kids two years older than him.'

Gerry was frozen in awe for a moment before he came back to his senses.

'You ought to play with Ronny more,' he said to Tom, who was watching the snowflakes fall.

'We get Gerry,' one of the kids from the hockey rink called out. They always called for him first.

'Any team I play on gets my little brother too.'

Nobody grumbled much because little brothers were a fact of life and Gerry would punch anyone who forgot it. I was on the other team.

I kept an eye on Tom during the game. He didn't do as badly as I thought he would. He stayed out of the way most of the time, and when someone passed him the puck out of kindness, he usually kept it on his stick long enough to get away a pass to someone else. He got into trouble once when he passed to me by mistake and I scored. It took a little explaining before he understood that an assist only counted if you passed to someone who scored for your own team.

'You did great,' Gerry said at the end of the game. Tom's fingers were too cold to undo his own skates. 'Did you have a good time? Do you want to do it again?'

'Okay,' said Tom.

'It's got to be more than okay,' Gerry said, looking up at Tom from his skates. 'You've got to want to win so bad that you'll do anything. It doesn't matter if you're cold or tired. You have to go in for the kill. You use your elbows or your knees, and if someone gets upset about that, you butt them with the end of your stick in a corner. And if it looks like they want to fight, always hit them first. Take them by surprise, and you won't have to swing twice.'

On Saturday afternoon, my father called us all down to the basement to look at the gym equipment he had made for Tom. For weights, he'd taken two tire rims and put them on the ends of a wooden stick. The dumbbells were two hammers each, with heads at opposite ends and held together with black electrician's tape.

'Are you sure that's not too heavy?' my mother asked. 'We don't want to give the boy a hernia.'

'Mother, please, sports are for men. Just watch.'

Tom did all right with the dumbbells. He curled the hammers again and again.

'Easy there, kid,' said Gerry. 'You need to warm up with weights so you don't pull a muscle.'

But he could not lift the tire rims.

'Too heavy!' my mother said, alarmed.

'What? I made these so even a small boy could lift them. He's just too weak from eating all those damn corn flakes every morning. Gerry, you try it.'

Gerry squatted down into position and began to lift. The tire rim bar bells were heavy even for him. First the stick bent, and as he strained, he finally got it up to his waist, but it broke in the middle when he tried to lift it higher, and the tire rims came crashing down onto the floor.

'Hey, I just laid those tiles,' my father said. 'You're going to ruin the finish.'

'What a stupid idea,' my mother said.

'Stupid? If you didn't feed him all that American garbage, he'd be all right. You're poisoning him with your food.'

'So what should I feed him, pork fat?'

'That would be good for starters. He should be forbidden to cut the fat off his food. Then lots of meat. No more soups. Cut down on the vegetables, and back to rye bread.'

'You don't like the food I make, you can cook for yourself. As for the kids, I feed them the best I know how.' She would have said more, but she started to cry and ran upstairs.

Tom spent the rest of the day fooling around with his electric train set and the scrap electrical wire my father had brought home. By evening, he had run the wires from his electric transformer along the baseboards to the basement where he hooked it up to an old door buzzer. Then he got another kid from the street to come over, and each of them copied the Morse code notation from a book. They would have kept sending messages to each other all night, but the hockey game began at eight-thirty and the buzzing was so loud, we could hear it all through the house.

'Young Marconi down there is driving me crazy with all that noise,' said Gerry. 'Dave, you run down there and tell them that's enough for today.'

'Run down yourself.'

'I'll smash your face.'

'I'll squeeze your head so tight, your brains will blow out of your ears.'

Life had become a lot easier after I started to bulk up. Gerry was still stronger than me, but I was faster.

'He taped the wires to the baseboards,' my father said. He was in a bad mood because he'd had to make his own supper. 'When he takes off the tape, he's going to rip off the finish as well.'

My mother was not in a particularly good mood either, but she went downstairs and got the boys to finish sending Morse code signals. She and Tom walked his friend home. When she came back, she put Tom straight to bed, and then came into the dining room to do her ironing while the rest of us watched the hockey game.

'How come you put Tom to bed?' I asked.

'He was tired.'

She seemed to bang the iron on the shirts a lot more than usual, but neither Gerry nor I had the courage to ask her to be quieter.

'Father,' she said after the second period.

'Uh-huh?'

'I've been thinking about Tom.'

'What about him?'

'Maybe we're doing the wrong thing with all this exercise.'

'The boy has to be strong. Do you want him to die young?'

'Maybe he was made to be something else.'

'Like what?'

'A priest.'

My father puffed on his pipe for a while. 'I don't know. In the old country, a priest was somebody. Here, he's not valued much.'

'He's smart. He might even become a bishop.'

'Sure. Why not Pope? Why not saint?'

'Saints usually have to be martyrs.'

'I was joking.'

'It's impossible to have a serious discussion with you.'

The iron banged all the way through to the end of the game.

'Could you imagine a priest in the family?' I asked Gerry after the lights were off in our room that night.

'You'd have to go to church every Sunday even after you grew up.'

'He'd make us go to confession every month.'

'You'd have to tell him if you screwed a girl.'

Gerry always raised the ante higher. It made me uncomfortable.

'We can't let it happen,' I said.

'No. We've got to toughen him up, and we've got to do it fast.'

We took Tom out to the rink with us after lunch on Sunday, but this time Gerry put him on my team. Tom must have been thinking about something else besides the game. He had trouble keeping his eye on the puck and once he stopped and just looked into the distance. It was beginning to get on Gerry's nerves.

'Christ, Tom, if someone passes you the puck, then keep it on your stick.'

'You're not even on my team. Why should you care?'

'Because I'm your coach, you sap.'

'You're on the other side. You're my enemy now.'

Gerry nodded. He could understand that. It was bad enough that I was too big to beat up any more, and now this little kid was giving him lip. A couple of times, Gerry hit Tom on the shins with his stick as he skated by. The third time he did it, Tom started to cry.

'Keep on playing,' Gerry shouted when the other players wanted to see what was wrong. Eventually, Tom stopped. He stood around for a while, looking dazed, the way little kids do. I thought he might start crying again or just walk off the ice. In the distance, I could see the Old Man standing at the chain-link fence and puffing on his pipe. He came down sometimes to make sure we were really at the rink and not smoking cigarettes in front of some drug store.

Tom finally started to skate with the game again, but now Gerry's eyes were on him. Gerry never looked at anything but the puck during a hockey game, but now he was watching Tom, waiting for the right moment. It was cold out, but Gerry's hair was plastered to his forehead and his face glowed with sweat. Twin streams of icy air puffed out of his nose. I knew I would have to be quick if Gerry went for Tom, and just as fast to defend myself if I got in the way of Gerry's hot anger.

The other team had just scored a goal and we were getting organized on our end after the face-off. Most of the other team's players were hanging back. It looked like a safe moment to give Tom a little play time. He was in a corner when I passed the puck to him. As soon as I passed the puck to Tom, Gerry came charging down from his end of the ice.

'Quick, Tom, pass it over,' I shouted, but he just turned into the corner when he saw Gerry coming. I had no time to get between them. I'm not even sure Gerry recognized Tom at that point. He had that strange look he took on when he was in the heat of a game and he didn't recognize anybody except for a basic distinction between friend and enemy. Tom was the enemy now.

My father was inside the park now. Some parental instinct alerted him to danger, and he loped forward through the deep snow with comic slowness, puffing on his pipe as he ran.

Gerry was going to skate around Tom to blind-side him. Then he'd knock the kid down and steal the puck. Just as Gerry turned into the corner, in close behind Tom, he dropped suddenly to his knees and slid cursing into a snow bank.

All the kids on the ice knew the sound of a real injury, and the game stopped dead as we rushed in to see what had happened.

'The kid punched me right in the balls,' Gerry said between gasps. No one had ever seen Gerry taken down before, and all the kids he had beaten over the years stood around to watch the terrible but magnificent sight.

'I did not punch,' Tom said. 'I used the end of my stick.'

My father finally made it to rinkside and took in what had happened. 'Thank God it's only you,' he said, and then he turned away from Gerry and put his hand on Tom's shoulder.

Tom never did go on to be much of a hockey player. On the other hand, Tom never became particularly religious either. He sang in the church choir for a while until Father Morrissey kicked him out for trying to look down the fronts of the older girls' dresses. And this was years before his voice broke.

The Fight

'WE'LL ALL GET ALONG REALLY WELL AS LONG AS YOU FOLLOW the rules,' said Mr Henderson. 'Isn't that right, Jack?'

Jack smiled out of the side of his mouth and nodded. He slouched so low that he lay in his desk more than sat in it. His Cuban shoes with the sharp tips pointed up to the ceiling at the end of legs stretched out in front of him. He was sitting in the front row, so much bigger than the rest of us that the room seemed to tilt slightly on the side where he was. He wore a black windbreaker and his hair was longer than anybody else's, and combed back slick on the right side above his ear.

'Jack broke every single rule there was last year. That's why he's back in grade nine all over again to take a second a run at things. What are some of the rules, Jack?'

'No jeans.'

'That's right. What else?'

'No smoking on school property.'

'All you kids leave your cigarettes at home or in your lockers. If I see them, you'll lose them.'

A titter went through the class. None of us smoked, but it felt good to be warned against it. Adults at last. That was the difference between elementary school and high school. No pictures of the Blessed Heart of Jesus either. It felt good to be in a public high school — like taking classes in Sodom.

Mr Henderson taught gym. We had him in home room in the mornings and at the end of the day when he checked the attendance record. He made Jack run through all the rules he could think of.

'You missed just one thing.'

'What's that?' Jack asked.

'Insubordination. I'll throw a week of detentions at you just for insubordination — like wearing the wrong look when I ask you a question, or sitting in the desk like a smart aleck.'

Mr Henderson sauntered over to Jack, and kicked at the Cuban shoes sticking out from under the desk.

'Sit up straight, Jack. It's better for your posture.'

Jack smiled out of the side of his mouth again, and slowly straightened himself up.

'Now our friend Jack here has just showed insubordination in the way he responded to my request. That'll be a detention tomorrow for you, Jack. Welcome back to grade nine. I hope you enjoy it better the second time around.'

We all huddled around Jack in the hall as he strutted on the way to the first class. He was the only one of us who wasn't a little scared on the first day.

'That Mr Henderson is pretty tough, eh?' said skinny Paul, the class prefect. He got to carry the attendance clipboard from class to class and hand it to each teacher. Nobody had elected Paul as prefect. Mr Henderson went to Paul's father's church, and he said he guessed a minister's son could be trusted not to fiddle with records.

'Naw, he's okay. He just wants to slap a detention on me right at the beginning to make a big impression. Are you a squealer?'

Paul had a heavy load of books, and he was having a hard time balancing the load and the attendance clipboard, and keeping up with Jack.

'Me? No.'

'Well, your old man's a minister, so that's one strike against you.'

'You can't blame me for my father.'

'Every class has got one squealer in it, and usually it's the kid who carries the board. You sure you're not a squealer?'

'I don't squeal.'

'We'll see about that. One of these days I'm going to have to cut class to see my girlfriend. When I get back, I'm going to fix up the attendance sheet.'

Jack stopped to talk to one of his friends in the hall. Paul looked sick.

'You'd better pay attention to what he says,' a blond kid with glasses said to Paul. 'He got into two fights last year, and he won both of them.'

Paul's first day of high school, and already the upcoming years were ruined. His dad had probably told him about the moral choices he was going to have to face in life, and now here was a textbook example.

Gerry was a year ahead of me, so I had it easier. All the coaches knew him, and when my name came up, they asked me if I was his brother.

'Play football or hockey?' they'd ask, and when I nodded back, they'd smile and say they'd see me at practice.

Gerry had even given me some tips before the first day.

'If anyone calls you a Mick, you punch him right in the face. Don't wait, don't discuss it. Doesn't matter if it's in Latin class and you get a three-day suspension. Once you let anybody get away with that, you'll be finished for the whole year. And don't cross yourself at the end of the Our Father every morning.'

'Why not?'

'Because Protestants don't cross themselves. And another thing.

Their Our Father is longer than ours. There's all this stuff about the power and the glory at the end, but if you don't like that part, you don't have to say anything. Just look down and act really respectful and the teachers will leave you alone. I think there's some kind of deal they made with the bishop about it.'

There was a new Catholic high school in the neighbourhood, and a lot of the boys from our grade eight class had gone to it. My father said he wasn't going to pay two hundred dollars a year extra just to have priests teach us biology. To make up for going to Weston Collegiate, he made us get up early and go to mass one morning a week. But since he was gone for work by that time, Gerry never went and I only did if there was a big test that day.

I didn't know a single kid in my grade nine class. Some of the kids from my class had gone to the Catholic school, and those who came to Weston Collegiate were spread out in the technical, business, or arts programmes. The kids in my grade nine class were from the Protestant school they called junior high.

I didn't mind being on my own, not really. Weston was a big school, and it was nice to be invisible in the halls. I didn't have to look at anybody who remembered me as the kid who crapped his pants in grade two when I got the stomach flu. Still, it would have been all right to have someone in my class to talk to.

Most of the men teachers were pretty tough, especially the ones who taught the technical subjects that all the boys had to take in grade nine. On the third day of class, Mr Thatcher threw a drafting board at a kid in the back row who had fallen asleep. It was a big drafting board, about two by three, and it only made it halfway down the class before smashing into one of the desks.

The electricity teacher made a loop of wire the first week.

'See this loop?' He wore a white lab coat and dark-rimmed glasses that made him look like the kind of doctor who might do experiments on you after he drugged your chocolate milk. 'Anybody steps out of line in this class, and we put a body part in here. Then we do this.' He pulled both ends of the wire so the loop closed tightly.

The only man who didn't scare me was Mr Doyle, the math teacher. He was a very big man, somewhere over six two, and he had a chest so wide it looked abnormal, like an armour breastplate had been stuck under his shirt. He had a square jaw and dark hair, but he talked like a girl. The voice was so funny that half of us laughed the first time we heard him speak.

'Some of you think you're tough because you know how to fight, and some of you think you're tough because of what you can do on the football field. But that's not tough. Tough is using your brains to figure out equations — it's forming a picture in your mind out of thin air and coming up with a conclusion that's applicable to the real world.'

None of us understood what he was talking about, but that high-pitched voice on the huge body was just too funny.

'Is Mr Doyle a wuss?' I asked Gerry.

'I don't know him.'

'Math teacher — big guy.'

'The guy with the squeaky voice — yeah. He's a new one. I saw him throw a medicine ball halfway across the gym. He's strong as hell. Henderson says he was a junior shot-put champion. He's no wuss.'

'But the voice on him.'

'Beats me. Maybe his underwear is too tight.'

The girls in our class were a lot different from the ones in grade eight the year before. They had done things I'd never dreamed of, like gone to dances. A couple of them wore makeup as well. The only girl who had ever tried that back in the Catholic school had had to stand at the front of the class, spit on a Kleenex, and let Sister Mary wipe the stuff from her eyes and mouth.

Girls with makeup were a little intimidating. I liked to look at them, if they weren't looking back, but they were as exotic as Afghanistan to me. The one girl I did start talking to was Mary-Jane. Some of the boys called her Plain Jane and Brain Jane. She *was* smart, but I didn't think she was plain at all. When she smiled at me, I didn't feel stupid. She'd spent the summer with relatives in Germany, and she told me about places that I'd only read about in books, like the Black Forest and the Alps. She even told me she'd seen the Eiffel Tower from the plane as she flew over France. She was the only person my age that I'd ever met who knew who Rasputin was, and she got me to join the drama club.

'Drama club? Are you nuts?' Gerry said when he found out.

'What's the big deal?'

'Last year they put on *Romeo and Juliet*, and the guy had to wear tights. Who the hell is going to want to share a dressing room with a guy who wears tights?'

'I'm not wearing tights.'

'They start you off in black turtlenecks, and the next thing you know, you're walking around memorizing Shakespeare and looking like a goof.'

'Jesus, Gerry, it's not like it's a disease or anything.'

'How did you ever come up with this idea?'

'Jane talked me into it.'

'Jane?'

'A girl in my class.'

Gerry looked thoughtful. 'A girl. Okay, that's different. But watch out for one thing. I've seen it happen to a couple of the guys in my class. When you start to go out with a girl, you can get sucked into her world, or she can get sucked into yours. Go on to the drama group if you want, but make sure she's out at all of your games. Make her come to the practices too.'

'She's not my girlfriend.'

'So what are you telling me, you decided to wear tights on your own?'

Jack picked up a couple of admirers over the first few weeks, a small guy with a pointed face, and a taller one who always wore crew-neck sweaters.

'Mouse and Rat,' said Mary-Jane. She was fast that way, and I liked it about her. On the way home one day we started to talk, and she asked me over to her house to take a look at her dog. I knew if anybody saw me going over to her house after school, they'd call her my girlfriend. I didn't care.

Her mother was in the back yard when we got there, sitting in a Muskoka chair with a wide-brimmed hat on her head because it was a very warm October. She was a thin, blond woman, with an ashtray on one arm of the chair and a highball glass on the other. The dog was a big collie that looked up at us and wagged its tail.

'Hi, Mom,' Mary-Jane said, in a voice flatter and deader than anything I had heard from her before.

'Did you bring home a friend? Should I set another place for dinner?'

'I don't know,' Mary-Jane said, sounding doubtful. If I stayed, they'd be calling her my girlfriend for sure. I wanted to stay, but I knew my father wouldn't like it. He'd say it was immoral for a young man to eat dinner at a girl's house unless they were planning to get married.

I made an excuse.

'Don't you think you'll like my food?' her mother asked. 'Doesn't the place look clean enough to you?'

'Mom.'

'What's your last name?'

I told her, and when she asked me the nationality of my parents, I told her that too.

'Ah yes, I know your people. We had some farm labourers from your country in Germany. They were all Catholics. What do they call them here, Micks? Are you a Mick too?'

Mary-Jane walked me to the end of the block when it was time for me to go. She tried to apologize for her mother, but I told her I had a father who was exactly the same. I didn't tell her that I had spat in her mother's glass when she had gone in to get a cigarette and Mary-Jane wasn't looking.

Some of the guys from class were having lunch in the cafeteria, and Paul, the minister's son, was talking. None of us were friends, really, but that didn't mean we couldn't talk. Paul knew he wasn't much good in sports, but he wanted to try something, and he was talking about basketball.

'I'm tall. Maybe that'll help.'

'You've got to be fast too,' I said. 'You can't just stand around under the hoop and expect someone to pass you the ball for an easy shot.'

Jack came down the aisle with Mouse and Rat, and he stopped beside Paul.

'I need a little favour from you, Squealer.'

'I told you, I'm not a squealer.'

'Whatever. I've got a little excuse note here I need you to sign.'

'I don't get it.'

'He doesn't get it,' Mouse said to Rat. The two hung around Jack all the time now, and they ran little commentaries off the sides of his conversations. Mouse and Rat had a talent for making anyone they talked about feel stupid. Paul already had the colour rising in his cheeks. I could sense the anxiety mounting in Paul as he looked nervously up at Jack and his friends. There was no sympathy in any of them. He had known some of the other guys at our lunch table since grade two, but none of them were going to help him out. As for me, it was none of my business.

'Let me explain it to you,' said Jack. 'I skipped yesterday afternoon, and I didn't get back in time to fix up the little pad you carry around. So my Mom wrote this note for the teacher, but she forgot to sign it. I want you to sign it in her name.'

Panic was shooting out of Paul like great bolts of electricity. I could just imagine his dad with him in some recreation room with a fireplace and a dog, telling him that moral choices were going to be hard. The only advice my dad ever gave me was never to pay the price on a tag, and cheap liquor got you just as drunk as the expensive stuff. It was at times like this that living with my father didn't seem so bad. At least he didn't lay out an impossible life plan.

'I can't do it,' said Paul. He'd sunk his head a bit between his shoulders, as if he expected to get some kind of blow.

'*Can't* do it?' Jack looked shocked. 'You mean you don't know how to write? I'd give you a little lesson if I had the time, but I've got to see my girlfriend. I think you're saying you *won't* do it.'

Paul could not speak. I'd never seen anyone so afraid before in my entire life.

'I think you're a squealer after all,' said Jack. 'I hate squealers.'

He leaned forward and gave a tough little shove against Paul's shoulder. Paul was so scared he lost his balance, and fell onto the floor. The chair fell over and made a big racket, and Mr Henderson, who was on lunch duty, was over by us in a second.

'I saw that. I saw the whole thing. Are you all right, Paul?'

'I'm fine,' he said. He'd scrambled right back up, knocking over some chairs and making more noise in the process. There was a kind of invisible wire that ran through all the high school kids in the cafeteria. Any little conflict, and the end of the wire tugged at the notice of the kids. The whole cafeteria was quiet now, and everyone was looking at us.

'What's that slip?' said Mr Henderson, and he snatched the note out of Jack's hand. 'Forging notes and pushing around other students. It looks like you're all set for a three-day suspension, Jack. I guess you didn't learn a thing last year. Two straight failures, and you'll end up in the two-year sheet metal programme, kid. You'll be making tin boxes for clothes-pegs for the rest of your life.' He led Jack away to the vice-principal's office.

Mouse and Rat stayed where they were.

'Jack was right,' said Mouse.

'You are a squealer,' said Rat.

'But I didn't even do anything!'

'Oh yes you did. You raised a big fuss, and now Jack's going to be out of school for three days. His old man is going to beat the hell out of him, and Jack's going to be awfully upset when he comes back. I'd watch my back on the way home if I were you.'

I thought Paul was going to puke.

'If he tries anything, he'll get expelled,' Paul said weakly.

'Unless he gets you somewhere away from the school,' one of the kids at the table said. 'They can't expel him if he does it out on the street somewhere. Last year this nut named Crazy George waited for a guy on his porch. I mean hours. Crazy George had a broken hockey stick, and he smashed the kid when he came out the door.'

We had math in Mr Doyle's portable right after lunch, and I sidled up to Mary-Jane to tell her what had happened in the cafeteria.

'Swift justice,' she said.

God, I loved the way she talked. I set myself up across from her at the back of the math class, and we talked a lot more. Mr Doyle's discipline was soft as his voice, and we could do just about anything we wanted in his portable. Mr Doyle would toss and catch a little piece of chalk while he looked at two kids having a shoving match at the back of the room, but he'd never say anything about it. I guess he didn't believe it was happening. Mouse and Rat looked at a *Playboy* during class, and all Mr Doyle ever did was turn back to the blackboard and keep working on algebra.

'That poor man just doesn't know how to run a class,' said Mary-Jane.

'Forget that. What do you think about what happened to Jack?'

'Serves him right. Half the boys in this class are terrified of him.'

'I'm not.'

'That's because he doesn't push you around.'

'If Paul stood up for himself, he wouldn't get pushed around either.'

'He's a sensitive boy. I was watching television at his house one time, and he started to cry right in the middle of a show.'

'You watch TV at his house?'

'Sometimes.'

'Are you old friends or something?'

'Not really.'

I thought I could learn to hate Paul.

'I've got a football practice after school,' I said. 'Want to come watch?'

'What do you do?'

'Mostly exercises, but we're starting a little scrimmaging.'

'Maybe I'll wait until you play a game. I'm not really all that interested in sports.'

Gerry was already home when I got there after football practice. He was so good that they'd moved him up to the senior team, which everyone knew was against the rules, but Gerry had been told to say he was in grade eleven if anyone asked. He liked playing with the senior team. Most of them were bigger than Gerry, but none were faster. Gerry was peeling potatoes and Tom was doing his homework so he'd be all finished before dinner.

'I saw you talking to this girl on the way to a portable today. Is she Mary-Jane?'

'Yeah.'

'No knockers on her.'

'What?'

'She doesn't even have any tits on her is what I'm saying.'

'I never noticed.'

'Legs are okay, though.'

'I never noticed that either.'

'So what do you look at, for Christ's sake, her chin?'

'Mostly I just listen to what she says. She's really smart, and kind of pretty in her own way.'

'Well, talk about beauty in the eyes of the beholder.'

'What's that supposed to mean?'

'It means you should drop her this minute.'

'I can't drop her because I'm not even going out with her.'

'Then stop hanging around her. Women make men bad in sports. Don't you know that? She's making you dopey, kid. I'd let that pass if she was a real looker, but let's face it, you're losing more than you're gaining.'

'What am I losing?'

'Your peace of mind. You'll be thirty yards out, running for a pass, and the next thing you know, her vision floats up in front of you and you miss the ball.'

I kicked over the basket with the potatoes in it, but Gerry just kept laughing.

*

A lot of the guys in our class seemed to take pleasure in telling Paul just how tough Jack really was, and how he was sure to smash up Paul's face as soon as he was back in school. It was strange how much pleasure they seemed to get out of these conversations, because Jack had pushed around most of them at one time or another. Just about all the boys were afraid of Jack, and just about all of them delighted in scaring Paul. He was as jumpy as a cornered rabbit, and Mouse and Rat weren't any help.

'Hey, Paul,' said Rat.

'Yeah?'

'You might want to take a different way home tonight. I think Jack's looking for you. Might be a good idea to bring along some friends as well.'

But when it came time to walk home, Paul didn't seem to have any friends at all. I had to stay late for football practice, so it wasn't as if I was running out on him. He wasn't really my friend anyway — just a kid in the class. Mary-Jane walked him home instead.

'You only would've made it worse if Jack came for him,' I told her between classes. 'No guy wants to get beaten up with a girl watching.'

'He wouldn't have got beaten up. I would've talked Jack out of it.'

'No way. That guy's something right out of *Alley Oop*. The only two people in the world stupider than him are Mouse and Rat.'

'I think Jack's just misunderstood. You know that girlfriend he keeps talking about? She works at Kresge's in the candy department and the manager's sweet on her. Poor Jack's heart must be breaking.'

'You've stuck your nose in books too long,' I said.

'What is that supposed to mean?'

'Just because you're smart in school, you think you're smart about people too. Well, you don't know anything about people. You can't see past the end of your own nose.'

'Why are you being so mean to me?'

'Because you don't understand anything.'

'I never want to talk to you again.'

'Fine.'

'Fine.'

That was on Friday, Jack's last day of suspension. Paul had a whole weekend to stew about the pummelling he was going to get on Monday. I didn't do too well that weekend either. I kept waking up in the night, and then I was dopey during the day. Brain Jane. Plain Jane. The others who knew her from the Protestant school had been right. The only thing I couldn't understand was that if she was so dense, how come it hurt me so much to find it out?

'Welcome back to Weston Collegiate,' said Mr Henderson to Jack in home room on Monday morning. 'Thinking of changing into the two-year technical programme? A boy like you could spend a lifetime on an assembly line some place. Not much chance you're going to make it through Latin next year anyway.'

Jack was quiet. The confident smile he usually wore had disappeared. Between classes, Mouse and Rat kept talking him up, though, and by lunch time, he was looking a little better. Rat managed to walk alongside Paul on the way to the cafeteria.

'Jack says you're going to get it, Squealer. Sometime in the future. You'll never really know when, but he'll be there for you one day. Maybe this summer. Maybe tomorrow. I wouldn't make any really long-range plans if I was you.'

The other guys at the lunch table were not much help.

'Do you really see stars when you get punched in the face?'

'I heard that if that happens to you, you go blind later in life. Twenty years down the line, the scars just burst and your eyeballs fill with blood — on the inside. There's nothing they can do about it either.'

'It doesn't matter,' said Paul.

Everyone looked at him like he was crazy.

'I talked to my dad about this. He said I have to stand up for my rights.'

'He's not the one who's going to get plastered in the face.'

The class in Mr Doyle's portable was wilder than most that day. Paper airplanes were being thrown by kids who never said 'boo' to a teacher before in their lives. Quiet Mr Doyle kept his back to us most of the time, and kept drawing algebra problems on the board and talking in a low mutter. I wasn't talking to Mary-Jane, who sat up front and tried to hear what he was saying.

Mouse walked across the floor to the pencil sharpener. On his way back, he gave Paul a little shove.

'Just a taste of what you're going to get later,' said Mouse.

Paul stared at his notebooks for a while, and then sighed. I could see his shoulders rise and fall. Then he put the cap on his fountain pen. He was the only guy I knew who used a fountain pen to do math. Then he closed up his notebook, and packed it carefully into his three-ring binder, and stood up.

Paul walked over to Jack's desk. Jack was doodling in his notebook, and he looked up at Paul and gave him a funny smile. It wasn't his usual smile, the cocky one, but a sad kind of smile, the kind you might give when you've been struggling against the current in a strong river, and then decided to give up.

'Let's get this over with,' said Paul.

'Shut up, Squealer. Go sit down.'

Paul shoved Jack, hard. Jack grabbed at the armrest to keep his balance, but those little wooden desks with the small armrests were never very stable, and Jack went over with it. He crashed to the floor and his books went flying.

Mouse and Rat were up in a minute.

'You're finished, Paul,' they said. 'You're meat. He's going to pound your face once you get outside. You're going to be on crutches for the next six months.'

It was strange, but Jack himself said nothing. Mouse and Rat helped him up, and straightened out his books, and whispered to him intensely.

Mr Doyle looked around at the loud crash, but then he just turned his back on us and kept on writing at the board.

'Who's going to hold my books for me?' Paul asked.

The words were like a drop of detergent hitting a greasy surface. The other guys in the class backed off him so fast I thought they were going to fall over themselves.

'You're just asking for it, Paul,' they said, making sure that Jack could hear them. 'What are you trying to be, a hero or something?'

'Hold his books for him,' Mary-Jane said to me.

'If you like him so much, you do it yourself.'

Mary-Jane took Paul's books for him when we stepped out of the portable.

Classes were changing, and there must have been three hundred kids outside. None of us from our class walked back towards the school — we all walked out towards the centre of the football field. There was that wire running through everybody again, and all the students from the other classes started to look towards us.

'Hit him first,' said Mary-Jane. She only had it half right. She should have told him to hit hard as well. I thought about standing up for Paul, but decided against it. Let her see the kind of guy she had fallen for.

Jack looked more serious than I'd ever seen him. No hint of a smile any more, and he was wearing a couple of rings on his right hand that he had borrowed from Mouse and Rat. They squared off at the centre of the field, about ten feet between them. Paul raised his fists, a sight pathetic to behold. He had his thumbs inside his fists, like a guy who'd never hit anyone before and didn't know you could break your own bones that way. And his fists were so wide apart you could throw a basketball between them. Jack held up one hand.

'Just apologize, Paul. Tell me you're sorry, and the whole thing will be over.'

'Kill him, Jack. Don't let him talk his way out of it,' said Rat.

But Paul wasn't talking. He moved in slowly, determined. It made me want to laugh, kind of. I mean, the look on his face was like he was bound for glory or something.

He must have remembered what Mary-Jane told him, though, because he came in close. Jack couldn't seem to believe what was happening. Paul threw a fast right that caught Jack by surprise on the side of his face. But the whole thing was pathetic. Paul came around wide on the swing instead of jabbing straight, and because he couldn't really bear the feeling of flesh against his fist, he pulled the punch a bit. It knocked Jack's head sideways, but it was no worse than a slap from a girl. And in the meantime, Paul had this goofy look on his face, as if he'd done the job, and stood up for justice. He thought it was high noon.

Whatever Jack had been thinking of before, his reflexes took over after the punch. He straightened himself out, stepped forward, and gave a sharp, powerful jab with his right fist that hit Paul's eye and nose at the same time.

You could hear the sickening crack as the cartilage broke, and the blow made him stagger back. There were bleeding scratches where the rings had cut his face, but that was nothing compared to the fountain of blood that shot out his nose. He was stunned, and didn't even know it was over. Nobody could keep up a fight when he was bleeding that badly. Paul raised his fists again and started to walk forward. But Mary-Jane was on him in a minute. She was pulling Kleenexes out of her bag and holding his nose and crying harder than I'd ever seen anyone cry in high school.

The rest of the guys in the class were climbing all over one another to congratulate Jack. It made me sick. He pushed them around every day, and they tried to clap him on the back. What Mary-Jane was doing made me even sicker. She was hugging Paul, getting blood all over her clothes and not making any sense in anything she said.

Jack pushed off Mouse and Rat and the other kids, and he tried to get a hold of Paul, to get his attention.

'Why did you make me do that? I'm finished in this school now. My old man is going to kill me,' and then he was crying too. Paul's eye was starting to swell up, and the fountain kept gushing out of his nose. The whole three hundred kids changing classes closed in to get a good look, and any second one of the teachers would show up and Jack and Paul would be swept into the high school justice system in the vice-principal's office.

I couldn't figure out all the tears. Jack was doomed anyway, and Paul was going to go home to a father who said he'd done the right thing. Mary-Jane would even come over to see him later that night to make sure he was really all right.

I was the one who should have been crying.

The Main Drag

GERRY SAT AT THE WHEEL OF THE STRATO CHIEF WITH HIS shoulders hunched, as if the world's biggest lineman faced him in a football scrimmage. My father sat right beside him, up tight in the middle of the front bench seat, close enough to grab the wheel if something went wrong. And something always went wrong.

'Your hands keep jiggling the wheel back and forth,' my father said. 'When you're on a highway, you lock your arms in position and then don't move them any more.'

'That's ridiculous,' said Gerry. 'There's wind and curves, and you have to keep making slight adjustments.'

My mother, Tom, and I were in the back seat, with a cooked chicken in a roasting pan at our feet, all the beach towels flat on the seat under us, a basketball on my lap, and a beach ball on Tom's lap. Tom had a Sherlock Holmes book balanced on top of the ball and he wore a deerstalker hat that brought him a lot of grief at school. Tom was not much of a fighter, but he fought anybody who touched his hat.

'It's safer if you all get in the back,' my father had said before we left. 'He's never driven on a highway before, and if he smashes the car, at least we'll be the only two splattered against the windshield.'

'There'd be some satisfaction in that,' Gerry had muttered, but my father did not hear him. His hearing had begun to fade.

Although this could be maddening at the dinner table, it had its advantages.

'Slow down,' my father said. The sound of his dentures clicking against the pipe stem was a sure sign of his frustration.

'I'm five miles under the limit.'

My father stretched his foot over Gerry's foot and pressed on the brake.

'Don't make comments. Just do what I say.'

Gerry hunched down lower in the driver's seat, but he did not slow down. He pushed harder on the accelerator. I could hear the brake shoes grinding against the drums in the wheels. When my father finally took his foot off the brake, the car shot forward in a small spurt of speed.

'Two dollars! That's what you just cost me with that little trick,' my father said. 'You've been wearing down the brake shoes. Next time you need money, it's two dollars off for what you just did.'

'You never give me any money anyway,' said Gerry. 'Two dollars off nothing means nothing.'

'Pull over.'

'The traffic's too busy. I'll have to wait for the next exit.'

'Discussion, discussion. This is not a debating society. Pull over now,' and my father reached for the wheel and tugged to the right. Gerry hit the brakes, and when we touched the gravel shoulder, the car zig-zagged and threw up stones and dust before it came to rest.

'Now you're ruining the finish of the car,' my father said. 'Get out of the driver's seat. Mother, you come here and sit with me in the front.'

It was deathly hot in the car, and I could taste the dust Gerry had thrown up. Gerry opened up the driver's door, the one close to the highway traffic, and got out. The cars were whizzing past him just a few feet away.

'The traffic!' my mother shouted, but Gerry just looked at the stream of passing cars and sauntered slowly along the side of our Strato Chief. He could have reached over and pulled the cigarette out of the mouth of a passenger in one of those cars.

'I think we should send him to driving school,' my mother said after my father managed to get the car back on the road.

'Fifty dollars! I'm not going to throw my money away.'

'It might be worth it for the peace it would bring.'

'It'd be like paying ransom. You can't buy off bloody-mindedness. You have to crush it instead.'

'You're talking as if he were a colt that needed breaking.'

'Somebody has to do something about him or else he'll end up in jail.'

'Don't be ridiculous. His marks are good enough.'

'But he's got to learn to follow instructions.'

'Maybe the best way to teach is by example.'

'What's that supposed to mean?'

'You get so hysterical every time he gets behind the wheel that he's bound to be edgy.'

'So now it's my fault.'

'Well, you might try to be a little calmer.'

'An unruly child has our lives in his hands and you talk to me about calm? He could dash us against a bridge abutment, or crush us under a transport truck. This whole family would be nothing but a stain on the asphalt, all because of his stupidity.'

'Now you're getting hysterical.'

'You never did take the marriage vows very seriously.'

'What?'

'You're supposed to honour and obey me.'

'Oh, *please*.'

'It's taken straight from the Bible.'

'You always get religious when it's convenient.'

'And you spoil those kids rotten.'

'There's more to being a father than swinging a belt.'

'They didn't get enough of that. That's why they're so mouthy.'

'They learned blathering from their father.'

They were just warming up, and we hadn't even reached Barrie yet. It was the July long weekend and it was starting off about the same as usual. There'd be another hour of this before we got to the cottage, them talking about us as if we weren't right behind them. Gerry had crossed his arms so tightly he looked like he was going to squeeze himself to death. Tom was unperturbed. He could read under any conditions. My parents had refused to buy him the curved pipe that he wanted, but sometimes when they were out, he took one of my father's pipes and read with it between his teeth. He would even suck it as he read his Sherlock Holmes, and the nicotine my father never cleaned from the stem would splutter sickeningly.

My father's cousin, Stan, had a cottage at Wasaga Beach where we stayed to clear the trees and the stumps from our own lot next door. We were going to build a cottage ourselves once we had saved a little money.

'We should have bought a lot somewhere else,' said my mother.

'This was cheaper.'

'You mean closer to Stan. Even dead drunk, you'll be able to make it to your own door. A few lots farther away and you'd spend half your nights in the ditch.'

'A little respect, woman.'

Stan was a bachelor. Sort of. He'd had a wife and kids, but they got separated during the war. Left behind the Soviet lines. It was no big deal to us. There were lots of our parents' friends who were bachelors in Canada. My mother told us she'd thought of leaving Gerry behind as well because they figured the Americans would push the Soviets back in a few weeks. Sometimes I wished we'd both been left there.

Stan had no family of his own in Canada, but he made up for it by taking in just about anybody he knew at his cottage. Sometimes the guests paid for their beds, and sometimes they didn't. His cottage had six bedrooms, and every one was filled on weekends by people who didn't have places of their own. He had a tent out back for times when there were so many guests he had to give up his own bed, and occasionally Gerry and I slept out there as well.

Wasaga Beach was a strip of yellow sand on the shore of Georgian Bay, where the water was shallow enough we could swim without freezing for five or six weeks each season. Back from the strip of sand were a couple of long roads that ran parallel to the beach with wooden cabins of cottagers. A fish-and-chip shop for Fridays, Percy's Snack Bar for ice cream cones, and the Red Door Knob for groceries, where old Mr Wheeler took my mother's cheques if she ran out of cash. On weekends, the motorcycle gangs drove up and down the biggest road, which we called the main drag, and sometimes we'd see their motorcycles parked out in front of the Lighthouse Grill where they had dances on Saturday nights.

It was a strip of ghettos. Further up were the Ukrainians, and then the Poles, and then all the other funny East Europeans from places we had never heard of before. The Italians were the day crowd — huge families hauling baskets and barbecues and bottles of homemade wine that they drank from until the police came around and wrote out tickets for drinking in public.

'Idiots,' my father called them.

'You managed to finish a whole bottle of whisky last night,' my mother said. 'What makes you so much smarter than them?'

'Wine is for women,' my father said. 'They must be a whole nation of women in pants if all they drink is wine.'

Every other nationality was made up of idiots. The Ukrainian men danced with men, and that made *them* idiots. The Poles all put on airs. The rest came from countries that no one had heard of. Who could tell Slovakia from Slovenia, or the Baltics from the Balkans?

Wasaga Beach had been English and Scottish and Irish before the war, and there were still a few WASPs around, looking dazed, like people who had been invaded without even knowing it, until they woke up one morning and suddenly there was a column of kids from the Latvian summer camp marching down the road to the beach and singing a song that made the woods echo with foreign syllables. Most of the original cottagers, the 'Anglos,' as we called them, had finally sold out, but a few lingered on, frowning.

The trick for us kids up at the cottage was to get out of the way before my mother or father found something for us to do. As if there wasn't plenty to do already up at the basketball court or down at the beach. It was only noon when we arrived at Stan's cottage, but Stan was already sitting at the round dinner table in the middle of the cottage with an open bottle of Five Star whisky and two other men I did not know.

'Clear four stumps out of our lot and you're free,' my father said. We had cut down all the trees we needed to clear that spring, but the stumps remained.

'Couldn't we do it tomorrow?'

'No working on Sundays,' and my father sat down with the other men, and accepted the half glass of whisky that Stan poured for him. Of course, Gerry and I were supposed to do all the labour. Tom never had to do any of the dirty work — we were the ones who would have to dig up roots in the muck and then hack at them with a dull hatchet and use a pole to lever up the stumps.

'We're not even building this year,' said Gerry. 'Why can't we do the stumps another time?'

'No arguments. I'll be out to help you later.'

Gerry let the wooden screen door slap back against the jamb with a satisfying bang.

'He just said that to get us to work faster,' Gerry said as we carried the tools out to the lot next door. 'The last thing we need is him after two glasses of whisky, standing around and telling us what to do.'

He had said four stumps, but he hadn't said which four, so we chose cedars, which were small and whose roots did not extend as deeply as the birch or maple. We even pulled out five for good measure by the time our mother showed up. She had come out the back door with bathing suits, beach towels and the basketball.

'How many have you pulled?' she asked.

'Five.'

'Small ones — but it doesn't matter. Take these things and be home for dinner at six. And for God's sake, Gerry, indulge him — will you? He'll be drunk by the time you come home, so don't sulk or anything.'

'Why don't you just stop him from drinking?' Gerry asked.

'You can't keep a bear from honey. I'll just try to make sure he isn't too ridiculous.'

'You would've had to get to his mother before he was born to do that.'

'That's terrible. You apologize right now.'

'To who? He's not even here.'

'He will be if you don't hurry up. Now get out of here.'

Saturday afternoons made the whole weekend bearable. Tom was off at Vaughn's, the only kid we knew with a last name for a first, and Gerry and I went to the basketball court where a pickup game was already being played. A hundred degrees and the heat was rising off the asphalt in waves, but we stripped down to shorts and ran a hard, fast game for an hour before heading down to the beach. We had to go into the woods when we passed Stan's cottage just in case the Old Man was outside and saw us. He'd be sure to call us back in.

The sand on the beach was so hot it burned our feet as we ran down to the water and then swam out beyond the last sandbar. The white Collingwood grain elevators were like distant fortresses on the horizon, and sometimes ships sailed along that line where the sky met the water. Tramp steamers. Sometimes I imagined swimming right out to one and climbing up the ladder. I'd never come back, and all the others would think I had drowned.

Wasaga Beach was full of teenagers, all of us playing out private versions of beach movies. Some girls danced to the music from a radio, and the guys played cards or threw a football around. Cars drove up and down the beach, and every weekend some genius drove into the shallow water to wash his car, and then got stuck and twenty of us had to push the car back up to the dry sand. Life without our father was glorious, but the afternoon was always too short.

He was deep in a pit on our lot when we got back, throwing up shovels of earth from a hole as deep as his chest, and his face and clothes were covered with muck.

'Cedar stumps,' he said. 'A woman could pull out five cedar stumps while the potatoes boiled. Why can't you boys take a little initiative?'

'Must have been some stump you dug out there,' said Gerry, ignoring my father's comment.

'I'm digging a well. That's what I mean by initiative. Don't just do what has to be done. Try to do better than that. I'm an old man with two strong sons who spend the day on the beach while I'm stuck digging a well. I could have a heart attack down here.'

'Need some help?' I asked.

'It's too late for that. Your mother will have dinner on the table in a couple of minutes. Go inside and change.'

Stan was still sitting at the table with the two other men. They were lumberjacks who had agreed to work in the forests for two years to pay for their passage over from Germany after the war. They'd never left the lumber company. They spent most of the year in the forests and only left to spend whatever they had earned when they came into town. One of them was called Onion. A real DP name. He didn't look much like a lumberjack to me. He was thin and bony, tall, and bald, like Ichabod Crane. He wore gold-rimmed glasses and he kept peering over the top of them because they fogged up from the sweat he worked up from drinking. His friend was barrel-chested and quiet, and Stan kept them both entertained with stories from his childhood. The lumberjacks must have been paying for the whisky.

Stan had a lot of leaves for that table, and there must have been another five of them stuck in because it extended halfway across the room. Three other families were spending the weekend at Stan's cottage, and there were chairs and benches for all the adults and the older kids. The little ones sat on a ratty couch or on the front stoop to eat. My mother had her chicken on the table, and there were cabbage rolls and sausages and 'DP burgers,' as Gerry called them — huge meatballs that were stewed in a pale sauce made up mostly of sour cream. The front and back doors were open, but the place was hot from the summer's day and the cook stove in the back kitchen that had had the oven and all four burners going for supper.

'I hope we get the tent tonight,' said Gerry. 'This place is going to be a hell-hole.'

We were just sitting down to eat, when the screen door flew open, and then banged shut, and Tom came in. He had a paper bag in his hand and tears were running down his face. Twenty faces turned to look at him and the room fell silent.

'I hate you,' he said to the frozen faces looking at him. 'Every one of you is a dirty DP. You're not fit for anything but hauling pig manure.'

'Hey, Tom,' said Gerry, using the lull to fill his plate with both chicken drumsticks, 'if we're all DPs, what does that make you?'

'Two loafers and one hysteric,' said my father. 'What a family.'

Tom went into the bedroom and slammed the door behind him.

'I wonder what happened to him,' my mother said.

'He wasn't wearing his hat. Maybe somebody stole it.'

The food was more interesting than Tom, and soon there was a great din of chewing, slurping and slopping and talking with mouths full. My mother went into the bedroom and came out with Tom a few minutes later. She believed that you could get powerfully ill if you did not eat regularly, and skipping a meal might be the first move on the slippery slope to death.

'So what happened, kid?' Gerry asked him.

'I was over at Vaughn's cottage. He's got this great collection of Sherlock Holmes comics. His grandmother was over to visit and she lives in London, so I was asking her all these questions, like what it's like to walk on Baker Street, and maybe if I sent her the money she could buy me a real hickory walking stick and send it over. I thought she was really nice, and then she turns to Vaughn's mother and says in this great English accent, "He's such a nice boy. You wouldn't even know to look at him that he's foreign."'

'Then what?' asked Gerry.

'That's it.'

'Some old bag from England calls you a foreigner and you start to bawl?'

'I know more about Sherlock Holmes than Vaughn does. He didn't even know Moriarty was a professor of mathematics. I know the kings and queens of England all the way from William the Conqueror. I'm the only one who knows what the War of the Roses was all about. It's not fair that he's English and I'm not.'

'You know how they can tell we're DPs?' Gerry asked.

'How?'

'We smell of cabbage rolls. The stink gets in your blood, and those English have really sensitive noses. That deerstalker hat of yours is useless if you stink like a DP.'

'The English eat cucumber sandwiches,' said Onion. 'Honestly. We were in this forest above Atikokan, and there was this Englishman on the crew. Twelve hour days, six days a week, and there were men there who could eat a whole turkey for lunch. And this English guy has cucumber sandwiches, dainty as can be. A big man, too. Look at him the wrong way, and he'd happily stick a knife between your ribs.'

'Then he couldn't have been English,' said Tom. 'They're not like that. He must've been Welsh.'

'No, no,' my father said. 'The English are a race of liars. Their manners are so fine that you think you're dealing with gentlemen. But they are ruthless people. They pat you on the back and then they put you on a truck to take you back behind Soviet lines.'

'That's not true,' said Tom. 'They're the best people in the world. They have the best writers.'

'What about Goethe and Schiller and Dante and Molière?' my mother asked.

'Sound like wogs to me. The wogs start at Calais,' Tom said.

Since nobody knew what a wog was or where to find Calais, this got no response from the table.

'Your father's right,' said Onion. 'With a German or an Italian, you know where you stand. The one is always straight and the other is always crooked, but with an Englishman, you never know.'

*

My father did not work after dinner, so there was no danger that he was going to snap us up for some project. Onion had put another bottle of whisky on the table, and Gerry and I walked down to the beach to see who was around. Alma and Francine were in the dunes, smoking cigarettes.

'Kiss me,' said Alma. Gerry never even considered that she might mean me. Alma was a big girl. Big breasts, big bones, tall, and pretty at the same time. A kind of cross between a cheerleader and a football player. She was wearing a white mohair sweater that was too warm for the early evening, and she had a bead of sweat on her upper lip. I would have licked it off quite happily, but Gerry moved in. She locked her hands around his neck, but didn't kiss back — just pressed her lips against his, and then talked out of the side of her mouth. 'Now hold this position for a minute. Put your arm around me, for God's sake.'

'What's going on?' I asked.

Francine kept exhaling smoke in long, thin streams, and she stared at the horizon as if she was waiting for her ship to come in.

'Ron just broke up with her, and he's hanging around behind the dunes to see how she takes it.'

'Rub your hands up and down my back,' said Alma, and Gerry obliged.

'How about kissing back?' said Gerry.

'How can you be so cruel? My heart's just been broken. Can't you feel my cheeks? They're still wet with tears.'

Nobody could see Ron hanging around, but Gerry kept on pretending to kiss Alma from time to time. They sat with their arms around each other when they weren't pretending to neck. Gerry didn't seem to mind.

'We're going to the Lighthouse tonight,' said Francine. 'Want to come?' Francine and Alma were the same age as Gerry, and they really didn't like talking to me all that much because I was a year younger. Francine had her eyes on an older guy. He was nineteen and smoked a pipe. Some of the other guys smoked cigarettes, but nobody else our age smoked a pipe. Francine might have looked like the folk singer Mary, of Peter, Paul, and Mary, if she'd had blond hair, but hers was brown. Down on the beach, she was always fussing with it to make sure she didn't get any sand in it, and the guys loved to watch her drape her hair forward over her shoulders — she could have looked like Lady Godiva if she'd taken off her bathing suit.

'I'd go, but we don't have any money,' said Gerry. 'It costs a dollar to get in when the bands play on Saturday night.'

It was the only time I was ever glad we were broke. It was bad enough that the bikers hung around there, but it meant the end of the world if our parents found out. Getting caught at the Lighthouse was worse than getting caught with a case of beer. The fathers we knew tended to confiscate any beer or liquor they found. Since there was nothing to confiscate when they found you at the Lighthouse, they got twice as angry.

'I've got money,' said Alma.

I looked fast at Gerry, but he just shrugged his shoulders.

'If you've got money, no problem. We'll just have to wait until after dark.'

'Afraid to be seen?' Francine sneered.

'Aren't you?'

'We can sneak in the back.'

When we came in, the band was already playing hard, five guys in ties sweating so badly that the armpits of their grey jackets were wet all the way down to their pockets. The Black Diamond Riders were up at the counter, Cokes in hand, backs to the bar, looking at the girls dancing.

'You get some Cokes,' Alma shouted, 'Francine and I will go to the bathroom to check for supplies.'

'What kind of supplies?' I asked Gerry.

'I don't know. You think the women's bathroom has rubbers?'

The Lighthouse was famous to all us ethnic kids because of our parents' prohibition. I'd never been inside. It didn't look like anything special — a low-ceilinged country restaurant that had been expanded with a concrete floor for dancing. The strange thing was, the Lighthouse sat right in the middle of our ethnic beach, where we had our own church and kids' summer camp, and I didn't know a single person in the dance hall. It was like another world existed right alongside of ours, and I'd never seen it until I walked in through the Lighthouse doors. There were lots of guys in there, mostly in crewcuts with the odd Presley haircut, but the really surprising thing was how many girls there were. They sat or stood around in little knots, looking at the guys, or dancing the twist in small circles. What would their parents say if they found them in there? Maybe other nationalities had other rules, or maybe these were just the ones who were good at sneaking away.

'You got the Cokes?' Francine asked. 'Give them here,' and she and Alma took the bottles and went back into the bathroom.

'Probably going to drop aspirin in there,' said Gerry. 'Gets you high.'

When they came back, the Cokes had vodka in them.

'Girl sells the stuff right out of a stall. If the cops come in, they never dare go into the women's washroom.'

We stood around for a while and sipped on the Cokes. I couldn't really taste much in mine except for something that felt a bit like medicine, but by the time Alma finished hers, she was wearing a lopsided grin.

'Come on, Gerry,' she said. 'They're playing the Everly Brothers. I want you to wrap your arms around me in a slow dance.'

'This is where I find out if she wears falsies,' Gerry whispered to me on his way to the dance floor.

Alma put her arms around Gerry's shoulders and pressed into him as the music played. Just watching her made me sweat.

'She's drunk already,' said Francine.

'You want to dance?' I asked.

She made a small grimace, but when she headed for the dance floor, I followed her. I went to put both my arms around her, but she held me off, and made me hold one of her hands between us to keep us apart. Every time I tried to lean in towards her, she locked her elbow.

'The vodka doesn't seem to have much effect on you,' I said.

'I can hold my liquor.'

For the next couple of hours, I watched Alma melt further and further into Gerry, and as this went on, Francine's elbow got stronger and stronger. I figured she could have joined the Olympic arm wrestlers and stood a chance of winning — on the men's team. The two girls went into the bathroom to buy more supplies.

'I think she's going to let me screw her,' said Gerry.

'I hate that word.'

'Make love. Whatever. Any luck with Francine?'

'Ice queen.'

'Alma says she likes you.'

'Could've fooled me.'

'She's just pretending. Wait until she gets good and drunk and then make each move really small.'

'What do you mean?'

'What I mean is you can't ask her to pull down her pants until you've necked for a really long time. I mean long. So long, you'd think it was enough hours ago. Then you work really slowly to the boobs. Put your arm around her waist and then work your way up until she's not sure if you mean to touch her boobs or just her side.'

'How do you know all this?'

'I read a lot.'

'Anyway, Francine's not drunk at all. Alma's the only one who's getting stoned on that stuff. I don't believe there's anything in those Cokes.'

'It must be something. She's melting in my arms.'

I wasn't sure I was going to get anywhere with Francine, but if we went back to the dunes and Alma and Gerry started going at it, maybe she'd follow their example.

I went to the bathroom to take a leak.

It was a long trough of a urinal — the kind they had at Maple Leaf Gardens, with mothballs thrown in to keep down the stink. I had just started when two bikers came in. They both had beards and the smaller one was wearing a Nazi helmet.

'Get out of here,' the one with the helmet said. They started to talk quietly to one another, but then they stopped and looked at me again.

'I'll be finished in a second.'

I wanted to be finished, I really did, but the yellow stream refused to stop. The bikers looked at me some more, and I could almost feel the bristles on their beards starting to bunch and rise like the fur on the back of an angry bear.

'Get out now.'

When bikers spoke, I listened, or at least I tried to. But something had gone wrong with my bladder and I couldn't stop the flow of urine.

'I said now.'

It was impossible to comply.

They lifted me up by the shoulders, turned me around, and marched me towards the door. I was still having trouble stopping the stream, although I was working like mad to get myself back into my pants. The big biker held open the door and the Nazi marched me right onto the dance floor. A couple of girls saw me fooling around with my fly and they tore away screaming. The lead singer stopped in the middle of a long 'ooh,' but his hands kept strumming at the guitar. The Nazi gave out some primitive shout of disgust and he threw me right onto the dance floor, where I landed on my stomach. I didn't give a damn for bruises. All I wanted to do was get my fly back up.

It was a show-stopper. The dancers scattered like cowboys in a Western movie when a gun-fight is coming. The music stopped and there was dead silence as I scrambled to lift myself off the floor.

'The bastard pissed on my shoes,' the Nazi said.

'What a pig,' said the other. 'Only a pig would piss on somebody's shoes. Get him to lick it off.'

The Nazi was practically snorting out of his nose by now. He had a chain hanging off his belt, but he didn't go for it. He kept clenching and unclenching his fists at the side of his body. He was the smaller of the two, but he had half a dozen years on me and at least fifty pounds.

'Yeah,' he finally said. 'Lick off my shoes.'

So this was how death came, I thought. Even if I managed to down him with a lucky shot, there would still be his friend. And then all the other friends at the counter. Of course I could always do as he said and maybe get a playful kick in the teeth. Maybe I would have thought about it more if Alma and Francine weren't there. But with them in the room, there was no way. I brought my fists up to the ready.

'Wait a second.'

It was Gerry. 'This is my little brother. He's kind of goofy. You can't hold him responsible.' Gerry had walked up and stood beside me. Not that it did much good. The big biker came up and stood just behind his Nazi friend. If Gerry got in the way, it wouldn't be just a fight, it'd be a rumble.

I guess the Nazi couldn't talk. He was all muscle and instinct. The big guy talked for him.

'You want to lick off his shoes instead?'

'Sure.'

I couldn't believe what I was hearing. Gerry walked up to the guy and then knelt down on the concrete floor like he was going to confession. I could hear laughing from the counter where the other bikers stood, and some titters from the guys with crewcuts. Even the Nazi started a slow kind of smile. He stuck one of his feet forward like he was about to get a shoeshine.

Gerry drove one of his fists straight up into the guy's balls. No expression on the Nazi's face — nothing. He just went straight down, and as he was going down, Gerry was coming up. Gerry elbowed the Nazi hard in the face and sent him backwards onto the concrete floor where his head stuck with a loud crack.

Gerry was fast. The big biker had his mouth open in awe, and Gerry would have slammed his jaw shut before he had time to react. That would have left the others at the counter, but I wasn't thinking that far forward.

But the second biker was saved by the Old Man.

'Did I raise you to be criminals?'

My father was standing at the door to the dance hall. I should have felt relieved, but this was even worse than what I had expected from the bikers. He was wearing a housecoat and slippers, but the knotting on the housecoat was loose and you could see that all he had on were boxer shorts and an undershirt — the kind with skinny straps over the shoulders that the bricklayers wore on construction sites. He didn't even own a housecoat, so he must have borrowed one from somebody at Stan's cottage. If he was in his underwear, it meant he had gotten out of bed, and if he'd been in bed it meant that he was drunk.

'The only place on this beach that I forbid you to go, and what do I hear from the neighbours? They come to my bed and tell me my sons are on the way to hell, and they're taking two fine girls with them. Francine and Alma, you should be ashamed of yourselves. I thought you girls would have more brains than these two dolts.'

A kind of titter ran through the crowd, and the bikers looked at him, unsure. The Nazi that Gerry had decked still lay on the ground, groaning. At least he wasn't dead. The biker, his friend, had regained his composure.

'Get out of here, old man. Me and my friends will bring you your kids in pieces.'

'I saved these boys from real Nazis. You think I give them to you?'

'Johnny,' said the big biker, and he looked to the counter.

'We're not done with these two,' said a voice. It was Johnny Beret himself — the head of the Black Diamond Riders. I'd heard the name before, but I'd never seen him. He wasn't wearing a beret, but he had an ease about him that made him stand out from the rest. No beard. Hair not really long either. The kind of face that girls in movies like to kiss.

'What you mean, not finished?' my father asked.

'They hurt one of our friends, and now it's their turn.'

'One on one, he win fight. Now over. You think you could do any worse than what I'm going to do? On their knees for rest of weekend — all three masses tomorrow and confession before that.'

People often laughed when my father spoke. They laughed now.

'That's not good enough.'

'You bet it's good enough. It's more than good enough. I'm taking them home right now.'

'No, you're not.'

'What you going to do, hit an old man? For fighting young boys, police charge you. For beating old man, police will hurt you and then lay big charges. And you!' my father pointed to the owner, a thin, wiry man in glasses who was hanging behind the counter.

'Why you don't phone police? You encouraging fighting here? You not protect an old man like me? I go straight to city hall and they close this place so fast you be bankrupt in six months. You should be ashamed of self. You called police yet? If no, you help crime. All here my witness. You call police already? Yes or no?'

If I hadn't been so scared, I would have laughed too. The owner had his eyes darting all over the place to avoid those of my father.

'Sure, I called them. They're on their way.'

Maybe he was lying. It could have gone any way at that point, but I guess Johnny Beret got to be leader of the BDRs because he had some brains. He started to laugh.

'Let them go, boys. Their daddy's going to spank them anyway.'

The others joined in the laughter. It was almost as bad as having to lick the guy's shoes.

The music started up again as my father led the four of us out. A lot of cars drove up and down the main drag on a Saturday night, and all of them slowed to look at the old man in the housecoat and slippers and the four teenagers in tow. None of the people in the passing cars could have known the details of the story, but it was clear the old man was taking some kids home. Somebody I knew was bound to be in one of those cars, maybe one of the older ethnic kids who was cruising the main drag for girls. Word of our humiliation would be up and down the beach by morning.

If only my father would be quiet.

'Alma, I tell you, your father is sure to be sending you to the convent school after this. He's been worried about you all year and now he's bound to send you up to North Bay. Convent school — right in the middle of the forest where there's nothing for the girls to do but pray and study. Don't worry, you'll get used to it. Maybe you'll decide to become a nun.'

'It was all Gerry's fault,' said Alma. 'He's the one who convinced us to go.'

'I'm not surprised. But girls are supposed to have brains! Your mother can speak Latin, for God's sake, and here you are walking around in a sweater that looks like it belongs to your little sister.'

The Old Man laid off her when she started to cry. Francine was a harder case. She just went silent. Then he turned on us.

'Are you crazy?' my father said. 'Those hooligans would have torn you apart.'

'They were picking on Dave.'

'Very noble to help your brother. Very stupid to be there in the first place. I want to see both of you in confession before early mass tomorrow.'

'The priest doesn't do confession up at the cottage. He's out drinking too late the night before.'

'A little respect for your elders! I'll have him make an exception for you. I want everybody to see you on your knees at mass. How am I ever going to live down two lumpheads like you?'

Francine was staying with Alma and he was taking them home first.

The Old Man was in fine form once he got to their house. Alma's parents had guests over, and he gave them all a speech from the lawn when they came out onto the porch. In the middle of his talk, the belt on his housecoat came undone, but the Old Man didn't care.

He just went on about the immorality of all us kids, and then he had a few things to say about parents who didn't watch their daughters closely enough. Worst of all, when he was finished, he took each of us by the hand as he led us back to our cottage.

At the corner of our street, one of the neighbours had a bonfire going, and some of my father's friends were singing. Kids let off firecrackers and a couple were screaming at one another.

'Want a drink?'

'You boys go inside. I'll deal with you in the morning.'

'Dad, do me a favour and put on some clothes,' said Gerry.

'Don't you go giving me advice.'

When we walked into Stan's living room, Onion and the other lumberjack were still sitting at the table. There was a new bottle of whisky. You had to admire the stamina of people from our part of the world — as long as there was something on the table, they could sit there all day and all night.

'Looks like you boys are in trouble,' Stan said, and the men at the table started to laugh until my mother shot them a look. Using the fewest words possible, she let us know we were sleeping on the floor in the bedroom. Tom was already asleep on the bed.

'It's a hundred degrees in here,' said Gerry. 'Why can't we sleep outside?'

'It'll be a good foretaste of hell, because that seems to be the way you're heading.'

There wasn't much room on the floor, and even in my underwear, I was still hot. On the side of me where Gerry lay, it was a couple of degrees warmer and I kept trying to push myself away from him and against the wall. The walls were made of paperboard, and there was a young couple next door. I could hear repeated giggling from them.

The men at the table in the other room were loud. They talked about working in the woods. Stan was trying to convince them to move to Toronto and get factory jobs. We heard the screen door slam as my mother went outside to get my father.

'Gerry?'

'Yeah?'

'You saved my life in there.'

'Don't get sappy on me. We both would've been smashed up if the Old Man hadn't shown up.'

'There's one thing I can't understand, though,' I said.

'What's that?'

'If he saved our skins, how come I don't feel grateful?'

'Because he's such a goof. I can't stand living with him any more. I'm leaving home.'

'You are? When?'

'In September. I applied for a job at a stationery factory, and they said they didn't have anything in the summer, but I could start in the fall if I wanted.'

'Not finish high school?'

'What for?'

'It'd break Mother's heart.'

'Yeah, well I'm not taking this kind of crap any more. I want to get a place of my own.'

'Then he'll have no one to pick on but me.'

'You'll survive.'

I wasn't so sure. I heard the screen door slam again as my mother brought my father in.

'Standing around outside in your underwear. Why didn't you just take off all your clothes?'

'Be quiet, woman. It was dark outside.'

'Not so dark that they didn't get a good look at your face. The story is going to be up and down the beach by tomorrow morning. We'll be the laughingstock of the community.'

'I had to save my boys.'

'I'm not sure which is worse, you or them.'

'Sit down and join us for a drink,' I heard Stan say.

'You get to bed right this minute,' my mother said. 'You've caused me enough grief tonight.'

'You go ahead. I'll be there in a minute.'

'I'm not going anywhere. I'm staying right here. If you step outside in your underwear again, I'll apply directly to the Pope for an annulment.'

We listened to them talk for a while.

'You think he'll really make us go to confession in the morning?' Gerry asked.

'Maybe he'll be so drunk tonight, he'll sleep in,' I said.

A big June bug was buzzing against the outside of the screened window. It kept flying back and taking another run at the screen.

'He never sleeps in.'

I sighed.

'Confession's going to be the worst.'

Gerry was quiet for a while. The big June bug was still banging against the screen.

'Except maybe Alma and Francine's parents will make them do the same.'

'What?'

'Go to confession. That would be all right.'

'What do you mean?'

'Then everybody will think we got to home base with them.'

Penance

I KNEW IT WAS MY FATHER AS SOON AS HE SHOOK MY SHOULDER. Even if she were angry, my mother would have been gentler, and said a few words. My father's hand was like a bear's paw, rough and insistent. There was no need for him to remind me that today was our morning for early confession. I had dreamt of it uneasily all night.

By nine o'clock, we were at the front door of the community centre that doubled as a church on Sunday mornings. The room was already stifling. It stank of the food from a summer camp that used it as a refectory all summer long. Two walls were made up of floor-length windows so the overflow from mass could listen to the service from outside, but no wind came in to freshen the air. The portable altar was already set up, but nobody was there.

My father was never sure if pipe smoke counted as food or not, but to be on the safe side, he didn't smoke before mass and communion on Sunday mornings. Instead, he kept the empty pipe clenched in his teeth at the corner of his mouth. He would have looked as stern as Moses if he hadn't been so bleary-eyed from all the drinking the night before.

'No priest, no people,' said my father. 'I feel like I'm in a dream.'

'A nightmare,' said Gerry. He crossed his arms, leaned back against the wall, and looked around him with an air of boredom.

'Get those arms uncrossed,' my father snapped.

Gerry uncrossed his arms and put his hands in his pockets.

Through the windows behind the altar, we could see men setting up folding tables on the freshly cut meadow. A couple of women were standing on the rectory steps, giving directions.

'Let's go out and see what's going on,' my father said.

'We can cut across the front and go out the back door,' said Gerry.

'What, use the altar for a short cut? Learn some respect.'

My father led the way around the back and stopped one of the men.

'What's going on here?'

'Father Mark's name day,' said the man. 'You know, he throws a party every year. We're roasting a side of beef on a spit.'

'What about the early mass?'

'Only one mass today, at eleven.'

'Will he have confession before?'

'I doubt it. He'll just want to get it all over with for the picnic.'

Gerry could not resist snorting in pleasure. My father looked at him hard, but passed on the opportunity for another tongue-lashing. Why bother? He had us where he wanted us already.

'I want both you boys in the front row of the church until mass starts. I'm going to help out here.'

It was a relief to get away from him. Gerry and I went into the church and sat down. I was already hungry and would have to wait until after mass to eat. The side of beef had been on the spit since four that morning. The smell was driving me crazy. At least we could look through the screened windows behind the altar and see the men working. My father would not be able to sneak up on us.

It was a strange new feeling to resent my father so purely without any remorse. That was usually Gerry's job, but if he was going to leave the house, I would happily take over for him. Gerry stretched out on the chair and put his hands behind his head.

We heard someone coming in from the back. Gerry snapped forward into a position of penitence, just in case my father or the priest was trying to sneak up on us. It was Alma's father with the two girls. He walked the girls up to the front row on the other side of the centre aisle from us. I could tell he didn't want to talk to us, but he was as confused by the absence of people as my father had been.

'No early mass today,' said Gerry as he slipped down onto his knees. 'My father's outside, helping to get the picnic ready.'

Alma's father was much smaller than her, so small it looked like she would be able to pick him up and toss him like a javelin if she wanted to. He was a thin man who used a cigarette holder and wore thick glasses. He'd been a schoolteacher in the old country.

'I'd leave the girls here to pray, but I'm not sure I can trust them after last night.'

'It wasn't their fault,' said Gerry. 'The whole thing was my idea. I'm sorry.'

The schoolteacher looked at him hard. He'd spent half of his life listening to liars, and he weighed Gerry's words carefully. But Gerry was an expert. He could lie his way into heaven. Alma's father nodded. 'I'm going to leave the girls here to pray. I want your word of honour that you won't speak to them.'

'You have it, sir.'

'You're sure?'

'I promise.'

The man gave stern instructions to the girls to pray hard for their sins. He paused at the back door, as if he had finally caught scent of Gerry's falseness. Gerry looked back at him quizzically. Surely this old man would see through the mock honesty on Gerry's face. But no. He was as stupid as the rest of our parents.

'Get down on your knees, girls,' said Gerry.

'You promised not to talk.'

'They can see in from outside, beyond the altar. As long as we're on our knees, we'll look good and sorry.'

The girls knelt down. Alma started to mutter a prayer.

'What are you, a nun or something?' Gerry asked.

'If my father doesn't see me praying, I'll have to go to that convent school.'

'Just look down and beat your breast a few times. That impresses the hell out of them. If you want, I'll beat your breast for you.'

'Doesn't your word mean anything?' Francine snapped.

'Not to parents. Tell them the truth, and they go crazy on you. It's not even their fault. They're all stuck in a time machine. Look at my Old Man. He's still back on the farm, around 1920. I figure your dad is about 1933. It's pathetic.'

'So you lie to them?'

'Sure.'

'Even your mother?'

'Mothers are different,' I said. The others waited for me to go on. 'You don't lie to them. You just don't say anything.'

We heard some steps around the back door and we all dropped our heads. Someone looked in and then left. Outside, some of the women were laying down tablecloths, and tacking down the corners to keep them from flapping up in the wind.

'Are you going to confession?' Alma asked.

'What do you think? The Old Man is making us,' said Gerry.

'What are you going to tell the priest?' Alma asked.

'I'm going to confess impure thoughts,' said Gerry.

'Don't you dare!'

'Maybe carnal knowledge.'

'That's a lie!'

'Who says I was talking about you?'

Francine started to laugh, looked up at the cross on the altar and then put her hand over her mouth and dropped her eyes.

'Gerry,' said Alma, 'if you say any of those things, the priest will think you're talking about me. Then I'll have to confess the same thing, and if I don't, he might refuse to give me communion. I'll be kneeling at the altar and my parents and all their friends will be looking at me.'

'Can't be helped,' said Gerry.

'Couldn't you just confess disobedience to your parents?'

I hated my father for making us go to confession, but Gerry didn't care. Everything was an angle to him. Now he'd found one with Alma.

'Not good enough,' said Gerry. 'I could make you a deal, though.'

'What kind of deal?'

'I could save that part of the confession for when I got back to the city. Tell some anonymous Anglo priest.'

'Would you do that?'

'On one condition.'

'What.'

'Meet me in the dunes tonight.'

Francine gasped. A date in the dunes was almost as explicit as taking off your clothes. And suggesting it in church! I wasn't too crazy about what he was doing either. It made me come close to understanding the idea of blasphemy.

'I can't even get out of the house. I'm grounded.'

'Then come with me for a walk during the picnic. Say, into the woods.'

Alma seemed to wait a long time before she answered.

'You mean into the bushes, don't you? We're kneeling here in church and you're asking me to go into the bushes?'

'Sure, why not?'

I envied Gerry his ease. Where did he find the energy to pick up girls when all mine was consumed with rage at my father?

'I'll see if I can get away,' said Alma.

We knelt in silence for a while. I couldn't believe Gerry's luck. Ask and it shall be given. I thought I would give it a try too.

'Francine?' I asked.

'What.'

'Aren't you going to ask me what I'm going to confess?'

Francine thought a little.

'Masturbation?' she asked.

From behind the altar we saw Father Mark come striding across the picnic yard. All of us looked down and started to mutter bits of prayers. Gerry was even saying bits of the Credo in Latin, but I knew he was bluffing. He'd failed the test to be an altar boy. Alma beat her breast with her closed fist. We heard Father Mark come in the back door and go into the vestry, and when he stepped into the church, he was wearing a stole over the shoulders of his soutane. He was a big man around the same age as my father, in his late fifties, and he had gold teeth and jowls over a barrel chest. Father Mark was a pastor of the old school, for whom a parish was like a farm. His priority lay in the buildings and the grounds. The sheep needed some attention, but the lambs were pretty much left on their own. He looked at his wristwatch, then at the four of us kneeling at the front row.

'I need some more hands out there,' he said brusquely, 'but your fathers say you need to go to confession. Let's do this as a group. What happened last night?'

'We went to the Lighthouse,' said Gerry.

'That's it?'

'Yes, father.'

'Damn foolish business. Disobedient to your parents, den of temptation, et cetera. Anybody take off any clothes?'

Alma gasped, and Francine turned pink.

'No, father,' said Gerry.

'Any funny touching through the clothes?'

'No, father.'

'Okay, so ten Our Fathers apiece. Say them later, during mass. Now get out there and lend a hand. Wait, any of you play the accordion?'

Nobody did.

Father Mark threw a good party, with plenty of food and bottles of whisky hidden under the soft drink table. The town issued no liquor licences on Sundays, the day of the Lord, but the police looked the other way as long as Father Mark was discreet. His parties were good, but not all were called to Father Mark's table. First, every single guest had to go to mass. Father Mark had an excellent memory and could tell who had been there. He had been known to chase out guests he had not seen at the mass before the party. More people showed on the day of the picnic than at Christmas and Easter. Maybe he should have thrown a party then too.

The summer masses were always full of layers. The serious, religious types like my father always tried to make it early enough to be inside the building. The semi-religious came a little later and sat on the chairs outside the building so they could listen to the mass through the screen windows. The ones who only came for a slice of beef and a few shots hung around the back door or the fringes of the chairs outside. These were the men and women who reeked of sulfur. The most brazen of them stood with their arms crossed and bored looks on their faces. Among them were men and women we saw at no other time of the year, lumberjacks like Onion or women in high heels and flashy clothes, the kind of women who did not take off their sunglasses even though the world of the mass was supposed to extend outside onto the sunny lawn.

On the day of his party, Father Mark always gave the sermon about the shame of dropping coins instead of folding money into the offering basket. Those who stood on the fringes of the outdoor part of the mass were especially vulnerable to the two offering collectors, bald men both. These two wore grey suits that smelled of mothballs and the sweat glistened on their bald crowns and grim faces. They were trustworthy men, religious tax collectors who thrust the offering baskets into the faces of those who stood on the edges of the mass. The basket could be discreetly overlooked by the regulars as it was passed along the row from one parishioner to another, but it could not be ignored when the collector was standing there in a full suit in ninety degrees of heat with the basket held right in front of an almost-atheist. This was always the test of their abandon. The weaker ones reached into their pockets and put in two- or even five-dollar bills, while the more deeply damned, like Onion, dropped in quarters.

All summer long we had played little delaying games with our father, forgetting handkerchiefs or having to go to the toilet in order to arrive late enough to have to listen to the mass outside. This time he had us, but even so we had won the game. Word of our sin was known to all, but to the parents we looked sufficiently contrite, while the ones our age suspected that at very least we had touched the bare breasts of Alma and Francine the night before, or maybe done better yet. I was a little uneasy before the communion, because of those old stories from the Catholic school about hosts that leaped off the tongues of sinners, but once the dry wafer was safely down, I was home free.

Towards the end of the mass, the smell of the roasting meat outside caused a rustle to go through the congregation. Many had gone to communion to please Father Mark, and that meant they had fasted for at least three hours, and most had not eaten since the night before. The tension started to build, and more than one eye was scanning a fast route out before Father Mark had finished the procession of altar boys back into the vestry. The more decorous hung back, the ones like Alma's father and the intelligentsia of doctors and engineers, but the majority stampeded out to where the side of beef was being turned on the spit by two men sweating freely at the hot handles on either side of the carcass. Mouths watered as the fat off the blackened side of beef dripped onto the fire and the smell of roasting meat filled the air, but the wiry chef, a veteran of the French Foreign Legion, held up his hand. The meat was not ready. Our people had a horror of under-cooked meat, so no one pressed him. The men would drink instead.

The fat and shiny organist stepped onto a wooden box, cracked a few jokes that were obscure to anyone under forty, and had the church ladies put a wreath of oak leaves over Father Mark's shoulders. Two accordionists (Father Mark had wanted three) started a waltz tune, and the whole mass of people crowded around the drinks table while the church choir sang East European pop tunes from 1937.

The trick at adult parties was never to arouse the attention of our elders. The men drank and the women talked, and we were always left on our own. The problem was, once in a while the men might say something interesting, or one of them might get drunk enough to offer us a cigarette or a shot of whisky, so we had to be distant, but available. A knot of men including my father and Onion had formed around a quiet man I didn't know, and it looked like there might be a fight starting, so I hung around the fringe to see what they were saying.

'I'm going back, and that's all there is to it,' said the man. He looked unkempt, with clothes that seemed to twist themselves around his belly, and strange bumps on his face that might have come from fat under the skin or a fight a few days before.

'You're crazy,' my father said. 'you won't even get to see your wife. They'll pick you up at the border and send you straight to Siberia, unless they shoot you on the spot.'

'Stalin's dead. Things are different now.'

'Khrushchev's alive. Look what he did in Hungary.'

'I've been in touch with the embassy. They say I can go back to my family.'

'What family?' my father roared. 'You've been gone over fifteen years! Your wife has some other man by now and your children are all grown up.'

'I owe it to them. It must have been hard.'

'So send them some care packages! Some winter coats and coffee, a few scarves to sell to old ladies on the black market. They'll love you for it. Go back now and you'll have nothing left to give when they strip you down at the border.'

'I have to do it — just look at me, all these bumps growing all over my body. I'm allergic to this country, I tell you. The beets are different here. You can't get a good borscht. And the cabbage here gives me gas. I never farted once before I came here, and now I'm turning into a wind-bag.'

'That's just age. Go back there now and you'll be farting as much as you do here. And do you think they have Tums behind the Iron Curtain?'

'That's not all.'

'What else is there?'

'It's the right thing. I have to do it.'

'Your only business is to survive,' my father said. 'All the ones with principles go to Siberia or die.'

'Then I'll do it.'

'Idiot. When your wife has no winter coat two years from now, she'll curse you through her teeth.'

My father got on my nerves. They weren't even fighting. It wasn't worth sticking around.

I found Gerry standing over by the basketball court, talking to some of the guys. They were being watched closely by six grey-headed ladies in the screened porch across the road. A retired nurse ran a convalescent home there for old ladies who didn't have a lot of money. Who else would want to live in an old summer cottage all year long? The ladies sat on the dark veranda all day. I even knew a couple of them because they had always called out to us when we were little kids to come over and have a humbug. It was a funny name for a candy — at first we thought the old grannies were witches who wanted to feed us insects. We kids had used to stop by the porch every couple of days for candies, but the invitations stopped after we reached a certain age. There must have been a height marker on the door jamb, and once we grew above it, they became suspicious of us. We might case the joint and come back to rob them later in the evening. These ladies feared alcohol above all else. One of our drunk countrymen had knocked on the door late one night, lost on the way to a party, and the old nurse had stuck a shotgun through the door. They were all grannies, but they were dangerous grannies.

Half a dozen guys were standing around Gerry.

'So did you do it or not?' Ron asked. He was the guy with the pipe, Alma's ex-boyfriend, but he wasn't smoking now because there were too many parents around.

'Do what?'

'You know what I'm talking about.'

'No, I don't,' said Gerry, but he had a smug look on his face.

'I want to know if you screwed her.'

'I could ask you the same question.'

'Don't be such a prick. I just need to know.'

'Look, all I can say is her old man and mine made us both go to confession this morning. You can draw your own conclusions. You dropped her anyway, so why should you care?'

'I care,' said Ron.

Ron looked worried. He always looked worried. He had a reputation for being smart, and things went on in his brain that didn't go on in anybody else's. You could see it in his face. He'd be looking off in the distance half the time, and the other half he was talking about people we had never heard of, like Atatürk or Neal Cassady. Sometimes he looked hurt, and nobody could understand what had set him off. I just thought he was an idiot who smoked a pipe to distract us.

'So what did you break up with her for if you care so much?' asked Gerry.

'Because it made the relationship more exquisite.'

'Huh?'

'In the tradition of courtly romance, the beloved is set on a pedestal.'

I looked at the ground and the other guys did the same. It was getting embarrassing. The only other guy I knew who talked like that was Tom, and he was still a kid. Gerry did not look down.

'Let me see if I've got this straight — you're saying it's better if you go out with a broad and *not* screw her?'

'Don't say *broad*,' said Ron.

'The priest must have got to you, Ron. Either that or you're pussy-whipped.'

They would have been fighting words to anyone else, but Ron was not a fighter. He just shook his head as if he was one of our parents.

'I'll tell you what,' said Gerry, 'anybody got a rubber?' Three wallets flashed open. Gerry chose the package that looked as if it had been in a wallet the shortest time. 'I'll see if I can use it this afternoon, and then we can talk about which is more exquisite, okay? You'll tell me what it was like to think of screwing her, and I'll tell you what it was like to do it.'

'You mean today? Now?' Ron asked.

'Wait and see.'

Just then, one of the church ladies stood up on the steps of the rectory and clanged a giant triangle one of the farmers had brought along, and the hundreds of us who had spread around the grounds started to come back to the food table. The only ones who hung back were the aristocratic families, two doctors, two engineers, and a City of Toronto clerk whose manners were so good they made me sick. The fast before communion always left me hungry after mass, and the wait for the beef while the smell of sizzling fat drifted in the air had almost made me crazy. I ate all the potato salad and greens on my paper plate while I waited in the crowd for a slice of beef, and when I finally got to the front of the line, one of my mother's friends was serving and she laid down a slab an inch thick on my plate. The top was covered with crisp, bubbled beef crackling, and so much juice ran out of the meat that it dripped off the edge of the plate.

Our people were changing. As a child, I had rarely eaten any beef but pot roast or hamburger. Beef was what the Anglos ate, but they ate it rare. 'Such good manners those people have,' my father would say, 'and then they eat like animals.' Most of the men had had three or four shots on empty stomachs, and now they tore into the beef as if they had spent the day marching across enemy territory. The accordionists had stopped their music and a whole army of ethnics sat down on the ground like an invading army on the eve of battle. The sun beat down hot on my head as I hacked the meat with a dull knife and sopped up the juice with a piece of black bread, and all around me was the clacking sound of denture meeting denture, and the sighs and groans of painful hunger eased.

I set aside the empty paper plate, closed my eyes and turned my face to the sun. I could see a field of bright red through my eyelids. In my dreams I saw Francine as if I were on the other side of the change room mirror in a department store, watching her through the one-way glass as she tried on bathing suit after bathing suit.

My jaw snapped shut and I awoke to three sharp chords on the accordions. Most of the fallen had risen and were brushing themselves off, and the men were around the drinks table again as the women poured themselves coffee and eyed their men to make sure they weren't getting too drunk. Pretty soon there were dancers out on the grass, doing the foxtrots and tangos. Some of the guys my age were playing basketball down on the court, but Gerry was not among them. I couldn't see Alma anywhere either. Father Mark still had on his wilted wreath of oak leaves, and he must have had a lot to drink because he was blessing the dancers and the cooks and any other group he happened to walk by. I could make out the old grannies on the screened porch of the convalescent home, still watching the show, and I thought I could make out the deerstalker hat among them. That would be Tom all the way, hanging out with the old ladies.

I wanted to go down to the beach, but I couldn't find my mother in the crowd and my father was in a tight cluster of men at the drinks table. My stomach knotted with anger when I saw him again. These men could talk. No awkward silences in this group, where men spoke over one another and the one who was the loudest held the stage.

I'd heard it all before. What if Hitler had won the war? Working the black market for food in DP camps in Germany. The Russians and the Americans were going to war sooner or later. Was it worth the risk to drop the bomb? Half the kids were turning into communists, and the others were juvenile delinquents. But then they started to talk about more interesting things, about lumberjacks in the woods.

'In the wintertime the wolves come in so close, you can see them in the forest,' said Onion. 'This foreman of ours keeps telling us that Canadian wolves don't attack people, but a wolf is a wolf, and I never go out in the forest without a revolver.'

'That's against the law,' said Stan.

'I keep it in my lunch box so nobody sees it. But once that wasn't good enough. It was spring, you know, after the snow was mostly out and before the blackflies came down on us. I was up ahead of all the others marking the trees to cut, and goddamn but this bear charges me out of the forest.'

'Where was your lunch box?'

'Back with the crew. I was so surprised, that it had its big arms around me before I knew what was happening. I was looking straight into the mouth of this creature with big teeth that were about to rip off my head.'

'What did you do?'

'I punched it in the nose. You've never seen such a look on an animal's face. Why, it was in shock, like its dinner was getting off the plate and biting it right back. Then I wrestled it onto the ground and hit it in the nose again and it ran off.'

My father had a throaty laugh that started deep in his chest before exploding into a high screech. It was not a pleasant sound.

'What are you laughing about?' Onion asked.

'You must have been drunk. It was probably a pussycat lost in the woods.'

'Are you calling me a liar?'

My father laughed again. 'Not a liar, just a fool. No man wrestles a bear and lives to tell about it.'

'Well, I say I did.'

'And I say it was a pussycat.'

Faster than I could have believed possible for a drunk man, Onion threw himself onto my father and put him into a headlock. All the others stepped back, except for one of the aristocratic engineers who saw it coming from a distance and came running to break up the fight.

'Stop this immediately,' he shouted. Stan punched him in the stomach and the engineer doubled over, his lips forming a silent 'o'.

The others were all standing back in a circle now, and I saw my father's face turning redder and redder in Onion's headlock.

'Call me a liar, will you!' Onion kept repeating.

'Idiot,' my father croaked in the choke hold.

I kept waiting for Gerry to show up, but when he didn't, I came in behind Onion, gathered my fists together and swung from behind my shoulder at the side of Onion's head. He must have been used to trees falling over him, because he staggered sideways but did not fall until I repeated the blow. Then his arms flew open and he fell onto the grass.

'Hit my Old Man, will you!' I cried, and I kicked him in the side. He groaned and I kicked him again and again until the crowd was finally on top of me and arms pulled me back, and soon people were swinging at one another and Father Mark waddled into the fight to break it up as the women screamed at their men through the melee.

First one blast. Everybody froze, and then for good measure, another blast.

The retired nurse was standing out on her stoop with the shotgun still pointing to the sky.

'I've called the police,' she shouted at us in a reedy voice. 'Now be gone with you while you still have a chance!'

My mother was down on us in a second. She grasped my father

and me by the collars, as if we were little kids, and she dragged us away between the cottages, across front and back yards to keep us off the streets that the police would be coming on.

'Like stray dogs,' she muttered again and again, 'mongrels off the street getting into stupid fights. And right on the church grounds! I should call the police myself and leave you both to cool your heels in jail overnight. I'll never be able to show my face at church again in my life.'

She dragged us right into the bedroom back at Stan's and made us sit on the edge of the bed. It was worth it to see my father sitting on the edge of the bed with me. Then we had to stand as she tore off the blankets and sheets and tossed all of our clothes into a bundle. She led us to the car, threw the clothes into the trunk and made us get inside.

'Keep all the doors locked in case any of them come back this way. I'm going to get Gerry and Tom and we're going home.'

We saw her storm up the street ahead of us, a Valkyrie in a flower print dress.

My father was in the front and I was in the back. He sighed, and rubbed his neck and then took out his pipe and filled it. He did not look back. We were quiet for a while.

'You hurt?' he finally asked.

'I gave better than I got.'

'I didn't raise you to be a fighter. Stay out of those things.'

It was hot in the car, and soon it was filled with pipe smoke as well.

I waited for him to thank me. I kept on waiting.

It was taking my mother a long time. After a while, I heard something from the woods. It was Onion, gesturing from among the trees.

'Don't open the door,' my father said.

Onion kept gesturing, and when we didn't get out of the car, he looked carefully up and down the street and then came over to the car window. My car window. He rapped on it with his knuckles and I lowered it an inch. I wasn't afraid of him. He had bruises on both sides of his face, but he didn't seem to have a revolver hidden anywhere.

'No hard feelings, boy. I respect what you did. Your father is an idiot, but you're all right.'

'Who's the idiot?' my father shouted, but Onion did not lose his composure. He reached for his wallet.

'Here's five dollars,' he said, slipping the bill halfway through the opening in the window. 'I want you to have it.'

I was suspicious, but I heard my father hiss, 'Take it. Don't be a fool. Take the money.'

I slipped the five-dollar bill into my hand. I wanted to say something, but just then my mother appeared at the top of the street with Gerry and Tom in tow. My father rolled down his own window a couple of inches.

'Onion, you better get out of here. If my wife catches you, she'll kill us both.'

Onion nodded and he slipped back into the woods.

If Onion and my father had cooled off, my mother had not. She made Tom, my father, and me sit in the back, and she put Gerry in front of the wheel.

'Hey, nice job, Dave,' said Gerry as he moved the driver's seat up so he could drape his hands over the wheel the way he liked. 'I heard about what you did.'

'Be quiet,' my mother snapped, and her anger kept us all silent for twenty minutes as Gerry drove along at seventy miles an hour. My father was under an interdiction against speaking.

'Hey, Tom,' I said after a while. He was reading in the middle seat between me and my father. 'Were you on that veranda when it all happened?'

'I'm the one who called the police.'

'What?'

'Mrs Bentley went to get the gun, so she asked me to make the call.'

'Traitor.'

'He's the only one with any sense in his head,' my mother snapped, and that kept us quiet the rest of the way home. My mother went to the living room to cry after everything was stowed away, and my father retreated to nap in the bedroom. Gerry got me to go into the back yard just as it was starting to get dark.

'You did okay,' he said. 'I'm proud of you.'

'Where were you?' I asked.

Even in the grey light of late evening, I could see the bright smile that illuminated his face. Gerry held something out in his hand. It was too dark for me to see clearly, so I leaned forward to get a better look. It was the wrapper from the rubber he'd been given by one of the guys.

The next day, my father borrowed the five dollars to fix the eyeglasses that had broken in his pocket during the fight. He never paid me back.

New Shocks

MY MOTHER AND I WERE SITTING IN THE BACK YARD OVER OUR third cup of coffee. The Old Man was late.

'I'm worried about him,' my mother said.

'Father?'

She nodded and put the spoon into her empty coffee cup before setting it down on the low table. She was wearing a summer dress, a little too formal for coffee with her son, but she had become more and more precise as the years went on. It was easier to do now that Gerry and I were out of the house. Her hair was steel grey, and not one strand was out of place. For the last fifteen years she had been a girl Friday for an executive in a Swiss chocolate company downtown. The Swiss were even better than the Czechs. She prided herself on her ability to plan for the future. She would have twenty years of service when she turned sixty-five, enough for a reasonable pension.

The back yard had changed from when I was a kid. Then it had been an expanse of scrub with a cucumber patch in one corner and struggling petunias in another. Now the lawn was a deep blue-green in the shade of a couple of maples. A dwarf cherry tree blossomed first in the spring, followed by the tulips and lilacs and climbing roses on trellises against the back of the house. She planted annuals whose names I did not know, and the Old Man kept a vegetable garden in the sunny part of the yard.

'Let's face it,' he'd said, 'flowers are for women. There's no profit in them except for the looks. To me, a radish is more beautiful than any flower.'

We were starting to get worried when the Old Man's station wagon pulled into the driveway. I heard the car door slam and he came around to the back.

The white hair on his head was thin; I could see the shiny skin under it. His eyebrows weren't bushy any more. Did eyebrows go bald too, or did my mother trim them? He wore a golf shirt with a small crest of crossed clubs on the breast, pale blue pants with a white belt and white shoes. It was still a shock to see him like that, like a retired banker. 'The Florida look,' my mother called it, and he wore the clothes she bought him on weekends to humour her. The pipe was gone. He was trying to encourage Tom to stop smoking.

'Will you look at this, Mother,' he said. 'The hockey star found time to visit. Can I get a signed puck?'

'How are you?' I asked.

'I'm old. Just take a look at me. Every morning when I see myself in the mirror, I'm not sure if I want to laugh or cry. I'm half glad that all my bones ache, because if they didn't, I'd know I was dead. On the way back from the muffler shop, I drove past a couple of houses being built and I stopped to look. These men were shingling the roof and my hand wanted to grab a hammer and join them. What a joke! These legs couldn't make it more than three steps up a ladder.'

'What took you so long?' my mother asked. 'I was getting worried.'

'The man at the muffler shop told me the car needed new shocks. Then he didn't have them in stock and I had to wait until another shop sent them over. Three hundred and twelve dollars. Some shocks!'

'Where did you go?' I asked.

'Fleet Muffler. The shop on Pine.'

'Those guys run a racket,' I said. 'Every time you go in to fix your muffler, they tell you need new shocks. You believed him?'

'Why not?'

'He just wanted your money.'

'And he got it, too.'

My father sat serenely on the chair and eyed his vegetable garden to make sure none of the leaves were wilting in the heat. Now I was worried too. Once the Old Man stopped caring about saving money, he'd lost his main reason for existence.

'You wanted to see me?' I asked.

'I did?' He stared at me like he didn't know who I was.

'Come on, snap out of it, you're not even seventy yet,' I said.

'He's pulling your leg,' my mother said. She turned to my father. 'Stop wasting Dave's time. He's been waiting for you for over an hour and all you want to do is make stupid jokes.'

'What's the rush? This is summertime — he's not even playing anywhere, just coaching kids at some hockey camp. He can't spare a few minutes for his old father?'

'Get to the point,' my mother snapped.

'All right, all right. Stop rushing me, will you?'

'So now it's my fault?' my mother asked.

I had to stop them before they got warmed up. Once their bickering reached a critical mass, it could go on for an hour at a time.

'Where's Tom?' I asked.

'Downtown at the library. Studying,' my mother said.

'Is he taking summer courses?'

'No, he just wants to get a jump on his reading for the fall.'

'As if the boy can't read at home,' my father said.

'Who can read with you in the house?' my mother asked. 'You're bothering him every ten minutes. The boy needs a little peace.'

My father ignored her. He leaned forward, clasped his hands together, and studied his nails for a few seconds before he finally raised his head to speak.

'I've got a plan,' he said.

'A plan?'

'All these years I've been laughing at the Italians, and it turns out they have the right idea after all. Men I knew who did nothing better than haul bricks up a ladder all day long are now living in big houses in Woodbridge. How do they do it? Family. None of this Anglo-Saxon business of the kids all flying off in different directions. They live together and pool their money. The grandparents look after the grandchildren.'

'You don't have any grandchildren.'

'Not yet I don't, but it's just a question of time. We could build an extension on the house — enough for everybody. We could do the same at the cottage. Maybe put a second storey on it. It wouldn't even cost that much — just the materials. All of my friends are retired, but some of them are pretty strong. You boys could do some of the heavier work, say hauling the shingles up to the roof, but some of these old geezers can still spend a day shingling. Maybe half a day, some of them, before the arthritis starts acting up. Think of it! We could live together again. Big meals together every night. And best of all, it would be far cheaper than building separate houses. So, what do you say?'

Some of the old light was up in his eyes. He reached reflexively for his breast pocket, but there wasn't even a pocket there, let alone the pipe that he had put away two years before.

'I'll think about it,' I said.

'What think? Is it a good idea or not?'

'Have you talked to Gerry?'

'He's afraid of Gerry,' said my mother.

'What do *you* think of this plan?' I asked her, but she only shrugged.

'I'll call you in a couple of days,' I said to my father. We talked for a while, and then my mother saw me to my car when it was time to go.

'Humour him for a while,' she said. 'He's got nothing to do any more. It's driving him crazy, and me too.'

I said I would.

'And another thing,' she added. 'I'm worried about Tom too.'

'What about him?'

'His feet are dirty all the time. I change the sheets on his bed, and three days later, the bottom end is filthy. I think he takes off his shoes when he's downtown and walks around barefoot.'

'You think he's turning into a hippie?'

'You're way behind the times,' my mother said. 'That's been over for years. He just wants to act cool with his friends. The thing is, I wish he'd wash his feet before he got into bed at night, but he's so touchy. I can't say anything to him. Your father's endless blathering has worn him down. He's raw nerve and muscle.'

'You want me to talk to him?'

'Could you? But be discreet. I don't want him to know I told you.'

'Sure.'

'Don't tell him I said anything.'

'I won't.'

Tom was already walking up the street from the bus as I drove away.

'Hop in. I'll buy you a beer.'

'I don't drink beer,' he said. 'I drink wine.'

'So I'll buy you a bottle of wine. Come on.'

Tom was fleshy and short. Not fat, exactly, but it looked as if he'd never lost his baby chubbiness. He had thick glasses and curly hair, and sometimes I thought he'd been picked up out of the wrong crib at the hospital where he was born. Either that or he was some sort of genetic throwback.

I drove down to the Central Restaurant in Weston. It was the place where I'd had my first drink, and for years before that the hangout where I'd filled myself up on French fries and gravy and butterscotch sundaes. I recognized men who had been sitting at the counter for decades. A couple of guys I knew from my high school days were warming the seats in a booth, practising. They were geezers in training.

'Hey, Dave,' one of them called out, 'are you moving up to the National League this season? I heard the Leafs made an offer.'

'You heard wrong. I'm still in Junior A. The only Junior with greying hair.'

'Maybe next season,' he said.

'Maybe around the turn of the century,' I called back, and they laughed.

'What did you pick this place for?' Tom asked. 'This represents everything I'm trying to get away from.'

'What's that?' I asked.

'The damn suburbs — the aridity of middle-class, white-picket-fence living. This place is such a wasteland, it makes me want to weep. Give me a glass of Blue Nun,' he said to the waitress. She didn't even ask for his fake ID.

He ticked me off. Every time he opened up his mouth, he said something stupid. Our town was no Manhattan, but it didn't pretend to be.

'I don't know about that,' I said. 'Weston was a good place to grow up. It's not as noisy as downtown.'

'I love noise. I don't want to get away from the maddening crowd. I want to live downtown, where the action is. I never even knew there was an art gallery or a symphony when I was growing up. We were raised in ignorance. I'm getting out of here as soon as I can, before I finish university if I can manage it, but right after if I can't.'

'Madding,' I said.

'What?'

'It's called the *madding* crowd, not the *maddening* crowd.'

'Are you sure?'

'Yeah. I looked it up.'

'You see what I mean? We're handicapped. We were raised like foreigners in our own country.'

I told him about the Old Man's plans anyway. I got about the reaction that I expected.

'He wants a DP dynasty. I can just see it, all his grandchildren learning to speak English with accents. Did I tell you I saw him downtown?'

'Where?'

'At a pro-war rally. All these old DPs were holding counter-demonstrations. The Old Man had this megaphone and he kept yelling that the atomic bomb brought us peace. I've never been so mortified. He doesn't even know it's the hydrogen bomb now.'

'Do you see Gerry much?' I asked.

'Bourgeois capitalist,' Tom spat out. 'Talk about a bottom-feeder. All he does is put house buyers and sellers together and he gets six percent. He doesn't add any value to the cost of a house, he just raises the price.'

Tom lit up a cigarette and looked at me defiantly.

'Mother wants you to wash your feet at night before you get into bed.'

'What?' Tom reddened.

'You get into bed with dirty feet and you expect her to wash the sheets.'

'I don't expect her to do anything.'

'Are you walking around barefoot downtown?' I asked.

'None of your business.'

'Yeah, well scrape the gum off your feet before you get into bed.'

I didn't say anything more. There was no use in pushing Tom. He just became more obstinate.

My mother called me a couple of days later.

'A big load of lumber came in today. The truck dropped it on the driveway and your father and his geriatric friends moved it into the garage. I think he's decided to go ahead with the extension on the house. Did you tell him you were moving back in?'

'I haven't talked to him.'

Once the Old Man got an idea in his head, there was no stopping him. I wasn't moving back into the house, but I didn't want to break it to him too fast. I thought I'd call Gerry. I had to leave a message at the real estate office where he worked, and he called me back that night.

'I think it's a great idea,' said Gerry. 'The Old Man's right. Run the family like a business and maximize the profits.'

'You were always dying to get out of the house. What makes you want to go back now?' I asked him.

'The Old Man really *is* old now. I'd take over. Everybody pours their money into one till, and I'm the banker. I could always save money better than any of you. I'd keep you all on a tight leash, and you'd be able to retire by the time you turned fifty. I could even train you in real estate. You know, give you a little edge. Let's face it, another year or two and your hockey career will be over. Besides, Tom's gone to hell since we moved out. This way, we'd be around to knock a little intelligence into him.'

A sense of dread descended on me. Now that my father was too old to do it, Gerry wanted to boss me around again. He waited for me to speak, but I didn't know what to say to him.

'The Old Man's already ordered the lumber. The garage is full of it.'

'Perfect.'

My mother called me again.

'Your father's friends are all measuring wood and cutting in the garage. He drove down to the retirement home and pulled a couple of old men from in front of a TV where they'd been sitting for two years. He even bought a radial arm saw. I've tried to tell him that it's all foolishness, but he keeps on measuring and sawing. He even brought in a skid-load of glass. He must be planning a glass house. I want you to put a stop to all this.'

'Gerry thinks it's a good idea.'

'Well, why didn't anyone think to ask me? I said to humour him, not give in to him. Tom keeps straining like an animal caught in a leghold trap. He needs to get away. And what am I supposed to do, give up my job and become a cook for all these men? I've cooked for men and held down a job for most of my life, and I'm sick of it. As far as I'm concerned, I never want to make another bagged lunch or roast pork until the day I die.'

'Why don't you tell him that?'

'He hasn't listened to me for thirty years. What makes you think he's going to start now?'

'Why don't you get Gerry to do it?'

'They'll just get into a fight, and your father will drink half a mickey to calm down his nerves.'

'He still drinks?'

'I said *half* a mickey.'

I wasn't crazy about doing it. I could picture the Old Man's face falling when I broke the news to him. All those old guys in the garage would have to be sent home, and then we'd have to think about what to do with all the lumber he had bought. He'd want to save it, stack it up in the back yard for a rainy day, and there it would still be ten years later. With nothing but empty days in front of him, he'd drink and drive my mother and Tom crazy. I knew what happened to old people without enough to do.

Even so, I thought about it for a while. I was away most of the winter anyway. Maybe it wouldn't be so bad. It just meant that if I met anybody in the summer, I wouldn't be able to bring her home for the night.

No. It was nuts. I had to talk to the Old Man.

Stan was standing outside on the driveway, smoking a cigarette. He wore a painter's cap and a carpenter's apron. The hammer was slung on a loop on the apron. Like most of my father's friends, Stan had shrunk. The robust shoulders and chest had started to sink in, as if he was living through a slow implosion. Where did all that bone and sinew disappear to in old people?

'Your father won't let me smoke in the garage,' said Stan. 'He claims the sawdust might catch fire, but I think he's turning into one of those health nuts. He pays all right though. Cash, so I don't have to worry about income tax.'

'He pays you?'

'Sure. You think I'd work for free? I'm getting four dollars an hour.'

In the old days, these men had helped one another build their houses for bowls of cabbage soup and half bottles of whisky. It saddened me to think they helped one another for money now, and it amazed me that my father was willing to pay it.

The lumber and glass had overflowed from the garage and lay stacked about outside. There was even a skid of sheet aluminum, and two dozen aluminum-clad windows were leaning against the fence. Maybe he planned to make the addition into a greenhouse.

The light inside the garage was poor from all the sawdust in the air, and the old men moved around like gnomes with respirators on. I hadn't known that my father knew what a respirator was. Maybe it was really just oxygen for the old geezers with emphysema.

The Old Man himself pulled down his respirator and blew a whistle hanging from around his neck. The sawing and banging stopped.

'All right, men. Lunch time. See you in an hour.'

'You give them an hour for lunch?' I asked the Old Man when he came out.

'Some of these old guys need to take a nap.'

'What do they eat?'

'The cheap guys bring bag lunches. The others drive out for some Kentucky Fried Chicken or McDonald's.'

'No cabbage soup?'

'Who has time for that? Come on, we'll sit in the garden.'

The Old Man led the way to the chairs out on the yard. He was followed by a cloud of sawdust. When he sat down, he reached for his breast pocket and pulled out an old leather zip pouch. He took his pipe from it and began to fill the bowl with tobacco.

'Are you smoking again?'

'I need it for the stress,' he said.

'Stress?'

'All the responsibility of this project.'

'That's what I wanted to talk to you about.'

'So talk. I haven't got all day. I need to get some food in my belly before the afternoon shift starts.'

'Look, Dad,' I said, 'I appreciate how important this house renovation idea is to you, but I don't think it's going to work out. This isn't the Old Country any more. When kids grow up here, they move out. I can't come back to live here, and Tom is dying to get away. It's not that we don't love you or anything. It's just that we need to live apart. We were born and raised in this country. It's different for us. We have to live the way people live here.'

The Old Man looked at his watch.

'Do you understand what I'm saying?' I asked.

'Of course I understand. I'm just hungry. Are you finished?'

'I'm telling you I'm not moving in.'

'I get the point. Is that all?'

'You're not mad?'

'Why should I be mad? One look at your face, and I knew you didn't want to do it. To tell you the truth, I thought about it myself some more and gave up on the idea. Gerry would be bossing me around all the time. Who could live with that?'

It had been easier than I thought. He puffed calmly at his pipe.

'Are you going to fire the old guys in the garage?'

'Not on your life. They do good work, and cheap too.'

He puffed some more. I felt strangely tender towards him now that it looked as if his mind was going. I spoke slowly and distinctly so he would understand.

'You can't keep these men working on a house addition if no one is moving in. You won't need the extra space.'

'Who's building a house addition?'

'Well, what the hell are they doing in that garage?'

'Don't swear at me. Show a little respect for your elders. I'm building windows. Listen, times have changed. When I was in construction, we built each window, custom, right on the spot. Now the windows get built in factories and installed on the site. The problem is, most of the windows come from union houses, but the builders are always trying to cut costs. This is a small operation — no picture windows, but the builders appreciate anything they can get. I pay the old men enough to make them happy and I undercut the union cost of labour by a third. The rest is all gravy.'

'But what about the bylaws? You can't run a workshop from a suburb. And if the revenue people ever catch you, they'll kill you.'

'Don't worry about the bylaws. The neighbours are away all day. That's what I love about this feminism business. Even the women work now, so nobody gets bothered by the noise. As for the revenue people, the trick is to keep the operation small. I do the deliveries myself, just a few at a time from the back of the station wagon. That's why I needed new shocks. Not getting greedy is the key. Just a nice sideline to keep me busy in my old age.'

'Why didn't you tell Mother about this?'

'To tell you the truth, she's getting a little set in her ways. But don't you worry. Once she sees the extra money coming in, she'll be happy. She might even want to retire early.'

I looked at him in wonder as he puffed serenely at his pipe.

'Anything else you want to know?' he asked.

'I guess that's just about it.'

'I haven't got time to talk much now. Stop by on the weekend when I'm free. Oh, maybe you could do me a favour.'

He reached into his wallet and pulled out a ten-dollar bill.

'I've got to make a few calls just now. Pick me up a Big Mac and some fries, will you? You can keep the change.'

Tempus Fugit

THE OLD MAN WAS DEAD, OF THAT THERE COULD BE NO DOUBT.

I was driving through Weston on the way to my mother's house. The town had changed. When I was a kid, it had already stopped being a little town and become a neighbourhood on the edge of Toronto. Then the years passed and the edges of the neighbourhoods got smudged. The boundaries were gone. Now that there was a mall up by the highway for the carriage trade, the old main street was full of cheap discount stores. Soon the continent would be one big strip mall. In old downtown Weston, there were no more dress shops where my Aunt Ramona could mortgage her future, and no more appliance stores where my father could buy on time.

The city was trying to save money on services, and it looked as if they had started their cuts in Weston. Candy bar wrappers blew down the street like something from a post-apocalyptic movie. Two kinds of housing project now stood along Weston Road. One type was for seniors, and the other was for families on welfare, which consisted mostly of single mothers and their teenaged kids. The old people walked around scared. They were fragile ships, easily broken on the shoals of some disaffected teenager. It was the kind of town planning you might find funny if you weren't ever going to grow old yourself.

No trace of the old apple orchards remained when I turned onto my mother's street. In the early seventies, the city had put in sidewalks and planted trees. Maples on one side and dwarf cherries on the other. Twenty years before, the brick boxes still stood in the churned-up mud, and the whole place felt raw and new. It held some kind of promise then. It was a time when we had floated wooden boats on the water in the ditches. The city had paved over the ditches, but the water still ran down there, somewhere deep.

The geography of my childhood was changing, and the neighbours who had peopled it were disappearing. Where the Lymes had once lived in a concrete house with unstuccoed walls, a lawyer now resided with his family. Old man Lyme used to kick his daughters off the front porch if they were sassy and he was beered up, and now the house held a lawyer who sent his kids to private school. The Italian grocery, which had seemed so exotic with its olives and prosciutto, had become a West Indian grocery. We had turbaned South Asians, and former Vietnamese boat people stared out of picture windows as if they were marooned. *We* used to be the foreigners in the neighbourhood. It was enough to give me vertigo.

'So what did you expect?' the Old Man said from his place in the passenger seat. He appeared irregularly, with no premonition. Not exactly 'appeared.' He was just a presence. He had the pipe stuck between his teeth, but the bowl was empty. I could hear the sputter of nicotine resin from the stem.

'*Tempus fugit*,' said the Old Man.

'You never knew any Latin.'

'Your mother always wanted a grandfather clock, but I never got around to buying one. Used to look at them, though. The grandfather clocks at Eaton's always had *tempus fugit* written on them. Besides, most of my life I went to Latin masses. You think some of that doesn't rub off? Latin is what they all use in the afterlife. They need a *lingua franca*.'

'You're nothing more than a bit of undigested beef,' I said to him.

'A quote from Dickens. You always did admire the English. Not as much as Tom, but still. Mr Taylor would be impressed.'

He had mellowed since he died. He still gave maddening comments, but at least he didn't drink any more.

My mother was wearing a charcoal suit when she answered the door at the house.

'Going out?' I asked.

'No. Why?'

'Just the way you're dressed. Fancy.'

'I'm expecting company.'

'Since when am I company?'

'You're not. I'm expecting someone else.'

The place felt different ever since the Old Man had died. No more smells of pork roast, cabbage, and hamburgers. My mother pecked at food. The house smelled like Pine Sol.

She went into the kitchen to make some coffee.

'I didn't put any sugar in it,' she said when she came back.

'Why not?'

'It's bad for you. The health food books call it White Death.'

'I don't like bitter coffee.'

'I think I've got some Nutrasweet.'

'Do you still make napoleon cakes?'

'You should know. You eat them.'

'More than one cup of sugar, if I remember the recipe right.'

'I use honey for most sweetening now. I buy it in bulk at a health food store.'

She didn't get up to get me some sugar for the coffee, and I didn't feel like getting up myself. I sipped at the bitter liquid.

'Gerry called,' she said.

'What's up on the coast?' I asked in English.

'What a ridiculous phrase. That kind of language went out twenty years ago.'

'Where's your sense of humour?'

'Your father used up what little I had.'

Somebody knocked at the door, and my mother went to answer it. She came back with Mr Taylor.

'Hello, Dave.' I shook his outstretched hand. 'My belated condolences,' he said.

This was her company? Mr Taylor was a neighbour, not company. He pulled his pant legs up ever so slightly before he sat down, and then he leaned forward, with his hands in his lap and his back very straight, not touching the chair. Maybe he was afraid he'd get his shirt dirty. Even in his old age, his shirts were crisp. He must have started sending them out to the laundry after his wife died. My mother went to get him some coffee too.

'Still coaching hockey?' he asked.

'Refereeing.'

'Oh yes, of course. It's so hard to keep track. I'm getting on, you know.'

His head had a very slight wobble to it as he spoke. Early Parkinson's, I guessed. But he carried himself like a man of substance.

'I can't even tell half the names of the people who live on the street. Weston is getting worse every day. The character is changing, if you know what I mean.'

'I got used to the old foreigners ages ago. As for the DPs, they've blended in,' I said. 'Now it's mostly…'

'Don't be rude,' my mother cut in quickly in our language. She'd come back with his coffee.

Mr Taylor looked at me very carefully, but I neither smiled nor frowned. His face was set in a polite smile. He was wary, but he acted like a man with the advantage. I just couldn't understand what that advantage might be. He talked for a while about my father, and then returned to how the neighbourhood was changing, becoming unsafe. He talked about how difficult it was to keep up a house on one's own, especially for a woman.

I watched my mother nod and smile a bit more than she had to. Why was she being so nice to this man?

'It's been, what, four months since your husband passed on?' Mr Taylor asked.

'Six.'

'Time passes so quickly.'

'*Tempus fugit*,' I said. Mr Taylor looked at me carefully again, and then addressed himself to my mother.

'I'm glad to see you haven't done anything hasty, but as the time passes, you might begin to think of other living arrangements.'

'I've been thinking about that a great deal,' my mother said.

This came as a surprise to me.

'Of course, of course. Only natural to think of the future now. You have many good years in front of you still. But that brings me to the point. This is a fine house, and if you ever think of selling, I'd like the favour of being allowed to put in a first offer.'

'You surprise me, Mr Taylor. At your age, a second house. Were you thinking of investing?'

Mr Taylor laughed ever so lightly.

'Hardly. My nephew married not long ago. He's looking for a house in the area. With a little renovation, this place might suit him and his wife just fine. I'm getting on, and to tell you the truth, I'm finding old age a lonely place ever since my wife died. It's hard to meet new people at my age. I'd much rather live with someone, but if romance is out of the question, then at least I can have some family nearby.'

'Why is romance out of the question?' my mother asked him.

'It's just hard to find the right person to share the rest of your life with.'

'I know what you mean,' my mother said, and she sighed and looked out the window.

Even in his dotage, Mr Taylor was dangerous. As for my mother, I was torn between a desire to protect her and to give her a good, hard shake. In the end I did neither. I felt like an interloper in some kind of geriatric mating ritual.

I went down to the basement to look over my father's tools while my mother finished talking to Mr Taylor. I rubbed my fingers over the worn wooden handle of the manual drill and made a few false passes across the work bench with the plane. I was thinking about asking my mother for some of the tools for my own place when I smelled pipe tobacco. The Old Man was back.

'Just buy power tools instead. Good brands, like Makita or Sears.'

Other ghosts gave important advice. My father worried about brand names.

'She's betraying you up there.'

'She's your mother. No insults.'

I went back upstairs after I heard Mr Taylor leave.

'I didn't know you were thinking of selling the house.'

'It's one of my options. I don't need all this space, and no one wants to rent a floor of a suburban house. If I took a condo in the city, I could use the subway more often.' The words *options, suburban, condo,* and *subway* were all in English. Our language was being wiped out by time. My wife and children didn't speak a word of it.

'What about selling the house to one of your kids? Did you ever think of that?'

'Gerry and Tom live out of town, and this house wouldn't suit you.'

'Suit me? It's not like it's a pair of pants. I could get used to it.'

'Come on. You always said you hated the suburbs.'

'That was Tom, not me. But selling to Mr Taylor? Gerry still hates his guts. Why sell to him?'

'Why not? His money is as good as anyone else's.'

We didn't talk about it any more. I went into the kitchen to wash my coffee cup and look out the window. The yard had changed. The garden was laid out differently from how it had been when I was growing up, and a couple of maples now shaded most of the lawn. I reached across the sink and rested my hand on the windowsill. The Old Man had built that, I thought, in the days before windows were all prefab. I might even have helped him nail it in. Most of my childhood had been spent standing around him while he worked, just in case he wanted me to hold the end of a board.

'I think we should shoot the son of a bitch,' said Gerry when I called him in Vancouver. He was a real estate agent, and in 1981, Vancouver was hot. He flipped houses faster than a short-order cook flipped pancakes, and the money rolled in with every turn.

'She's lonely,' I said. 'What are we supposed to do, take away the happiness of her last few years?'

'I'm not talking about making her unhappy. What do you think I am, Hamlet or something?'

He waited for a moment, but I didn't say anything.

'What's the matter,' he said. 'Didn't you ever read *Hamlet* in school?'

'That was years ago.'

'You should have studied more.'

'Will you stop talking about my education and get back to the point?'

'Okay. I'll tell you what. I'll fly into town and take care of things, but I want you to know that this really pisses me off.'

'What do you mean?'

'The solution is obvious, but I'm going to have to fly across the country to take care of it. Why didn't you think of this?'

'Think of what?'

'Oh, Christ.'

He hung up the phone.

My mother found it strange that Gerry was coming back to visit so soon. Ordinarily, he only showed up once a year. But she was happy enough to see him and she made up his old room.

'What am I supposed to do?' I asked when I had him off on my own. 'What's the plan?'

'Just be ready to come over at a moment's notice. I've got it all worked out.' I did as he asked, and came over on a Tuesday evening after he called.

'What's going on?' my mother asked me furiously when she opened her door. This time she was wearing a navy dress and pearl earrings.

'I don't know. Gerry told me to come over.'

'He's bringing over some mystery guest. I cleaned the house and made canapés, but I don't know who's coming. I feel like I'm on *What's My Line?* and he's bringing out the mystery guest.'

We heard Gerry's car pull into the driveway and both looked out to see who he had brought. Gerry got out first and then walked around to the passenger side and opened the door. A bony hand reached up to the door frame and then stayed there. Whoever it was had to be an invalid. Gerry finally reached into the car and extracted an old man who almost fell into his arms before he found his balance. The man had thin white hair. He wore a baggy suit and carried himself with a slight stoop to his shoulders. Gerry was going to keep his hand on his arm, but the old man waved away the assistance.

At the front door, Gerry introduced him as Mr Batas, a resident of our parish retirement home, who had come to pay his respects. Mr Batas barely waited for the introduction to end before he walked past us and sat down in my father's old armchair.

'Sorry,' he said. 'My legs are bad and I can't stand on them for very long. I've got new shoes on and my feet are killing me. What do you think of them?'

We followed him into the living room.

'Very nice,' said my mother. They were black Oxfords that had a strange shine to them. They looked as if they were coated with Saran Wrap.

'Taiwanese shoes. Eighteen dollars, and they look like they cost eighty.'

'Can I make you a cocktail, Mr Batas?' Gerry asked.

'Cocktail? I haven't had a drink in eight years. Doctor's orders.'

'A cup of coffee?'

'Keeps me awake at night.'

'A soft drink?'

I can't stand bubbles. Just give me a glass of water and hold the ice.'

I followed Gerry into the kitchen.

'Who the hell is that guy?' I asked.

'A suitor. I thought I'd give mother a chance to pick someone more appropriate.'

'He must be fifteen years older than her.'

'Ten, but what's the difference? Get this. He made a bundle on real estate decades ago. He owned a few boarding houses right on the new subway line, and the city paid him well when he got expropriated. Then he played a few penny stocks and made a killing. The guy is loaded.'

'I don't think he's right for Mom.'

'This is just my opening bid. The retirement home is full of old guys like this. One of them is sure to be a hit.'

We took our drinks and Mr Batas' water back into the living room. The conversation was all one-sided. My mother talked while Mr Batas looked her up and down like a new heifer.

'What,' Mr Batas finally said, 'is your opinion on women's rights?'

My mother looked at us accusingly.

'I'm a little old to have gotten really caught up in that. But I think I approve. I got dirty looks from so many neighbours when I went out to work thirty years ago. They accused me of abandoning my children.'

'You went out to work?'

'That's right.'

'Oh, that's what I love about ethnic women. Raise the children, keep house, and work as well. They don't make them like that any more. Now the women get cleaning ladies and nannies. Spoiled rotten. Wasting money when a little sweat and organization would make them rich in their old age.'

'Are you married, Mr Batas?'

'In a manner of speaking, I was. I married in the old country, but I got separated from my wife in the war. She remarried. Now her husband is dead and she writes me letters begging me to bring her out to the West. Hah! Wants me to bring her children out as well, I'll bet. Women look upon me as a moneybags, lady. I've had more offers of marriage than a pretty young woman. What do you think this house is worth?'

The evening was not a success. After two hours, Mr Batas asked Gerry to get him his briefcase from the car, and then the old man took the briefcase and hauled himself up the stairs to the bathroom. The rest of us waited. We waited a long time as my mother glared at Gerry and me. A very long time.

'Maybe he's had a heart attack on the toilet,' my mother finally said. But a moment later we heard the door of the bathroom open, and then the toilet flush. I wondered what kind of man opened the toilet door before he flushed. Mr Batas struggled down the stairs, but he did not come back into the living room. He stood at the doorway instead and asked Gerry to take him home.

'Lady, thank you for the water. I'll let you know my decision in a week.'

Gerry ignored my mother's poisonous looks. I left at the same time because I was afraid to be alone with her after the visit.

'There's a dance at the church basement on Saturday night,' Gerry said on the phone. 'Be there. I've taken tickets for the three of us.'

'Joan and I are going out.'

'Cancel it. Tell her we're at a crisis point here. Something's got to be done, and fast. Every time I slip out to buy something, Mr Taylor is over here in a flash. I'm tempted to leave a tape recorder on in the living room to hear what they talk about.'

'Maybe you'd have to leave it in the bedroom.'

'Say that again, and I'll smash your face in.'

'You're almost forty years old. You might have a heart attack.'

'Just don't get smart on me, okay? I'm losing thousands by being here.'

'What did she say about Mr Batas?'

'That son of a bitch is incontinent. He changed his diaper up in the bathroom and left the old one sticking halfway out of the garbage can.'

I hadn't been to a dance in the church basement for twenty years. Except for the teenagers who served dinner, Gerry and I were the youngest ones there. Some of the women were wearing floor-length dresses that had gone out of style fifteen years before. The music was played by Randy and the Good-Time Boys, who polished up their saxes and accordions, and let fly with polkas, waltzes, and tangos that would have sounded old-fashioned on *The Lawrence Welk Show*.

'What are we supposed to be doing here?' my mother asked.

'Having a good time. Come on, let me take you for a spin.'

The band was playing a Viennese waltz. Gerry always wore good suits, and he looked like a prosperous son doing the right thing by his mother on the dance floor. I could almost hear the ladies at the tables talking about how remiss their own children were. Gerry danced in a wide circle on the outskirts of the dance floor, so he passed by each table. My mother didn't look bad either, and he was making sure that every table got a good look at her.

The parade started soon after that. I wasn't sure if Gerry had spoken to all the men or if they came up of their own volition, but my mother barely had a chance to sit down, and when she did, men sat beside her.

Dr Diuda was a prosperous urologist whose wife had died only two years before. His hair had gone back to its original colour shortly after that, and he grew a pencil moustache. His specialty was the tango, and he came back to our table after he'd thrown my mother about the dance floor for five minutes.

'Hello, boys,' he said. 'Long time no see.' He had been Tom's Boy Scout leader, so we knew him pretty well. My mother beamed at him, and he went to the bar to get a round of drinks.

'Such a nice man,' my mother said.

Gerry beamed too, and he winked at me just before Dr Diuda got back with the drinks.

'Now Gerry,' Dr Diuda said, 'your mother tells me you've been having some problems with your prostate. Let me give you a little piece of advice. Don't let the problem drag on. Come in and see me. You're too young to have something like this. Now it might just be an infection, but it could be cancer as well, and that can be cured if we catch it early enough. As for standard enlargement, all we need to do is have the prostate reamed. The techniques are getting really good. Impotence is hardly ever the result any more.'

My mother looked like she was having a good time.

'It's not working,' said Gerry over the phone. 'Mr Taylor's around more than ever. Mother keeps disappearing into town. She won't talk to me. She's hiding something. Maybe they're getting married.'

'Can't you get it out of her?'

'She never did confide in me much.'

'Tit for tat.'

'It's time for us to go big-time. I can't spend the rest of my life here, trying to make her see what's sensible. We'll have to call in Tom.'

Our brother Tom taught at a private high school in Massachusetts.

'What good is that going to do?'

'She was always a sap for him. We sit him at the table with us. I provide the brains and the drive and he softens her up and then she'll confess.'

'What am I supposed to provide?'

'What do you mean?'

'Never mind.'

'You're so goddamned sensitive sometimes. I'm calling Tom. We'll get him up this weekend and it better work, because I've got to get back to Vancouver. This little family episode is costing me thousands.'

*

'Jesus Christ, it's enough to make you want to puke,' said Gerry as I drove up to the airport. Tom was already standing outside the terminal door. Our kid brother was wearing corduroy pants and a tweed jacket with leather elbow patches. He was blowing smoke from a bent pipe.

Gerry was out of the car door before the car stopped moving.

'What are you, Sherlock Holmes? You're dressed like some damn English teacher.'

'Master.'

'What?'

'I got a job at a private school. I'm called a master now, although the title is getting controversial. Not full master, of course, but that will come with time.'

'You're already full.'

'It's nice to see you too.'

'Don't take him seriously,' I said to Tom. 'He's a little edgy about this thing with Mom.'

We all got into the car. Gerry turned on me.

'Don't *little edgy* me. Tom's making some kind of point with this getup. He's trying to look like *an English*.' He spoke in our language.

'What did you say?' Tom asked serenely in English.

'You heard me.'

'Speak in English. I don't understand that language any more.'

'What do you mean?' Gerry asked.

'I mean I've forgotten the language.'

'That's impossible.'

'Well, I never get a chance to use it, and it's not as if it were French or something. It's never going to get me a raise. I just let it drop.'

Gerry thought for a while.

'You know what I hate about the name of the homeland?' Gerry finally asked.

'What?'

'The name.'

'It's just a name,' I said.

'Yeah, but it sounds corny.'

I said it out loud. 'Lithuania.'

'Gerry's right,' said Tom. 'It's embarrassing. And nobody knows where it is. It's one of those nonexistent countries.'

'And it's going to stay that way,' said Gerry. 'The iron curtain is going to last another hundred years. Even the sound of the name bugs me. It's the ending. All the funny countries have funny endings on them. Bulgaria, Albania, Estonia, Lusitania.'

'The last one was a ship,' I said.

'But it was named after a Roman province,' Tom said. 'Gerry means it sounds like we're from some kind of comic opera. Like we're from Ruritania.'

'So Norway sounds more serious than Moldavia?'

'Right,' said Gerry. 'Think about it. Germany, England, and France sound serious, but Tanzania, Romania, and Mongolia don't.'

'We come from a ghost country,' said Tom.

'Never mind all that stuff,' said Gerry. 'Every time I say something, it turns into an argument. We have to talk fast. Our dick-head brother here has got to turn the charm on Mom, and pronto. Today is the only chance we'll get.'

Gerry laid out the plan. We would confront our mother with the evidence of her attraction to Mr Taylor after dinner. Then we'd appeal to her not to marry him.

'Appeal how?' I asked. 'Beg her not to get involved with Mr Taylor? What if she tells us to go to hell? I'm a little uncomfortable about the whole thing.'

'We have to save her from herself,' said Gerry, and he crossed his arms.

Mr Taylor was standing on his front lawn, staring at our mother's house as we drove up. He gave us a quick look and a guilty wave, and went back inside.

My mother fussed over Tom when he came in. She always fussed over her out-of-town children. It was enough to make an immature person want to live far away. She had set the dining room table and made a big meal with soup and roast goose and cabbage.

'The goose has a lot of fat,' she said, 'so take it easy. Maybe you should pull off the skin.'

It was tense at the table. We knew the general plan of attack, but we had not decided who was to fire the first volley. My mother had baked a napoleon cake, and she set it on the table along with liqueur glasses into which she poured Cherry Heering.

'Mr Taylor was out there, looking at the house when we drove up,' I finally said when neither Gerry nor Tom opened their mouths. 'We wonder what he's up to.'

'You boys are just like children. I didn't want to say anything until Tom showed up, but if you wanted to know, why didn't you just ask?'

'We thought you might be in love,' I said when the other two stayed mute. 'It's kind of a tough subject to talk about.'

'With who?'

'Mr Taylor.'

She laughed. It was a funny kind of laugh. It started out like a schoolgirl giggle and then became so loud I thought the neighbours might hear her.

'That dried-out old prune? You know what he did to me once? He picked a piece of lint off my collar. The nerve. After all these years, it'll be good to get away from his snooping eyes across the street.'

'Get away?' Gerry asked.

'I sold him the house. I was afraid I was going to have to kiss the old fool to get him to write up an offer, but when I agreed to the first bid, he ruffled himself up like a rooster and strutted back across the street. Now have some cake.'

'Sold it?' Gerry asked. 'Without consulting me?'

'That's right.'

'The market's still getting hotter! This is the worst thing you could have done right now.'

'Father built this house with his own two hands,' said Tom, puffing furiously on his pipe and looking like nothing so much as an enraged don. 'His sweat and his blood are in every brick.'

'I think I helped build this house a little too,' my mother said.

'What did you get for the place?' Gerry asked. She told him.

'Oh, you could have done better than that.'

'I wanted a quick closing. Sixty days. Cash.'

'Sixty days from when?'

'Two days ago.'

I was already sitting in someone else's house. The sense of vertigo returned.

'This would break Father's heart,' said Tom.

'I still don't get it,' I said. 'Why didn't you tell us?'

'I couldn't trust you boys to keep your mouths shut. You were all so upset about your father's death. I was too, but I had to get this done, and fast. I was afraid you might crow a bit and spoil the deal.'

'So what's so good about the deal?'

'This house needs some work. And I've seen carpenter ants. Not too bad yet, but when they get in, the problems never end and you need to hire experts to get rid of them. That costs a lot of money. I felt a little guilty about it, but Mr Taylor has a good pension. Probably good savings as well, and his nephew is going to inherit it all anyway. They'll be able to afford it.'

Tom and I were still in shock, but Gerry was beaming. 'Mom, I never knew you had it in you.'

After we ate some of the cake and had a few drinks, Gerry and Tom and I went out for a walk in the old neighbourhood while my mother washed the dishes. For the two of them, it might be the last time they saw the house. As for me, I could drive back into the old neighbourhood any time I wanted. I wasn't sure I would want to all that much once my mother moved out.

We walked for a while and talked about the house, and our mother and father. Then we ran out of words.

One thing that had not changed over the years was the sky. Even in the dark, it still hung big above the old suburb of Weston, and although I had not looked for it in years, for all I knew the old Canadian Gypsum factory still sent a single white plume of smoke up into that sky. All the changes in the world could go on in Weston, but the sky was constant and big.

'I wonder what the Old Man would think of all this,' said Tom.

'He'd love it,' said Gerry.

'It's finally sinking in that he's dead,' Tom continued. 'As long as Mom was there in that house, I kept expecting him to come up from the basement with that heavy step of his.'

'Once in a while I have to saw a board,' said Gerry, 'and I get all tense and press too hard and the saw binds. And then I remember him telling me to let the saw do the work for me and not to force it.'

Ah, yes, I thought to myself. Now that the past was about to disappear, we were going to make it into some kind of fairy tale. Sweet and romantic.

'The Old Man drove me crazy,' I said, and that put a stop to some of the fond remembrances for a while. We walked the streets some more.

'You know,' Gerry finally said. 'We may have come out even on this.'

'What do you mean?'

'I think we drove the Old Man crazy too.'

Tom was still puffing on his pipe, but for a moment I thought I could smell another tobacco smoke, the coarser smell of the green-packaged Sail tobacco that the Old Man had smoked. And I was almost sure I could hear the sputter of nicotine resin from the stem of his pipe.

A House in the Country

A Prequel

1952

MY OLDER BROTHER GERRY WAS HOLDING OPEN THE ICEBOX DOOR and staring into the dark interior.

'You think ice is cheap?' my father whispered hoarsely. Whispering didn't come naturally to him.

'I'm hungry.'

'Keep your voice down.'

Gerry slammed the door shut.

'Idiot,' said my father. My mother was startled by the noise of the icebox, more afraid than angry.

We had been tip-toeing around the second-floor flat in our socks for an hour, my mother wincing at every clatter of dishes and squeak of the floor. Gerry had all the squeaky spots memorized — he stepped on them on purpose. The place was stifling. My father closed all the windows at night, and since we were going to be out for the day, he had seen no point in opening them that morning.

I'd waited long enough. I needed to get out of that cramped, airless city flat.

We'd moved to Toronto the previous fall, Gerry and me shouting ourselves hoarse in the two days it had taken to travel from Fort William in the back of Stan's pickup truck. But me and Gerry took a while to get used to the city. Walking on the sidewalks. Crossing at the traffic lights. Last fall we'd still had traces of accents and some of the kids had laughed. Gerry took care of that. A few bloody noses and nobody laughed any more.

My father moved us to Toronto because he said he did not come to Canada to be a farm hand. Now he'd changed his mind about living in the centre of town. The city disagreed with him, and so did our landlord.

Mr Grymes was a veteran of the Pacific campaign, a crewcut soldier who'd gone back to tailoring in Canada. He was nothing like the tailors in fairy tales, who started out meek and ended up being heroes. Things bothered him. He didn't like the smell of cabbage, fish, or roast chicken. Lighters and strike-anywhere matches made him nervous. He declared a curfew on noise between nine in the evening and nine in the morning. He was not the kind of man who should have taken in boarders, but he needed the money. As for us, the town was full of DPs and flats were hard to find. We needed a place to stay.

My mother rummaged in one of the picnic baskets. 'Have a piece of sausage,' she said to Gerry. She wore a kerchief tied over her head and a thin spring coat that I remembered from the refugee camp. She was ready to go — two picnic baskets with tea towels on them at her feet, and her shoes on top of one of the tea towels. My father's dirty rubber boots stood beside two new pairs for Gerry and me. There was a new shovel leaning up against the wall. My father was taking us out to the edge of town, practically the countryside, to start work on the lot he had bought. I don't know where he got the money.

The beeping of a car horn and a series of shouts threw my mother into a panic.

'It's Stan. Hurry up, hurry up. Mr Grymes will be furious.'

We all grabbed for boots and shoes. Except Gerry.

'I have to go to the toilet.'

'Well, hurry up.'

I took one of the baskets, and the three of us flew down the steps in our stocking feet. Well, two of us flew. Father was like a mountain, far too heavy to fly. At the bottom of the stairs, my mother opened the door, and we stepped out onto the porch. We put on our shoes and boots there. My father's cousin, Stan, was sitting at the wheel of the rusted pickup, leaning on the horn and shouting out the window in our language.

'Come on, you DPs. Get on the train to Siberia!'

My mother said hello to the three men in back, and then got inside the cab with Stan. The men in the back were quiet, aged farm boys who still found words too hard to assemble, smokers with faces made rough from working outside all year round. They already wore their carpenters' aprons.

Gerry shot out the front door, slammed it behind him, and leaped from the porch onto the sidewalk. He already had his new boots on.

There wasn't even time for my father to yell at him. The door opened right behind him, fast, and Mr Grymes stuck his head outside.

'I've told you a hundred times, that boy is not to run down the steps with his shoes on. Shoes are forbidden upstairs!'

My father turned to him and shrugged, like a farmer before the inevitability of bad weather.

'You old soldier,' my father said from the city sidewalk out front. 'You listened machine guns and bombs. One boy not so bad.'

It embarrassed me whenever I heard my father speak English.

'I told you before, the floors creak and the steps are worse. No shoes upstairs.'

'Boy is boy. Boy forgets. I beat him for you tonight.'

'No. I've had enough.' Mr Grymes ran his hand over his bristly hair. 'I want you out of here, understand?'

'Mr Grymes, we gone all day. You sleep. Quiet today.' My father had his arms open wide, and shovel in hand, he was the very picture of reason with a foreign accent.

But Mr Grymes was far beyond reason.

'I didn't want to let you in right from the beginning. I could have rented this place to anybody. But you promised. You said you'd be as quiet as sheep. I can't take this damned noise any more. I want you out, you hear?'

My father stepped up onto the bed of the pickup and turned to speak to Mr Grymes.

'We build new house. Gone by September. In few months, you rent to old lady. You tell her, no whistling kettles.'

Mr Grymes ran his hand over his hair again. He was working up a head of steam.

'I mean *out*. Right now. I won't stand for it. I want you out before tonight!'

'You give little time.'

'I've warned you before. It's too late now. Twelve hours. Move your furniture out now, or you'll find it on the street tonight.'

He stopped suddenly, as if he had just noticed the pickup truck. One of the smokers in the back had just stood up beside my father. Gerry picked up a rock from the yard.

Mr Grymes withdrew quietly and closed the door behind him.

'Honestly, that man is as nervous as a woman,' said my father, fluent and insulting again in his own language. Stan and my mother got out of the cab.

'You want us to help you move instead?' Stan asked.

My father sucked on his pipe for a while.

'We don't have any place to go and we don't have any money to pay rent if we did. Give him a few hours to cool down and we'll take our chances.'

'That man is unbalanced,' my mother said. 'Our things will be on the street by tonight.'

'Don't get hysterical.'

'Who's getting hysterical? I'm just pointing out the obvious.'

'Get in the truck.'

'A problem doesn't go away just because you ignore it.'

'Get in the truck.'

'Say something sensible to me. Think.'

'What is this, a school? Get in the truck.'

I could see Stan take the weight off one of his legs. He was getting ready to wait a long time. Our people knew how to argue, especially husbands and wives. But my mother cut short the fight by turning suddenly and getting back into the cab. She slammed the door behind her.

As Gerry jumped onto the back of the truck, my father swiped him gently across the head.

'I told you to be quiet,' my father said.

'I'll stick a potato in his tailpipe.'

'A waste of food,' said my father, and he sucked hard on the pipe so I could hear the sputter of nicotine resin in the stem, 'better to use a rock.'

Father tamped down the burning tobacco in his pipe with his thumb. No nerves at all. Whenever I pulled a sliver out of his finger, I had to pierce the thick skin with the needle, and then rip away parts of the flesh. It made me sick, but he would just stand there, impassive. Now I sniffed the air to find out if his skin burned against the ember, but he was as insensitive to heat as the devil.

Gerry sidled up to me in the back of the pickup as soon as we were on the move.

'Mr Grymes is taken care of,' he said.

'Huh?'

'I turned on the tap in the kitchen, just a little. It's going to drip all day. By the time we get back, he'll be in the loony bin.'

'From a dripping tap?'

'He hates noise, right? It'll be like the water torture.'

This was not the first time he'd tried to do in the landlord. Mr Grymes had a horror of insects, so Gerry sprinkled sugar on the earth along the side of the house to attract ants. He left empty books of matches on the lawn so Mr Grymes would think the local juvenile delinquents had been trying to burn down his house. But although Mr Grymes raged wildly sometimes, he refused to go off into the deep end of madness where Gerry had hoped to drive him.

We drove for a while through city streets and on into downtown Weston, not much more than a block of stores. Then on through quieter streets with houses and trees until we made it out past civilization.

There were many dirt roads, laid out in grids. In the distance there were some fields and the occasional farm house, but in our section, only rows of apple trees. Stan stopped the pickup at the top of a low hill. He and my mother got out of the cab.

'This is it, our new home,' my father said, waving expansively at the orchard.

Gerry let out a whoop. 'A cherry orchard!'

My mother turned to my father in alarm.

'Not a cherry orchard. That would be bad luck.'

'What are you talking about?'

'It would be a bad omen. It's in Chekhov.'

'I don't care if it's in the Old Testament.' My father spat. 'Anyway, these aren't cherries. They're apples.'

My mother put her hands on her hips and surveyed our piece of the orchard. She still looked unsure, and the low anger that always simmered in her might still have boiled over.

'Will you have the house built by tonight?'

The men laughed.

'Lady, today we'll just take down the trees and start digging the cellar.'

My mother turned on my father.

'We'll get back and find our things on the front lawn. That horrible man will have us out on the street. Then what are we going to do?'

'Our house will be ready by the fall.'

'But what will we do tonight? Live in a tent?'

'You worry too much.'

'Somebody has to.'

'I say we'll be in the new house by winter.'

'Hmph. Another tarpaper shack.'

'Sure, tarpaper first, and then bricks.'

She looked across the trees in the lot for a moment as if he was telling a fairy tale. She sighed. I read her sighs and gestures as if they were a weather vane. Her anger was gone, but I was not yet sure what mood had come to replace it.

'We'll never live in a brick house.'

'Two storeys.'

'And a garage, I suppose.'

'A double garage, solid. I'll build that out of concrete blocks.'

She laughed. 'You've been watching too many movies.' She walked over to where Gerry had climbed into a tree.

'Come here,' my father said to me, and I followed him to the corner of the lot where a survey stake with numbers poked out of the ground. The others were unloading the truck.

'Your eyes are better than mine. Look on the neighbour's side of the stake. Feel around in the ground. Any holes?'

I did as he told me, and after I felt around with my hands, I found a piece of field sod that looked funny, and it came away easily when I pulled on it.

'Aha!' said my father. 'The neighbours have been stealing our land already.' He pulled the stake out of the ground, and then pushed it back into the hole I had found. The stake fit perfectly. We regained a foot of our lot.

'How did you know about that?' I asked him.

He shrugged.

The men fanned out with axes and began to fell the apple trees.

I felt like running. For months I had waited for school bells to release me at the end of the day and then tip-toed around the flat in Mr Grymes' house. Now there were the long corridors through the orchard and the open fields beyond. There might be streams there, and ponds, and abandoned houses with windows waiting to be broken.

The first trick was to become invisible to my father, and the second was to get beyond the range of his voice. He did not like to see us standing around — it made him think of things for us to do.

'Gerry! Dave!' My father called us to heel with our English names. Gerry and I had rechristened ourselves in the new country. My father took us to a corner of the lot where he had rammed four sticks into the earth, making a square about three by three. He handed a shovel with the handle broken off at the top to Gerry.

'I want you to dig a fox-hole here.'

'Fox-hole?'

'That's right. It looks peaceful around here, but you never know. I want it deep, too, as deep as you are tall. That way you'll be safe if a tank runs over you.'

'This is Canada, Dad,' said Gerry. 'We don't have to worry about tanks running over us here.'

'You never know. When the Germans retreated across my father's farm, they lit up the whole place. Fields, house, barn, everything. We would have been happy to have a fox-hole to crouch in. Now get to work.' He strode off to the men who were cutting down the trees.

'I don't get it,' I said to Gerry.

'What?'

'The war's over. There are no tanks here.'

'He's nuts. Start digging.'

'Why me?'

'There's only one shovel.'

We spoke English to one another when our parents were not around. I cut the sod in a square, and then started to chop out hunks of it. It was hard because the field grass and the roots were long. The shovel was dull. Gerry sat down on a piece of log and watched me.

'I'll bet you the other one's nuts by the time we get back tonight too,' he said.

'Mr Grymes?'

'No, the Virgin Mary. What do you think?'

'He won't go nuts from a dripping tap.'

'Then I'll use other methods.'

'Like what?' I was already starting to sweat.

'I could take some of the mouse poison and mix it up with his cereal. Grape Nuts. He'd never tell the difference. I could make a hole in his muffler pipe. The guy drives to work with his windows closed, even in the summer. The carbon monoxide would get in there and he'd be dead before he got to his job. I could hide under his bed with a bayonet and stick it through the mattress while he was asleep.'

'He'd feel the point coming through and wake up.'

'Not if I was fast.'

'You might kill Mrs Grymes by mistake. She's OK.'

That was a problem. Gerry thought about it. Mrs Grymes slipped us fudge wrapped in wax paper. She was always quiet when Mr Grymes was around, but with us she talked about the dances she used to go to before the war. She'd met Mr Grymes at a dance at the Palais Royale. It was hard to imagine him at a place like that.

'You may not have a chance,' I said. 'We could get back tonight and find our stuff on the sidewalk.'

'I'd come back. I'd get a tarantula out of a banana box and slip it through their window at night.'

I dug for a while until I had a hole halfway up my calves. The soil was mostly clay, still wet with spring runoff, and it was hard to work inside the hole. Half the soil slipped off the shovel as I tried to lift it out.

'You've piled the earth too close to the hole,' said Gerry when he took over. I had to pull it farther away with a piece of board. Gerry was smart. Whenever I worked, he was resting. Whenever he worked, I was working too.

The lot was clear of trees by lunch time. The men cut them into pieces and hauled them into a pile at the corner farthest from the road, and then lit a bonfire. The green wood did not burn very well, but one of the men lay down dry grass in thick bundles, and eventually the mass of trees caught fire and burned with a lot of hissing and giving off of a sweet, white smoke that rose in billows into the sky. There were two other columns of smoke in the distance where others were burning trees, and if we had had a blanket big enough, we could have signaled to them.

The men had knocked together a rough table and benches. We had to be careful sitting down because the nail heads were not driven all the way in. Later, the table would be pulled apart and used for the joists and walls of the house. My mother spread a green tablecloth and laid out boiled white pork sausages, whose colour was uninviting but whose smell made my mouth water.

'You can put them on sticks and brown them on the fire,' my mother said, but we were too hungry for patience. Cooked cabbage, sliced cucumbers, horseradish, hard white cheese and black bread and butter, and a bottle of beer for each of the men. The men kept the beer bottles between their legs on the seats in case a police car came by. Cold, sweet tea for Gerry and me. My father grew expansive over the food.

'Just breathe in that air,' he said. 'Clean and fresh out here. There's a farmer who still keeps cows a mile down the road. We'll have fresh milk for the boys. No criminals out here. No dirt and dust.'

Stan laughed.

'You grew up on a farm. You should know better than that. You'll be hauling a pound of muck on each boot. If you want to live in Siberia, that's your decision. I want a place where I walk to the corner to buy a newspaper or a package of cigarettes.'

'Life out here will be much healthier.'

'The factories are still in the city. Two buses and a street car each day to get to work.'

'I'll buy a car.'

Mother laughed bitterly. 'A brick house, a garage, and now a car. Where is all this money going to come from? If we get back and find our furniture on the street, we don't have the money to pay for the first month's rent. Then you can knock these boards together and we'll live in a tarpaper shack, right back where we started. We may as well be in Siberia.'

They were all quiet for a while, which was unusual for our people. They could always find something to talk about, like the coming war between Russia and America. Sometimes they would talk about their lives before the war and someone was bound to cry. It made me sick. Behind us the bonfire hissed and crackled and the heat from the flames made us sweat. The men were tired, but when the wind shifted and smoke began to blow across the table, they all stood up to return to work. Gerry and I had to finish the fox-hole.

The men fanned out along a string line my father had tied, and they began to dig the cellar. By the middle of the afternoon, our fox-hole was as deep as I was tall. Gerry wanted me to dig it deeper, but he wasn't willing to dig it himself. The men had stopped to smoke cigarettes, and my father came over to study our pit.

'That's enough,' he said, and then he called over the men and they brought along some boards.

'Out of the way, boys. The men take over now.'

'What's to build?' asked Gerry. 'It's supposed to be a fox-hole.'

'Nope,' my father said. 'It's an out-house. We have to build the essentials first.'

Gerry threw down the shovel, even though I'd been the one who'd used it the most.

'You lied to us.'

'Don't you dare use that kind of language to your father,' he said, but the words were said serenely between puffs at his pipe. 'I just needed to motivate you.'

I thought we'd be free of him then, but I should've known better. We were never free of him. The field beckoned, but he made us go over the lot and pick up the sticks and branches and feed the fire. It seemed to take forever, and we didn't even get any credit for it when it came time to go.

'Just as dirty as farm children.' My mother scolded us, and she beat the dust off our clothes and wiped our faces with a damp towel before we got back into the truck.

The men were quiet on the way back. They were tired. Even my father, who was often angry and even more often irritated, sat on a tool box with his hands clasped between his knees.

'Don't worry,' one of the men finally said. 'If the furniture is outside, we'll pack it up in the truck and toss a tarp over the top. There's an empty room in the house where I'm staying. I'll put in a word with the landlady and you can throw down a couple of mattresses on the floor.'

My father just nodded.

We came back to the smells of the city, car exhaust and concrete. Everyone tensed as we drove up the street to our flat, but when we pulled up, there was nothing on the sidewalk outside. Some kids still ran around the street, but all the adults were back inside. It was too cool to sit on porches once the sun had gone down.

My mother hissed at us to take our boots off on the porch, and we were apprehensive when my father threw back the bolt of the lock. Mr Grymes might be waiting inside.

But no. The lights were all off, except down in the kitchen where we could see Mrs Grymes sitting at a chair with a book and a cup of tea. She slipped her reading glasses down her nose as we came in, and waved. We walked upstairs quietly, cringing at every creak, took off our coats, and went into the tiny kitchen where we sat around the table. There was only enough room for three chairs in the room, and I carefully pulled out the lidded garbage can and sat down on that. My mother put on the kettle for tea. She twisted shut the tap and the dripping stopped.

The fresh air had sapped our strength, but Gerry still had enough spark left in him to be angry. He was always angry. Maybe he was just disappointed that Mr Grymes had not been carted off to the lunatic asylum.

'This is like living in a prison,' he hissed.

'Three, four months, and then you'll be free,' said my father.

'Will the house be finished by then?' my mother asked.

'Enough for us to live in. We'll move into the basement and work on the rest of the house as the money comes in.'

'How long?' she asked.

'I'll have the walls up before the first snow falls.'

'Then we'll live like peasants,' my mother said. 'We'll grow potatoes in the back yard.'

'Sure,' my father said. 'And radishes and cucumbers too.'

My mother's good humor had faded with the sunlight. She unpacked the picnic baskets and set the dishes by the sink to wash them in the morning. She took a newspaper and went to her bedroom.

'Can we at least listen to the radio?' Gerry asked.

'Are you out of your mind? Don't make any noise tonight. Don't even flush the toilet.' He took a section of the newspaper and went into the living room that doubled as a bedroom for me and Gerry. He turned on the light, sat down in an armchair, and began to read.

There was nothing to do. It was too late to go out and too early to go to bed. I got the checker board and Gerry and I played a couple of games on the coffee table. Gerry wanted to play a third game, but he punched me in the shoulder every time I took one of his men, and the shoulder was getting sore. The light was already out in my mother's bedroom when my father put down his paper and gingerly folded open the couch that Gerry and I shared as a bed. Gerry and I crawled in under the sheets.

I wasn't ready to sleep, but my father had a rule of silence once we were in bed. We had to wait until he was finished in the toilet and went off to his own room before we could be sure he was out of earshot. I could hear him run a thin stream of water in the bathroom sink. Gerry was uncommonly still. He was already starting to fall asleep and there would be no one to talk to once my father was done.

Then it started, the way it did sometimes.

First we heard the groans, loud and deep. Fast footsteps as Mrs Grymes went to him, but not fast enough. He shouted in a full-throated voice, scared. My father came out of the bathroom and went to the landing at the top of the stairs. There was no door between our living space and theirs down below. We followed.

Mr Grymes shouted and screamed, and then there came the words, hardly words, in sharp barks, half angry and half pleading. Mrs Grymes had to speak loudly to him to calm him down.

It was a bad night, maybe the worst. We heard her make him get out of bed, and walk him to their living room. From my angle, I couldn't see their heads but I could see their feet. She sat him down on the couch and poured him a glass of brandy. But sometimes the world of his dreams refused to leave him so easily.

We saw my father hesitate at the top of the stairs before us, and then start down in his undershirt. I sensed my mother behind us in her nightdress.

My father walked to their doorway without going any further into the room.

'War over now, Mr Grymes,' he said. 'Time to forget.'

He must have looked at my father then.

'You don't know what it was like. We had defenses all around the hill. Hong Kong is a mountain, you have only so far to fall back before you make it to the top,' Mr Grymes said. His voice was different, somehow, as if it belonged to another man.

'You move to country, Mr Grymes. Breathe fresh air and it clears brain.'

'We had machine guns trained on them, down the hill. Plenty of ammunition too, but they kept on coming. The bodies piled up so much that the guns couldn't be cranked up high enough. We pulled back and started it all again. So many of them, coming and coming.'

'You drink milk from a pail in country,' said my father. 'Fresh from cow. You watch birds go away in fall and come back in spring.'

'Almost four years,' said Mr Grymes. His wife continued to murmur, her words nothing more than cooing in the background. 'The men died slowly. Just enough to eat so it took years to die. We ate ants and beetles. At night, I could hear the insects scrabbling along the wooden floors. We ate them by day and they came to try to eat us by night.'

'You build new house, Mr Grymes. No creaking floors. No time to think when you build. Time to forget, Mr Grymes.'

It got quiet then, and Gerry and I leaned as far forward as we dared. We crouched low on the steps so we could see his face. He was looking at my father as if he did not recognize him, looking at him like a stranger. Mrs Grymes was at his side, still cooing, petting his shoulder repeatedly.

Something came over him then, some kind of return to the man we knew by day. But it was a hard transformation. He smiled at first, caught himself, and frowned. Face wet with tears and a frown on his lips. It took him a moment to find his voice.

'Good night,' said Mr Grymes.

My father looked at him for a moment longer. Then he shrugged.

'Good night,' my father answered, and he turned to come back up the stairs.

Acknowledgements

With thanks to George Galt, who made this happen, and to Ned Seager, who brought it to fruition.

About the Author

Antanas Sileika is the author of six works of fiction and two personal histories, including most recently the novel *Some Unfinished Business*. The first edition of *Buying on Time* was nominated for the City of Toronto Book Award and the Stephen Leacock Medal for Humour, and his novel *Provisionally Yours* has been adapted for both film and television. Beyond writing fiction, Sileika worked as a journalist and taught for many years at Humber College, eventually becoming director of the Humber School for Writers. He is now retired and lives in Toronto.